ALICHAN

Facing the Shadow of Doubt

by
Al Epifanio

ALICHAN

Published and packaged by
Illumify Media Global
www.IllumifyMedia.com

Print: 978-1-949021-07-3
eBook: 978-1-949021-08-0

*Dedicated to my parents
and my brother, William Paul.*

CONTENTS

AUTHOR'S INTRODUCTION

WHEN YOU WRITE A book these days, you're supposed to come up with a clever elevator pitch to grab the reader's attention and summarize the whole story in under twenty seconds. Unfortunately, life is not that simple.

In March of 2003, I began exploring my family history. With no idea where this journey would lead, my first destination on the map was identified as "NOT RECOMMENDED FOR TRAVEL." Still I needed to know where I came from and where to go next. Everyone comes to a similar fork in the road where they must discover what's real in their life and what is myth.

Soon I learned that delving too deeply into your past can be a dangerous proposition. Entering the terroir of El Narco, exposed many uncomfortable truths. The fables of lost treasures and ancient monsters that my grandmother Rosita shared with me long ago, now seemed less incredible.

Looking backwards is especially disastrous in my favorite sport of cycling. Over the last few years I've spent a lot of time recovering from old wounds and digging into some of the bigger questions in life. Now join me on this adventure into the past, along with the primary fictional character of this story, Alan Martin. He is very much like most of us, wandering around in search of answers and freedom from the stupefying effects of this media-driven age.

Before you jump into this race against time, you should understand that much of this tale is based upon actual historical events. Though many of the characters in this novel represent real people, some of the names have been changed to protect the not so innocent.

Most of the places and creatures described in this narrative are also very real. So whatever preconceived misconceptions you may have about this book or its contents, please wash them all away right now and let's tear down any walls of misgiving that may divide us socially, politically, or spiritually.

The Alichan raises doubts in life that hold us back from becoming everything we should be. What is your Alichan? Ultimately finding an answer to that question is what this story is all about.

Alan Martin had no idea what he was looking for when he went out in search of the long-lost beauty in his life. Encountering the Alichan challenged everything he always believed. Now if you dare to face the shadow of doubt, let's go for a little ride . . .

PROLOGUE
THE RACE BEGINS

"In the midst of life's journey I found myself in a dark wood,
for the right path was lost."

—*Dante*

Race Day — Durango, Colorado

I LOATHE MY LIFE. The pain is unbearable. My legs are burning and there is a fire in my lungs. What is the point of all this suffering?

Minutes ago, the fanfare of a cheering crowd spurred me forward from the starting line into first place. A picturesque Rocky Mountain landscape of pines and junipers quickly seduced me into its snaking switchbacks. Now, every muscle screams for mercy as the first wave of doubt begins to flow over me. There's an orange jersey closing in. I'm not moving fast enough.

At a fork in the trail, there's a sign to take the narrow path. It is steep, rocky, and treacherous. The pounding drumbeat inside my head almost drowns out an orange-clad rider as he rushes past shouting, "ON YOUR LEFT!"

A small ichthys logo on the back of his shorts asks, "How Can We Pray for You?" What kind of cruel deity would test this common man so harshly? I should be praying for the strength to overcome the anguish of life and for the faith necessary to win this race. Instead I shout, "You better pray I don't catch you and kick your ... AYE!"

Hey! He's already around the next bend. Now another mountain bike is closing in from behind. Holy crap! It's another orange jersey. He's breathing hard, but a position on the podium may be slipping away, so I accelerate with all my might while glancing backward to measure the gap. What did I ever do to deserve this much torment?

Most people dream of winning a race or becoming the best in their field. Right now, I just want a shot at redemption. For this weekend warrior it's getting harder to keep up with the twenty-somethings in this category, but there's not much passion left for anything else in life. I'm almost twice as old as some of the kids out here, so finishing within the top three positions and winning a medal would be a special reward.

Fighting on, I tear through a thick spider's web and wonder what could be in it—a huge wolf spider? Struggling frantically to shed the discomfort of my own skin, I want to be free from all misgivings. No matter how hard I try to wipe it off, a sticky feeling still clings to my chin—the web's creator must be angry. With one hand still on the handlebars I swipe at something that probably isn't even there. It's so easy to fall into the shadow of doubt without even realizing it's there.

A small prickly caterpillar slinks rapidly across the path. It seems harmless, but you must respect the purpose of a creature so blindly determined to reach its destiny–something greater than itself. In a few short months the ugly worm will be a beautiful monarch butterfly; but where will I be? My own monster of anger and uncertainty begins to creep up again, but by the time I fully grasp the danger –it's too late.

In the twinkling of an eye, the larva distracts me from the real obstacle on the path –a huge stone. My bike swerves automatically, barely enough to avoid the collision.

Losing control in this startling instant, I see myself flying over the handlebars down a steep embankment. The firmament appears above, conifer walls on every side, and a lot of cold air between me, and the steeply sloping earth far below.

Merely seconds ago, I was climbing boldly towards a personal El Dorado; now heaven and earth are about to collide. They say that in the final moments of life, countless memories flash before your eyes. Whoever "they" are, they're right.

As my body strikes the ground for the first time, I'm taken immediately back to that devastating moment in life not so long ago when something important was lost, a thing once thought so valuable yet was actually a hindrance to growth: it was my job.

Rolling rapidly forward through life, the second big blow came a few months later with the loss of some places in my heart even more dear: a home, a younger brother and my father.

Then, my torso strikes the ground with a thud that takes my breath away. I stagger to my feet searching for answers to this predicament. There's a lot of blood coming from somewhere. Stumbling forward, my head strikes an unforgiving pine branch that falls upon me like a gavel. The third and final blow is the loss of love for life itself. Just let me lie down in the dust where people will search for me, but I will be no more.

Something rustles in the bushes and my imagination goes to work. Is it a snake, a mountain lion, or just a spotted towhee with auburn eyes? The last clear thing I remember is the flash of a bright orange jersey on the trail high above. A nearby creek whispers its fading song into the darkness surrounding me.

Where am I now? Is this really the end of the road? Wait! There are still remote places on this Earth and in my heart yet to be explored . . .

GENESIS

In the beginning God created the heavens and the earth. Now the earth was formless and empty, darkness was over the surface of the deep, and the spirit of God was hovering over the water.

Genesis 1:1

1

The Call — Littleton, Colorado

IN THE BEGINNING, LIFE was good. When I first met RuMa, it was as though she was made just for me. We said, "till death do us part," and we meant it. That's what we said and that's what we believed. We shared the first years of our marriage naked and free to explore the limits of the paradise in which we lived. Then we wanted more. We wanted more education, more money, better cars, a bigger house, children, the world. We thought we could have it all.

Then she left, and her disappearance disturbed me more than the agony of our last days together when we either argued to points beyond despair or avoided each other altogether. There should have been some sense of deliverance when she departed, yet there I was, irretrievably broken.

A few weeks before that race in Durango, I woke up alone in my bed, tortured by RuMa's absence. I missed her soft, warm skin next to mine. My world was formless and empty. Dawn hovered over the purple majesty of the Front Range refreshing my spirit, if only for a few fleeting moments. The mountains were my refuge and strength, an escape from the reality of a love lost.

Often, I rode far into the forest on my bicycle hoping to find answers to the biggest questions in life such as: Where has my passion gone? When will this dysthymia end? Or, is it possible to ever love someone without doing irreparable harm? In the distance a stream whispered an answer that I could not understand.

After my early morning ride and a speedy shower, another busy workday was about to begin when the phone rang. The soft familiar voice on the other end of the line immediately sensed my fatigue and said, "Happiness is . . . *Mi hijito*, I'm afraid I have some urgent news for you."

No matter how dismal the occasion, Mom always prefaced every conversation with: "Happiness is..." and the words *mi hijito*, which in Spanish mean, "my little son." When merged together, they sound like honey to the ears and get pronounced as one word: *mee-heeto*. The tone of her voice meant that whatever shock she was about to deliver, I should gear down for it.

"I just got off the phone with your cousin Jose in Culiacan and he sounds very upset. He thinks they may have found RuMa somewhere near El Rodeo."

The fog lifted from my brain just enough to inquire anxiously into the whereabouts of my missing spouse. "What is RuMa doing in Mexico?"

"They think she was doing research, diving into some old mines or a cave for something, I don't know. Anyway, Jose heard on the news that they found a body in the area where RuMa was supposed to be."

Oh no, my worst fears were about to be realized. "But, then," she continued, "he got a call yesterday from a priest we know named Padre Arres. He said that the Father thinks RuMa may still be alive. He has a message from her about some important word that he needs from you. Do you know what he's talking about?"

I had no idea, but being a devout cynic, I asked, "How do they know this message came from RuMa?"

"Well, because your cousin was talking to the priest a few weeks ago and El Padre said he met with a lady named Rosa Martinez, but Jose said it must have been RuMa." I recalled that RuMa occasionally used Rosa Martinez as an alias when traveling in foreign countries. Oddly enough, most people fell for it because of her dark hair, high cheek bones and comfortable Spanish accent. So many thoughts at once caused electricity to flow rapidly into every circuit of my body.

I've felt helpless before, but this took me far beyond the comfort zone. My vocation is to evaluate commercial real estate, to determine the value of places and things. RuMa, was an archaeologist who tried to discover the nature of peoples through the analysis of their things. Although her maiden name was Ruth-Marie Andersen, our kids had trouble saying her Midwestern name of Ruth-Marie. Thus, *Mom* was affectionately slurred into *RuMa*. To me, she just became Rue.

After years of struggling through a difficult relationship, there was nothing left of our marriage once the kids moved out. Endless battles over finances and debates over how to spend our time together eventually drove us apart. Busyness could never satisfy the constant demand for more peace and more security. Though we tried counseling and therapies of all sorts, nothing was able to overcome the void between us. We legally separated over a year ago, trying to make the most of life by putting all of our energies into respective careers and interests.

Then about two weeks ago, RuMa completely disappeared, and despite my best efforts, we have been unable to find each other. Though it wasn't unusual for her to disappear from me for a few days or even weeks at a time, a few of her friends and distant family members were wondering whether we should get the police or detectives involved.

At this point I was looking agitatedly for a note pad to write on, "Do you know if Mark is home right now?" Mark was RuMa's older brother who lived in Los Angeles and the only living member of her immediate family. Scribbling out a to-do list, it began to make sense that RuMa, with all her degrees in science, would go back into old Mexico to explore the hidden demons and treasures of my family's past.

Mom sounded troubled but not quite frantic yet. I only thought about my workload for a moment while trying quickly to make travel arrangements in my mind, "Maybe I can take a few days off and get down there to find out what's going on."

"Ohhh, that would be wonderful! Happiness is . . . a family adventure." Mom's voice was back to normal. I had to hold the telephone a few inches away from my ear. She was relieved for the moment, but now I had to figure out how to make this all happen. Trying to escape from client obligations for more than a few days could be financially disastrous. Unfortunately, living from project to project makes sudden cash demands like this even more challenging.

"Well, I can't take you with me, but I may need to stop over on the way to find out more about where she might be. Hopefully Mark can explain what RuMa was up to and we can bring her back." I thought about calling the police first, but if they asked what I thought she was doing in Mexico, the cops would probably lock me up in an asylum. At the very least, I'd probably be a murder suspect with no chance of ever getting out of the country.

"Before you call anyone else, better let me talk to Mark first."

Then the phone went silent as Mom began to catch up. It didn't take long. The somber tone she originally called with returned, "You know I wonder if she was looking for the Alichan's treasure?"

I almost laughed out loud, but instead just chuckled softly and shook my head. Realizing the sincerity of her beliefs in our ancient family myths kept me silent for a moment before replying, "I'm sure RuMa is just fine. She's too smart and mean to be in any big trouble."

It took a full day to get my travel plans in order and get through to Father Arres via telephone. He is the priest of a church in the remote Mexican village known as Tamazula, a name which comes from the Nahuatl word for "lagoon of the toads."

"Father Arres, my name is Alan Martin, and I understand that you may have some important information regarding my wife. She sometimes goes by the name of Rosa Martinez or RuMa, but her real name is Ruth-Marie Martin. We believe she may have been somewhere in your area doing some archaeological work, digging for bones, and we have not heard anything from her in a few weeks."

The tone of his voice was far more urgent than that of my Mom's. In spite of a poor connection and el padre's thick Spanish accent, I could clearly understand that he needed to see me immediately, "Mr. Martin, your wife Rosa was here recently, and we just received a message from her that your mother has something you need to bring here right away. It is called the *La Palabra de Dios* (The *Word of God*). She also said that your mother knows exactly what that is and where to find it."

Before I could catch my breath to ask a question, the Father rushed onward, "Your wife has discovered a very important Scroll here in the Sierra that she will only allow me to give you when you bring the Palabra. We have someone here who can guide you to her and explain this more clearly once you arrive, but it is *muy complicado*. You must get to here right away. RuMa said you are the only one who can bring this Word to her in time."

"Okay, I'm not sure I understand, but do you know exactly where we can find her? Is she all right?"

There was a pregnant pause that seemed to last forever as the priest searched for the words in English to finally say, "I think she may still be alive, but in grave danger. There was a body found in the area where she was working but we don't know for sure that it was hers. There is nothing more I can tell you at this time. There is nothing more you should say to anyone. The police here are just as dangerous as the bandits looking for her. If she is still alive, the place where she is hidden is about 45 kilometers from here. That's almost two days by mule."

Dazed and confused by the father's odd statements, I did some quick math in my head. Thinking that I could ride faster than a mule and remembering the need to train for an upcoming race in Durango, Colorado, my naïve reply was, "I can ride my bike."

That got the priest to laugh gently before he replied, "You do not understand, the terrain here is very steep and rocky. There are no maps to where you must go; nothing more I can tell you by the phone. The rivers are rising rapidly here, so you must come at once."

Apparently, there was no time to refuse this request for action. Father Arres knew the legends of the Rios family well enough to leave them alone. Others were not so fortunate. This is a story that I didn't want to tell, but according to the priest, a great conflict was about to occur, "A war is about to begin that all of humanity needs to prepare for," he said.

Before that fateful call, I was focused, resolutely climbing toward my own selfish goals. Then suddenly this great shadow of doubt attacked . . . an enemy that we could not see was preparing for its big invasion.

RuMa must have discovered something near the tiny Mexican village of El Rodeo that she wasn't supposed to find. My family always warned us never to go any further than Tamazula de Victoria. Though I cautioned RuMa on numerous occasions that the Federales and drug cartels did not want anyone exploring their territory, she must have gone into the Sierra anyway. When Father Arres heard about a body that turned up near a new church construction site, he did not ask any further questions; that was now my problem.

At this stirring merger of fear and anticipation, there were rising rivers to ford. Searching for any glimmer of hope, I grabbed a recent picture of RuMa and packed it into a bag. Even if she was still alive, what was the probability of ever winning back my mate and convincing her of my true worth as a man?

I've heard that Einstein once said, "The true value of a human being can be found in the degree to which he has attained liberation from the self."

That day I wasn't planning to search for a lost love, discover some ancient legend or a priceless treasure; I just wanted to be free from all the prevailing wounds in life — free from myself.

2

Sunday Morning — Southern California

MY ITINERARY ONLY ALLOWED for a brief stop in L.A. to find La Palabra, and to recruit Mark and his hiking gear. First, I'd have to absorb as much information as possible from my mother, Leonila (aka Lenie) Rios Martin. For decades, Mom's stories went untold or blinked away as merely old wives' tales. In light of recent events however, her yarns now warranted further exploration. Apparently, I was about to enter a remote realm of dangerous mysteries where any further ignorance could potentially bring real harm to myself and others.

For too long Mom's fables, like our neighbors and native relatives to the south, remained courteously neglected. How did I get so deracinated from my motherland and from myself?

Birds and cats scattered as my rental car pulled up the long driveway. Mom rushed out to give me a big hug. For that fleeting moment, I was home again. There was so much to talk about, but we only had a short while to dig up any useful information for the journey ahead. My Mom is the ultimate storyteller and collector, perfectly suited for her job as the curator of a local history museum. Unfortunately for Dad, who passed away recently, every item of memorabilia she ever came across was cherished and collected until the garage door bulged.

As soon as I asked about La Palabra de Dios her face grew pale. Shuffling through dusty piles of priceless junk, she finally found what she was looking for. Together we struggled to lift a heavy stone sword onto a nearby table. While capturing the object with my cell phone I asked, "Why would a short sword like this be so heavy and made of stone?"

Mom explained, "This is called a Macana. It was used by the Aztecs to stun their prisoners with this blunt tip, so they could be sacrificed later to their gods. You can see here the handle is made of wood; the blade was probably made of wood too. For some reason most of it has turned to stone." Over the ages it had obviously become petrified.

On one side of the sword near the hilt was a small inscription which read, "La Palabra de Dios." On the other side were several symbols or designs that just looked like some unrecognizable ancient hieroglyphics to me. A red light came on as my phone began recording the anecdotes of my mother's childhood memories, "Anyway," she went on, "this pre-Columbian sword came from the place where your grandmother was born. There were so many beautiful, cascading waterfalls there when we went many years ago. Everywhere you looked, lots of rivers in the Sierra de Durango, Mexico ..." An hour flew by like a minute. Regrettably I did not have any more time to hear her fantastic tales and rumors of a great war coming soon. RuMa had been there often, always taking time to listen to my mom's stories, and she probably even believed some of them—but I never could.

Soon it was time to meet with Mark, just a short drive from my parents' house. This would be my last chance to convince him that he had to come along with me. At the very least, I needed to find out much more about the technical aspects of RuMa's expedition.

Mark's background as a chemical engineer gave him a solid understanding of the many facets of his sister's work. With his wife and kids out for the day, the place was less chaotic. Over the years we had been on a lot of backpacking adventures together in the Sierras of California, so I knew where he kept most of his lightest camping gear. This international adventure however, would not allow for many of the amenities we had grown used to such as huge pop-up tents, propane stoves and Bowie knives.

"Too bad I'd never get this across the border," I said as I came across one of the old classics.

"No way" he said, "but I do have something to wrap around that old sword . . ." his voice trailed off as he continued to dig through piles and drawers of stuff.

Except for the constant background buzz of traffic noise, it was relatively quiet for a place right under the LAX flight path. My departure time for Mazatlán was rapidly approaching, so there wasn't much time for small talk. Mark poured me a beer as we packed a few more items he thought necessary for the trek. He also came across a few photographs of RuMa standing next to some skeletal remains that she found on her first visit to a proposed church site in Durango, Mexico.

"So, on the phone you told me you had some more stories about that mission trip you went on last year with your sister." Flipping through the incredible photos of what seemed to be a fairly complete skeleton, I asked, "Why didn't she tell anyone she was going back?"

"You know how she is, once she gets an idea in her head she just goes with it. I was just as surprised as you were to hear that she may be down there again.

"So how did she find these old bones?" I asked.

"Actually, it seems more like *they* found *her*. When we went down to work on the new church near El Rodeo, we kept hearing about a big cenote not too far from the construction site and since none of us had ever seen one before, we asked some of the natives to take us to it. We had a great time. Probably one of the most amazing things I've ever seen." Mark noticed the puzzled look on my face, so I didn't even have to ask what a cenote is.

"A cenote," he explained, "is a natural sinkhole that gets exposed to the groundwater underneath, usually when limestone collapses above it. That's where we came across this group of scientists digging and diving for something. Here, check this one out." He handed me another incredible photograph of the cenote they explored the prior year. A spotlight through the ceiling of this cave shone brightly into an aqua and tourmaline pool below.

"I'm not sure what they were looking for, but on one of our hikes, we found some old bones in a washed-out ravine. This is Grace Nakamoto." He pointed to the attractive Japanese lady in a safari hat, khaki pants, and sunglasses, hugging RuMa in a photo taken beside some important find, "I'm sure you've heard about how crazy that was for us to meet her there out in the middle of nowhere and find out that she was a paleontologist from here in Southern California. When she heard about this possible skeleton find, she was pretty interested. They called this place the Valley of Dry Bones. I couldn't believe how fast news traveled there without cell phones. Anyway, Grace did some digging and thought it might be some kind of animal she had never seen before."

Walking back to his garage, Mark lowered his voice, as if he didn't want the cars to overhear, "Do you ever think about going back to church? I mean, they really could have used your writing skills on this project." He knew that in addition to development consulting, I also enjoyed creative writing for local magazines and newspapers.

A few months earlier, Mark encouraged me to attend some early morning Bible studies as a way of healing from years of chronic depression. RuMa also coaxed me to see a local pastor for the resulting anger issues. That pastor asked me to try some creative writing for the church, but I wasn't even ready to take a short hop of faith, let alone a giant leap. Instead, I poured any writing abilities into my day job as an attempt to recover a once peaceful soul.

Mark realized I was not up for any further church chat, "You know I would go with you to Durango if I could, but there is absolutely no way we can get a full-time sitter for who knows how long; and even if we could, you probably have the best chance of rescuing my sister if you go alone. A gringo like me would stick out like a sore thumb. And even though this would make a great story, you probably don't want to attract too much attention. If the local banditos or Federales figure out what you're up to, they just might follow you to RuMa and that won't make for a very happy ending."

Mark continued, "We heard so many strange legends that even the local people were frightened by the idea of outsiders building a new church. In fact, the priests down there perpetuate some pretty crazy fables just to keep their flock from heading for the hills, if you know what I mean."

This was not news to me. As a kid, I heard some wildly insane stories from my grandmother. Mark said, "For a long time, I used to think your mom's stories were just made up by the drug cartels to keep curiosity seekers away from their crops - but here, take a look at this." He showed me a news clipping with a yellow highlighted conclusion that I read aloud, "Experts believe that the recent skeletal find may be of this prehistoric animal over 260 million years old; however, further tests are still pending."

"Apparently," Mark said, "RuMa went back to help Grace find the first-ever Gorgonopsian skeleton on this continent."

Walking back into the kitchen, I spotted a dark-covered book with the picture of some hideous skeleton on the cover, "What kind of dinosaur is this?"

"Oh, that's a Gorgonopsian. That's what RuMa and Grace are looking for in Mexico."

"So, what exactly is this gorga . . . gorgi-nopsian your sister is looking for?" I asked. He picked up the book and handed it over to me. On the cover was the skeleton of a frightening creature crouching beneath an orange moon.

"They're called Gorgons for short, but they were around way before dinosaurs." I began to read the short description on the back. Since they existed so long ago, they belonged to an assemblage of land animals completely unknown to modern culture. They were mammal-like reptiles; carnivores about the size of a big lion, with huge heads, lizard eyes and a long tail. They also had saber-like teeth and claws like those of a wolf.

"At any rate," Mark said, "here is Ron's cell number. He said not to call unless it's an absolute emergency, but he will meet you at The End of the World tonight at 9 p.m. It's a bar down in Mazatlán where he can tell you the rest of the story."

As it turns out, Ron was an old fraternity brother of mine who also happened to be married to RuMa's new best friend, Grace.

"Whatever the latest news is about RuMa. I'm telling you Alan, they must have found something pretty weird, because he didn't even want to talk to me about it on the phone."

"RuMa didn't want anybody to know about this, but she's been working with some of the bigwigs at your old alma mater, because she's probably one of the few expert rock climbers in the world with a PhD in archaeology and tons of deep-water diving experience. I guess they were trying to reach a fairly complete and well-preserved specimen that's inside a really deep cave."

"How deep are we talking?" I asked.

"She mentioned one crater that's about 350 feet, but inside that there's another steep drop that leads into a whole series of chambers and sumps over a mile deep. They're pretty close to setting some kind of record for depth but the re-breathers can just barely keep up with their depths and dive times."

"I don't get it, Mark. What makes this discovery so important that people are willing to risk their lives over it?"

"Well, if you read the book you'll see how they thought this animal might provide some clues as to what caused the mass extinction of life on Earth 250 million years ago." Mark noticed my interest waning, "The thing is, Grace wasn't so sure what they found really was an ancient discovery."

"What do you mean?" Suddenly, he had my full attention again.

"Well, we probably won't know for a few more weeks, but based on some of the information that she got from RuMa, Grace thought the remains could be less than 100 years old."

"What!?! That doesn't make any sense. Can I borrow this book for a while?"

"Sure. Take it with you."

"Thanks!"

In early spring, the best way to catch up with RuMa would have been via helicopter from Culiacan; but a foreigner with any kind of money or expensive equipment would draw too much attention. Even the laptop would have to stay behind for this adventure. Not to mention, my budget was paper-thin.

We finally agreed that a better method would be to slip into the high country as quietly as possible, like some aimless tourist or a lost soul returning to visit family, friends, and ancient roots. Indeed, that was more truth than fiction. Though many of my relatives were still there, I had never met one in person.

The long wait in the airport gave me time to read up on the Gorgon. According to the book, Gorgons ruled the world long before the Age of Dinosaurs. They were the T. Rex of their day until an environmental cataclysm 250 million years ago annihilated them, along with 90 percent of all plants and animal species on the planet, "in an event so terrible even the extinction of the dinosaurs pales in comparison."

What exactly was I getting into here? The picture on the cover was hideous but what must it have been like to encounter one of these monsters face to face?

The flight from L.A. to Mazatlán lasted only a few hours, but it gave me a chance to prepare for the terrain ahead. The Colorado River, from its mighty origin in the Rockies, faded to a trickle as it stretched toward the Gulf of California below. Depleted by millions of manicured lawns, the flow trickled into dust and sand before it could reach the Sea of Cortez. The sand was the color of a pale gray corpse drained of all life and trampled by scores of dream seekers. Most dreamers were heading in the opposite direction of my flight.

The plane was scheduled to land in Mexico soon, but the ground still showed no signs of life. A few fishing boats cut white swathes into the distant Gulf waters. Then, as we began our descent, giant figures began to emerge from the sand. At first, they appeared ominous and foreboding, either warning or taunting me. The foothills of the Sierra Madre Occidental finally appeared out of the haze. It was hard to believe these desolate mountains were the same Sierras that fork northward into the crowded Sierra Nevada and Rocky Mountains I knew so well. Eventually, the dry landscape gave way to the tropical images of Canary Island date trees and cabbage palmettos.

There was a gentle rumble as the landing gear unfolded below. Somewhere out there, RuMa may be hiding in some deep, dark cave, waiting for a hero to save her life. What was she thinking?

3

Sunday Evening — Mazatlán, Mexico

I ARRIVED ALONE IN Mazatlán with only *muy poquito* (very little) Spanish, and a distant uncle's telephone number. There was hardly enough time to notice that the beach was magnificent. Frigate birds soared like colossal fork-tailed kites above the surf as the sun set behind Bird Island.

A cab driver from the airport took me directly to the Chilean-themed restaurant at the end of the bay called *Fin Del Mundo* (End of the World). No matter how urgent the situation, there were no buses to Culiacan until tomorrow, so this new environment required me to take a deep breath and slow down for just a bit.

It was obviously a favorite watering hole for expats, and although there were a few authentic-looking dishes on the menu, they were playing country music and served a house drink called Make Me Disappear. Ron Nakamoto was the only Asian guy in the bar, so he was easy enough to find. After sharing a few intense beer stories with this fellow Trojan alumnus, about his recent encounters with El Narco, I began to understand why we couldn't just rush in to rescue our wives without a small militia.

Instead, we decided that I should go into the Sierra as soon as possible with the one local guide, as recommended by Father

Arres. Meanwhile, Ron would get back to the States to round up a better-equipped search party if necessary.

Ron said, "It could take me a few days, weeks, or even months to get enough support and firepower to attempt a rescue mission with the help of U.S. law enforcement, but by then the girls could be . . ." then he paused to consider the gravity of his next word ". . . dead."

Ron's countenance was grim but determined. He had spent the last several days just trying to get himself out of the country, and this was as far as he had come.

"So here is what the girls are facing up there, Alan. Some of the locals know that Grace and RuMa have been hunting for the skeleton of a Gorgon, but as you may know, there is also a legend that suggests that along with the remains of an ancient red dragon, there also lies the treasures of El Dorado."

To me that was just another one of my Mom's old wives' tales, so my response was nil. Then Ron added a new twist, "The problem is, the girls just discovered a scroll that gave them a pretty good clue as to where the Red Dragon rests and that news leaked out to a few of the locals. Now all of a sudden, the gangster warlords in the area are quite interested in this expedition. Of course, not only do they want the fame and fortune of discovering the gold; more importantly, they don't want anyone else coming into their territory to find all the illegal junk they produce in there. Either way, the girls are in big trouble. When I left them about ten days ago, we agreed to meet again at a certain cave that is only known by a few of our friends in the church who will keep their secret safe."

"So, if they are in a safe place, what's the big hurry to get there?" I asked.

Ron was all business now, "The caldera where they are hidden is a natural cauldron that has been slowly filling with boiling hot water from an underground spring, and based on the recent weather reports, there is a pretty good chance they could be flooded out within the next few days. Once they are out in the open, the locals will have no mercy. Everyone wants that treasure."

"Including the girls, right?" I asked cynically.

"Of course," Ron replied frankly. "A find like that would float their research for decades. But here is the really ironic thing. In addition to Federales, drug cartels, local bandits, and boiling waters, the very thing they are looking for may find them first ..."

"What are you talking about?" I asked.

Now Ron leaned in, and as quietly and seriously as possible said to me, "Grace thinks that some of the fecal matter they found in the cave they're studying may be from a living Gorgonopsia."

I was completely stupefied. Shooting upright in my chair, I shouted uncontrollably. "Holy crap!" A few people glanced at us for second, but for the most part, in this raucous place, it was still just another warm evening on the beach.

For the next hour or so, we tried to calm down by puffing Cuban cigars as we reviewed plans carefully. He was eager to see La Palabra, but I told him that since it could be considered a weapon, we had to disguise it as a toy and send it directly to the church in Tamazula. Luckily, Mark had a friend at the airport who was able to get it on board the same flight I was on.

When Ron looked at the picture of the sword on my cell phone, he seemed fascinated but confused. He was a business major like me, so we had no idea how these symbols could translate into fame or fortune for anyone. At that point we were just trying to avoid any serious misfortunes.

Ron said, "Those hills look like Swiss cheese from all the mining done over the years so I'm not sure exactly how to find them, but the priest should be able to direct you to La Caldera."

Ron needed to draw a map on something so that I might be able to find the right caldera in case anything happened to my guide. Apparently, there were more than a few calderas in that area. The best thing I had was a napkin in my pocket from the airplane.

As our Romeo and Julietas began to burn out, so did we. It was time to get some rest for the journeys ahead. When Ron finished up his map and handed the napkin back to me, the ground began to rumble and sway gently. Looking around we noticed lamps swaying and heard liquor bottles clinking. No one seemed nervous, as most of the patrons were already swaying gently. Ron said calmly, "Oh that reminds me, I almost forgot to tell you, this *X* where the girls are may be a dormant volcano. With all this seismic activity lately, some people are thinking La Caldera may be coming back to life."

On the way out, I wrote RuMa's name on a dollar bill and put it on the wall with all the others. Hopefully, she'll be here with me next time we come back to the bar at the Fin del Mundo.

4

Monday — Sinaloa, Mexico

EARLY THE NEXT MORNING I took an open-air cab to the bus station for a three-hour ride northward to Culiacan, capital of the Mexican state of Sinaloa. Always mindful of social and economic linkages, on the way to Culiacan I noticed that in addition to being a major hub for drug traffic, the city is also a rail junction and commercial center for nearby gold, silver, copper, and cobalt mines. There was also a huge variety of tobacco, fruits, and vegetables being exported from the surrounding areas.

Along the smoggy, dusty route, a group of the dreaded local policia stopped our bus. One stout officer came aboard and asked a young family from the back to step off the bus. I watched anxiously as the group in ragged uniforms outside my window interrogated our fellow bus passengers with great vigor.

The policia came aboard again and looked right at me before turning abruptly to the man in the seat across from mine. The barrel of the machine gun strapped loosely to his chest was now pointing directly at me. Apparently growing up in East Los Angeles and having guns and knives pointed at me on several occasions helped me remain calm.

Eventually the police allowed the young family back on the bus and it was my turn to show papers. The California birthplace raised an eyebrow and he told me to get off the bus. When I hesitated, he began to tap the rifle stock. Outside there was a brief debate with his superior, but since I wasn't carrying much cash and the passport was in order, the voyage proceeded without further incident.

Luckily, they didn't check the seat in front of me where I stuffed the napkin with the identification of La Caldera on it. Seemed like in order to get to the *X* on the map, there may be many more perils to face soon.

Reading what was printed on the front side of the napkin made me laugh, "*El que quiera azul celeste, que le cueste.*" The rough translation printed below said, "You have to work for what you want." To me it sounded more like, "If you ever want to see blue skies again, it's gonna cost you."

***

Upon arriving at the bus station in Culiacan, I placed one local call, and my cousin Jose appeared so quickly it was startling. Though we had never met, he spotted me immediately and it was obvious he was a Rios. When our similar dark brown eyes met for the first time, even from a distance our thick wavy hair and long eyelashes gave us away to each other instantly.

He called out "Señor Martín?" It almost sounded more like a statement than a question so as soon as he finished introducing himself formally I said, "Please, you can call me Al."

In this bustling city of almost 800,000 people, there were so many intriguing ancient and modern things to see. Yet, when a big flatbed truck full of military men in black face masks and full body armor pulled up alongside us, Jose warned me not to make direct eye contact.

By then the outside temperature was over 95 degrees Fahrenheit, and I just had to take a quick peek at the intriguing soldiers apparently preparing for some type of skirmish. At a glance I remember seeing fear peering out through the eye holes of a few, but intense bravado glaring from most. Black automatic rifles glistened in the perspiring hands holding them. When one soldier turned in our direction I immediately returned my focus to the map book in my lap.

For a long while I pondered what that soldier may have been thinking. Where was he going and why? Though our DNA may be similar, that man's life was so different from mine, it was hard to imagine the world from his perspective. He probably had a wife and children waiting at home. What motivates a man to dedicate his life to the destruction of another? Is it a sincere quest for righteousness, a paycheck, or something as evil as pride? The truck lights came on and let out a loud whooping siren to move traffic out of its way. The masked raiders rolled hastily on to battle or perhaps some other charade in a civil war against the sorcery of narcotics.

On the way back to his house, Jose pointed out a few points of interest as we crossed the bridge where the Tamazula and Humaya Rivers come together to form the Rio Culiacan. It was great to finally meet the welcoming faces of so many cousins. Their two-story home was immaculate. Jose's family lived on the ground floor with extended family on the second level. The younger children arriving home from school were all dressed in uniforms, and they spoke perfect English as well as their musical native Spanish. Their physical beauty went beyond my mother's descriptions. They all had olive skin and warm brown eyes unspoiled by any unfulfilled dreams. Their courtesy and hospitality went far beyond expectation.

It did not take long before a delicious meal was served: steak with rice, beans, fresh salsa and corn tortillas. Of course, in order to avoid any suspicious water, it all had to be washed down with a local cerveza. The raucous family gathering reminded me of the happier days of my childhood in Los Angeles where I grew up in my grandmother's Mexican restaurant, Rosita's Café.

Jose wanted to know all about how my family was doing and we both bragged about our kids for a long while. They already knew how worried I was about RuMa's safety and how we had grown apart lately. For some reason, she always had a special affinity for my family in Mexico and spent a generous amount of time with them whenever she could. In many ways, she was much closer to them than I was.

Jose also wanted to know more about where RuMa was and when I planned to see her again. Aside from the truth of not knowing exactly where she was, my feeling was that the less Jose and his family knew about what was about to happen beyond Tamazula, the better.

Following the meal and friendly conversation, we had to make plans for our trip on the following day. My specific destination could not be located on any map. The AAA guide only described the area as "NOT RECOMMENDED FOR TRAVEL." Still I felt led to go there, even if some family members acquainted with the terrain wondered aloud, "Why?"

Jose's daughter, Dora, arranged for the next day off from her job at the bank to drive us up to Tamazula. She said her little blue car had been overheating lately, "But I think it should make it there and back."

The only one who really wanted to go on this venture was one of Jose's little granddaughters named Blanquita. She was petting a lifeless white dove found earlier that day in the street. Blanquita's lovely aunt, Dora, kept telling her over and over, "Take that outside." The little girl could not accept that her new pet was not going to awaken any time soon.

Just then the room gave a little shimmy and candles on the ofrenda clanked gently. The gentle quake was not enough to cause any damage other than rattling a few nerves.

"Aye Dios Mio!" Dora shrieked.

The ofrenda is a colorful offering altar where Mexican families honor Jesus and their deceased love ones. Typically, this is done with a crucifix, portraits, statuettes of various saints, the Virgin Mary, pictures, candles, and flowers. On the Dia de los Muertos (Day of the Dead) one tier is covered with the deceased person's favorite food, drink or other gifts.

Blanquita was not startled at all by the tremor. Instead she took great solace in her aunt's promise to place a picture of the white dove upon the ofrenda. Though their reverence to family traditions was quite impressive, such blind faith in archaic rituals made me a bit uncomfortable.

When the kids were finally all asleep, Dora and one of her sisters paraded down the stairs in their party dresses, ready for a night on the town. They invited me to join them, but I was exhausted just watching them strut across the room in such short skirts and high heels. I tried not to stare at the revealing necklines, but just like the soldiers in the truck Jose warned me about that afternoon, these girls were dressed to kill. Their long, lean dancing legs, playful eyes, and bright lipstick made me miss RuMa even more.

"Don't be out late!" Jose called to them as they pranced out the door. "We have to leave early!" Jose said they would not go beyond the church at Tamazula. I would have to learn on my own why not, later.

5

Tuesday Morning —
Tamazula de Victoria, Mexico

EARLY THE NEXT MORNING, Dora drove Jose and I up to the small town of Tamazula de Victoria. Scenery along the way changed dramatically from the bustling city of Culiacan with its diesel buses and towering cathedrals to humbler populations and outdated thorps. Incredible tropical plants and birds appeared unlike any I'd ever seen before. Crested caracaras, white-winged doves, and astounding black-shouldered magpie jays flew about freely in abundance. Huge iguanas strolled casually back and forth across the hot pavement. I was definitely not in Colorado any more.

As the highway began to climb, so did the temperature, and suddenly a bright red engine light appeared on the dash board. I won't translate exactly what Dora said in Spanish; however, she was not happy to say that we needed to pull over right away. Fortunately, today Dora was dressed in an inconspicuous baseball cap, dark sunglasses, old jeans, and a long-sleeve shirt. Jose quickly helped her find the extra water and coolant fluid containers that he'd wisely packed in the trunk. They insisted that I stay in the car and within a few seemingly endless minutes, we were back on the road again.

Far beyond La Presa Sanalona reservoir, we inevitably came to the small town where this story all began generations ago. Tamazula is where my great-grandmother Dionicia first learned to dance. On special occasions, she performed at a pavilion in the center of the plaza. For some reason, the brightly colored tropical trees and flowers surrounding the plaza felt like home.

The town was named after the first President of Mexico, General Guadalupe Victoria. Before then, it was a part of New Spain known as Nueva Vizcaya. It is the gateway into a long narrow valley that leads to the base of the High Sierras beyond.

Narrowing streets led us straight to the little church beside a small lagoon full of croaking toads. Inside we found Father Arres kneeling alone before the altar. The smell of incense in the tiny cathedral reminded me of a smaller version of Junipero Serra's first missions along the California coast.

Those churches seemed built for exhibition. This building was not for show. This was strictly a place for worship and deep prayer, the kinds of petitions that cry out for a response. Though I had appraised many churches with greater monetary value, this one seemed to have a deeper intrinsic value than most.

The altar showed no signs of gold or conquest. Still there was richness in the aging walls; the texture of the wooden pews and the interior light were stained by colorful glass. Each Rios dipped their fingers into the holy water and crossed themselves before bowing deeply. Though familiar with all these rituals, I followed clumsily from the narthex into the nave.

When Father Arres finally noticed us standing nearby he rose slowly. Though we had never met, he greeted me warmly with both hands, "Señor Marteen, mucho gusto, y bienvenidos a Tamazula." His smile broke down all language barriers and we embraced as though we had known each other forever.

He told us that he came to this town over forty years ago from the upper valley and it took much effort to get the building restored to its present condition. Floods, earthquakes and ages of neglect had taken their toll on the stones that held these walls together.

Now in his frail years, he said that he knew my grandmother Rosita Coronel Rios very well and even her parents, my great-grandparents, Dionicia and Francisco Coronel. As we strolled across the plaza, Father Arres pointed out the school where Jose Rios used to teach many years ago.

In Spanish, the word, *rios* means rivers. The town of Tamazula lies near the union of several large rivers, including the Tamazula, the Humaya, the Sianori, and their many tributaries. The family name was so prevalent that walking through town we needed to stop several times to meet distant cousins in their brightly colored adobe buildings. Everyone was preparing to celebrate El Grito de Dolores (Mexico's celebration of independence from Spain). Dora and Jose however, were eager to get back home before dark. Soon after a heartfelt hug goodbye, they departed in hopes of a cooler engine for the downhill drive home to Culiacan.

Father Arres and I continued walking slowly together back towards the church. At a small café, we sat down for a cup of coffee and began to prepare for the journey ahead. Although his English was fairly good, I tried to speak in Spanish whenever possible, to the best of my ability.

While my first concern was to find RuMa, Father Arres seemed more interested in learning more about me. He was especially inquisitive regarding my disillusionment with the church and life in general. Something was certainly absent from my soul, and the father must have immediately sensed that misplaced spirit. He stared at me quietly for a long while, then said, "Before you go up to look for RuMa, your personal beliefs must be strong." Struggling for the right words in English, the father asked, "What will you be taking with you as your deliverance?

I wasn't exactly sure what he was asking for but took a shot at an answer anyway. "Well, I was baptized in the Catholic Church and made my communion when I was about eight. After I got confirmed and married we went to a Christian church for a while."

"No, I'm not interested in your religion, tell me what you believe in your heart to be your true salvation. For example, who do you believe Jesus was?"

"Father, I know who Jesus was. I've read the Bible, but I just don't understand what that has to do with the story of my life. What kind of god would put me through what I've suffered in the last few years?"

By then I had already shared the recent loss of my father to cancer and a younger brother to some inexplicable mental illness.

"I am a sinner. I know that. I've confessed my sins to priests before. I've even prayed for forgiveness directly to Jesus, but it just didn't work. There is no response, and we are not growing any closer. I'm not getting better, only angrier. One doctor said that I may have something called Dysthymia or PDD, which stands for Persistent Depressive Disorder."

I'm not sure if the priest completely understood as he replied, "Your RuMa was missing something in her heart also."

Of course, I already knew that. I had failed to provide her with the financial security or emotional peace she always struggled to find in our relationship. Now I had to at least attempt to find some way to bridge the years of separation between us. Perhaps the old priest was much more discerning than I thought.

It seemed like forever before we finally got around to talking about my most pressing dilemma: How in the world was I ever going to be able to rescue the joy of my life?

"So, please tell me, Father, what have you heard about RuMa?"

Padre Arres recognized my growing impatience and said, "Aha, yes. Thank you for sharing your anxious thoughts with me. It sounds as though your heart is suffering a great deal and from that sorrow, you may be growing closer to Jesus than you realize. I did spend a brief time with RuMa about two weeks ago. She came into my church and wanted to know all about your family history. She insisted on visiting a certain cave near El Espinazo Del Diablo (The Devil's Backbone) that is very deep and dangerous. I warned her not to go there, but she went anyway."

"Do you know anything about the body that was reported near the El Rodeo church site?" I asked.

The amiable tone in the cleric's voice subsided, and eye contact was lost. "No, sometimes people here get confused when reporters ask questions, or they mix one story with another. RuMa was fine when I saw her last. A messenger that arrived here just a few days ago from near El Espinazo said that RuMa and her friend Grace did make it to La Caldera, and the remains found near the church could be of a distant relative. But who knows; in that area bodies are found in ravines and caves all the time. That is not uncommon. If all went well, RuMa should be back to her hiding place by now. She had to escape from some desperados that have been threatening her and Grace. Tonight, after the sun sets, Gabriel will begin guiding you towards La Caldera. He is a strong Rarámuri and one of my brightest acolytes. He will make sure that you stay on the pathway of blessing. The Rarámuri or Tarahumara, are known as 'those with light feet'. In fact, your great-grandmother Dionicia was an indigenous Tarahumara. They are well known for their long-distance running ability. I would love to go myself, but the flesh is weak."

At his age, the father's ability to get around town was impressive. Given my very limited equestrian skills, I was more than a little worried about getting myself over the obstinate-looking mountains that even the locals feared. He said that "To get to the Caldera, you must take a detour through El Rodeo (which means a roundabout way or evasion in Spanish). It's the safest way.

"Do you see those mountains way over there?" He pointed to a chain of peaks far off on the horizon to the northeast. "Oh, yes," I replied.

"That is called El Reino del Cielo (The Kingdom of Heaven) and the Caldera is right below that. Hopefully you won't find any more bodies on your way there or back."

At first that seemed like an odd thing for the priest to say, then considering the volume of narcotics produced in Mexico it's no mystery why so many bodies are lost and found in this remote locale. For further clarification I had to ask, "How serious is the drug problem up there now?"

The priest replied somberly. "For a long time, the valley was quiet, but now the descendants of a man named Ismael Bertran have returned and they are producing an incredible amount of contraband. I've heard they built a private airfield somewhere up there, but most good people do not go beyond El Rodeo any longer."

"So, Father, please tell me how RuMa and Grace ended up in this Caldera. Weren't they supposed to be building a church?"

Padre Arres then went into more detail on the little side trip that became a huge distraction from their original mission.

"At first, she was just curious, but once RuMa found the bones, everything changed. That other lady, Grace went nuts—*loca!*

"We heard they were still doing some more tests or diving but my young scout Gabriel, who was working with them for a while as a guide had to get back. He said there were other items in one cave that she wanted you to have but needs to explain their meaning to you directly."

The priest lowered his voice to barely a whisper and said, "The cave where she is hidden is called, The Devil's Cauldron. Gabriel knows exactly where that is, and the Palabra that you sent should provide him with the details he needs to help RuMa and Grace find what they are looking for. By the way, your package arrived at the church this morning, just a few hours before you did. I'm looking forward to opening it with you."

Before our coffee cups could empty, they were filled again and again. I tried to learn as much as possible about the logistics of getting in and out of the Caldera; however, Father Arres seemed more concerned about my state of mind, "Before you travel out into the Sierra, it's very important that you not only understand *what* you believe, but also *why* you believe—because your faith *will* be tested. What is it that you truly seek here in Durango?"

There are some questions we may never be able to answer in this lifetime. I was only hoping to rescue the beauty of my life. Seeing that I could never answer that question, Father Arres continued, "If you are only here for your own purposes, you will never find your wife or whatever prize you pursue. However, if you seek first the Kingdom of God, then you will find victory. Sometimes to fully understand what we believe, we must step into the darkness for a while to find our purpose and bring light to others." He paused to let that sink in for a moment before continuing, "What will you do if you discover that everything you now believe is wrong?"

The sun was falling fast, so we began the slow walk back to the small, dark rectory of the church where Father Arres had stowed the package containing La Palabra. As my departure time was rapidly approaching, we unwrapped the box with great anticipation. The stone sword was wrapped in foil and shaped into a giant candy cane, with a few toy car wheels and Bibles for diversion. Carefully peeling back each layer of wrapping we were both overjoyed to find that the Palabra was completely unharmed in its travels.

After carefully placing the sword into my pack, we walked to the edge of town where we had to cross a long, swaying rope bridge over the Tamazula River to meet Gabriel. Ahead of us in the distance his trumpet sounded a greeting call for our arrival. The shanty where he lived alone on the far side of the river was built into the side of a hill and covered in palm leaves. Surrounded by a tiny corral full of animals, his home was almost invisible until we walked through the gate. In addition to chickens, a goat, and a few small pigs in a smaller enclosure, there were three mules, a jack donkey, and one tall white horse that kept every other animal at a distance.

El Padre introduced me to the sturdy young man who would guide me into the Devil's Cauldron. As he dusted himself off and shook my hand, I was going to say that he reminded me a bit of Enrique Iglesias, but he didn't seem like the type to be affected by any Hollywood hero. His greatest concern in life at that moment seemed to be the disturbing behavior of his honeybees. He motioned us over to one of the hives where he was closely studying their activities.

"For some reason, Padre" Gabriel said, "the bees are not buzzing properly this year. They're not huddling around their queen the way they usually do. Father, why are they not preparing for winter?" He seemed inordinately despondent over their performance. To me there were so many more important questions to answer.

For example, how was my grandmother ever able to leave such a desolate yet captivating place in order to raise a family in the United States? Father Arres alone was uniquely qualified to answer all my questions, as he knew my grandmother well when she was a precocious young girl growing up in this challenging environment.

Father Arres sensed my growing excitement as we prepared three mules for the journey. Gabriel took the frayed rope bridle of the first animal in the line and called him by the name of Reno. The tall and fiery sorrel stud mule carried the heaviest load.

The second in line was my dusty black molly with no name. She had a makeshift sheath of some sort for La Palabra on her right saddle bag. The third and smallest mule in our convoy was a pale gray mule named Palomita. She had a feathery, light brown tuft of fur rising from the center of her head and followed us dutifully out the gate.

Wrongly assuming the last mule was for RuMa, I wondered out loud. "Why aren't we taking another mule for Grace?"

Gabriel then informed me that Palomita was for Grace. RuMa would ride my mule on the way down. Though Gabriel planned to ride Reno on the way up, he said that he would rather walk or run on the way back. Later I learned that while mules can cover this terrain at an average speed of about two miles per hour, a well-conditioned Tarahumara could travel on foot at around six miles per hour. At that pace, I would most certainly be riding Reno on the way back.

Before we went any further, El Padre reminded us that "There is only one true Pathway of Blessing to stay upon. In order to succeed on this journey, you must first understand where you came from. I can only begin to prepare you for the journey ahead. If at any time you are not sure where you are or what you are doing here, trust in the Lord with all your heart and let him be your guide. Gabriel knows the more recent history of your family very well, so he can share the rest of the account with you along the way."

As the shadows began to lengthen, we gathered around a table near a patch of grass where the three mules nibbled serenely on the fuel for their journey. To make best use of the cover of darkness we had to wait at least another hour or two. Luckily, I took enough micro memory for my phone to store the entire story that Father Arres was about to tell.

I have to admit that due to some choppy language along the way, a few liberties were taken in transcribing my notes and tapes into the pages you are about to read. However, as Father Arres began to relate the incredible history of my family with seemingly complete omniscience, it was almost as if the nearby rivers were speaking directly to me. Finally, there would be a clear purpose to wake up in the morning - a battle to fight, a beauty to rescue, an adventure to live and a story to tell.

"Alan, in 1910, your grandmother was only six years old; yet she told me later in her life that even then she often wondered, 'What am I doing here?'"

Through this Rios tale, my past and future were finally about to be revealed . . .

6

The Spring of 1910—La Galancita, Durango, Mexico

"WHAT AM I DOING here?" Rosita used to ask her mother. Staring out the kitchen window towards the rising sun, Rosita always wanted to know what hovered beyond that glowing horizon. Each day, as distant waterfalls slowly emerged from the peaks of El Reino, roosters woke everyone up to watch God paint the Durango sky.

"Mama is every morning always going to be the same?"

Before Dionicia could answer, her daughter already had another question, "Don't you think those peaks of El Espinazo look like sharp teeth trying to take a bite out of the sky?"

Dionicia, too, wondered what the icy mountain caps might feel like as she dried her hands on a soft, freshly pressed apron, brighter than the snow she never held.

Rosita's auburn tresses were already long and wispy like her mother's. Washing their hands together before preparing breakfast was a ritual they shared every day. Their long thin arms worked together like sinewy branches of the great crystal willows standing proudly at the entrance to La Galancita, the hacienda where the Coronels lived.

Beyond the courtyard, several rows of poplars drank from the rivers and streams flowing around La Galancita. Currents whispered through the property, babbling back and forth between themselves, always arriving, never leaving. Their minerals nourished brightly colored poppies and the green gardens that provided an endless variety of fresh vegetables and exotic fruits. Bright morning glories climbed the thick and sturdy adobe walls bordering the hacienda.

Far beyond those walls in Mexico City, the nation prepared to celebrate its 100th anniversary. After surviving 50 military regime changes in its first dozen years of independence from Spain, Mexico hoped for a belle époque. Plans were made for a series of 16th of September centenary fiestas, including parades, banquets, and lavish balls. But the Porfiriato was over, and little did the country realize that it was about to undergo another great revolutionary period.

Every age of innocence is fleeting. Rosita was too young to understand the reason for all the pomp and circumstance taking place, but she was sensitive to the magnitude of events going on in a world beyond her reach. In this remote tropical village of the high Sierras she felt isolated from society, detached from all the big cities and happenings she could only read about in school books or newspapers.

Yet, she was old enough to understand that the most important things in life were: food, family and faith. Her father taught the family all about faith. Her mother taught about preparing the meals and without faith or food, there could be no family. Thus, family was always at the center of their civilization.

The crisp autumn air in the kitchen was thick with apples and cinnamon. Hot empanadas stuffed with fresh fruit were set at each plate. Rosita's mother Dionicia warmed a separate batch for the men filled with beef for their day in the fields. She waddled carefully from the table and then back to the oven. Any day now she was expecting to deliver her tenth child.

When the scents of fresh chorizo and huevos rancheros escaped from the kitchen, they became irresistible to the younger children who began to stir. Three-year old Timoteo wobbled into the kitchen first, wiping his sleepy eyes as he crawled up to the table for a cup of ponche. "Where's my ponche?" he cried. The rich, thick breakfast drink of warm milk was whipped together with eggs, vanilla, honey, cinnamon, and other spices, but by far the most important ingredient in every family recipe was the love.

Dionicia's first child, Rosa, died shortly after birth from influenza. Mateo was the oldest of seven mischievous boys and, though he was only 10, he was already out helping his father, Francisco, saddle horses for the day.

Don Francisco Coronel was known to his friends as Cisco. He was an irreproachable man of great strength and intelligence, yet he also held a meek, quiet spirit. His favorite horse's name was Lily. She was a rare black Andalusian. Stronger and taller than most every other horse in the valley, Lily was a symbol of loveliness.

Unlike most other landowners in the area, Francisco was raised in the Lutheran tradition. He learned to read at an early age, and his greatest wish was for his own children to have even greater opportunities for a better education someday. When Francisco made his first communion at age seven, his father gave him the greatest gift. It was a Bible. Since it was the only book he owned until he was seventeen, he read it repeatedly. Francisco's German father taught him to speak German as well as English and Spanish. Therefore, Francisco's appetite for reading was insatiable when he finally had access to other books.

Some of the other gifts Francisco received from his father included a sharp acumen and thick, muscular limbs. He could reel in a stray calf and drop it to the ground in the blink of his thick eyelashes. Fair skin and bright blue eyes were some of the other attributes that attracted Dionicia to Francisco when they married just before the turn of the century.

Dionicia was prized for her loveliness. Her high cheekbones and dark bronze skin were typical of her Maya and Aztec ancestors. In youth, she had loved nature and its beauty. She was a renowned dancer in Tamazula and the townspeople there always enjoyed watching her perform on a stage built exactly to her liking. In Dionicia's upbringing, there were many gods. Since Francisco would not allow idolatry in his family, the Catholic Church provided her a tolerable compromise. Though many saints were revered, only one God was worshiped.

In a few more years, Mateo would be old enough to ride out on the range with his father to round up cattle for the big drives into town. In those days, there were no nearby rail lines, and the herds needed to be driven for at least 50 miles along the treacherous trails of the Espinazo down along the Rio Tamazula into Culiacan.

When the ice melted on the nearby peaks of the Espinazo, fresh streams would quickly swell and reach La Galancita. The wells then filled again and sang songs to quench the thirst of a long hot summer.

The jagged peaks of El Diablo were named for good reasons. The sheer faces of the Espinazo rise and fall thousands of feet on either side. Their steep cliffs and narrow trails were treacherous to negotiate for sure-footed burros; clumsy cattle were even more susceptible to an occasional tumble, so only the smartest creatures made it over the backbone to their summer feeding grounds.

Nevertheless, with such a large herd, the loss of a few animals was not a particular concern for a major hacendado, (landowner of a large farm, plantation or ranch) such as Don Francisco Coronel. With over 700 sheep, 300 cows, 150 bulls, 50 mules, and too many pigs, goats, sheep, chickens, and roosters to count, he felt truly blessed with one of the largest ranches in the entire state of Durango. In addition to the livestock, there were thousands of acres of land that Francisco held for grazing and raising feed throughout the foothills of the Durango Sierras.

More important than all the land and personal property, he had won the respect and favor of many of the other farmers and ranchers in the area. They all helped protect his fields and herds from the numerous opportunistic bandits roaming the hillsides. Throughout the country, Francisco's beef and milk products were known as the very best.

The Galancita was a hacienda of modest size built at the dawn of the 20th century. The children's favorite part of the structure was called the tapanco, a storage area above the house where dry fruits and candies were stored.

The days were long and hard, but the rewards were great. While many of the Coronel's neighbors suffered from recent economic downturns, Francisco was always able to provide for his own family, as well as those in need. There always seemed to be a protective hedge that kept La Galancita, a gallant place.

Don Coronel often hosted huge fiestas to honor his parents and in-laws whenever they came to visit. Since they lived in El Rodeo and Tamazula with other children and grandchildren, the elders only made it occasionally to La Galancita as their health and weather would allow.

The prior three years had been especially tough on the Mexican nation as a whole. So, when little Apolonio Rios came running into the kitchen from the hacienda up the hill, the lady of the Coronel household thought that perhaps even their most prosperous neighbors might need some assistance.

"Nicia! Nicia!" The dusty little Apolonio screeched. Though he was just a few months older than Rosita, he was already pretending to be a man, "Did you hear what happened last night?"

Dionicia prepared her table as the young man caught his breath and prepared to organize a sentence, "Papa saw a falling star crash into the mines last night and it made a loud explosion. Did you hear it?"

Young Apolonio's father owned the gold and silver mines hidden deep inside the base of El Diablo, not far from the Galancita. He also owned the mines on the opposite side of the valley known as Coluta. Although they weren't producing much rich ore lately, their lucky strikes from prior years still made the Rios family one of the wealthiest in the Sierras.

Apolonio was known as Api. He had two younger brothers named Lazaro and Miguel and they had two even younger sisters – Florentina and Juanita.

"What are you talking about Api?" Dionicia inquired casually.

"Didn't you feel it? Our whole house shook!" More animated than usual, little Timoteo nodded his head. This gave Dionicia pause to consider her own restless night.

Little Paulo and Pedro Coronel, ages 4 and 5, had been listening from their room nearby and joined their little brother for ponche at the table. Then they all chimed in together, "Yeah, Mama, I heard it," said one.

"I thought Señor Rios was working late," said another, "or maybe it was an earthquake?"

"No, no," Apolonio insisted "my father doesn't blast in the middle of the night, he was home. He only woke up because I saw the flash and woke up when it crashed into El Diablo."

Soon Juan, Lucas, and Marcos, ages 7, 8 and 9, were all up and clamoring on in the excitement of the mysterious big bang.

"What did it look like?" asked one of the older Coronel boys.

"How big was it?" asked another.

All the questions overwhelmed little Apolonio, but he sure enjoyed all the attention for a change. Even the wise young Rosita took a seat as she poured the last glass of ponche for her mother. Once Api could finally get a word in he said, "Papa told us that if we didn't behave and get back to sleep El Diablo himself may come back here to look for his gold."

Normally Rosita just thought of Apolonio as another one of the rascal boys, but he apparently had something of real interest to talk about. This was not going to be about frogs, ponies, or toy soldiers; this could be something important. Api was pleased to have everyone's attention now, especially Rosita's. He was just about to provide a full oration when little Timoteo burst into tears. He too awakened to the bright flash of light but was too afraid to tell anyone until then.

"I don't want El Diablo to come here," he cried "I'm almost four".

"Ohhh," Dionicia rushed to her youngest son and poured a portion of her remaining ponche into his empty cup. Though she could barely bend over, she was still able to give him just enough of a hug that he could feel her words, "El Diablo is nowhere near us mi hijito. Besides, La Virgen would never let anything bad happen to us. And look, Jesus and all his saints are here to protect us from all harm. You have nothing to fear."

As she waved her arm towards their ofrenda altar near the front door, the little boy could almost feel the warmth from all the candles. Then his mother's warm body collided with him. Finally, the hot, frothy ponche reached his tummy and the tears subsided.

The sweet, magical blend of all these gifts helped clear Timoteo's blurry little eyes. Food, family and faith. The kitchen's oven and nearby candles were second only to the warmth of his mother's passionate embrace. The natural ritual of the embrazo was an important part of the comforting relationships in this highly emotional and familial culture.

Apolonio temporarily lost his spotlight, but he was not interested in frightening his little neighbor any further. Instead, he quietly and calmly began to talk about how his father was planning an expedition into the mines today to find El Diablo.

Timoteo did not want to hear any more of this so he tucked his head under his mother's arm and held one open ear tight with his hand. Paulo and Pedro pretended to be brave, but they were wishing their mom had enough room under her other wing for the both of them. Juan, Lucas, and Marcos were beyond pretending to be brave. They were almost old enough to pretend they might want to join in the hunt for El Diablo. Rosita was barely amused at this point, but willing to listen if Api had something more to say on the subject.

"We don't know exactly where it landed, so Papa needs to make sure the mines are sealed tight and no bandits can steal our gold," Api explained.

Normally during this time of year, the mines were too cold and damp to work. Thunderstorms and flash floods could fill a cave in moments without warning. At the end of each summer, a team of mules rolled boulders in front of the cave entrance to deter bandits from pilfering during the winter.

"Does your father need any extra hands for his trip today Api?" Dionicia offered.

"I don't know, but he's leaving pretty soon. I must get home now. Maybe he'll let me go too." Seeing the fear in their eyes, Api just had to ask the oldest Coronel at the table, "How about you Marcos, do you want to come along?" Knowing what the answer would be, it was just one more chance to show some bravado in front of Rosita. "Me and my brothers will probably go. Only the girls are going to stay home."

"I have to milk some cows today, or else I would," said Marcos. Before any more challenges could be offered, Lucas and Juan both concurred that for once chores were more important than adventures. "Me too," they announced together. Pedro and Paulo cautiously began clearing their plates to the sink lest someone get the crazy idea that they might be old enough to ride up to the Espinazo. Timoteo just buried his head deeper and deeper into his mother's breast until he finally heard Apolonio move towards the door to leave.

"Oh well, if I get to see him, I'll tell you what he looks like." With that, Apolonio waved so long and slammed the door behind him. After all the commotion, the house was strangely still for a moment. Dionicia rocked Timoteo as she said in a soothing tone just loud enough for all to hear, "We don't need to know what El Diablo looks like."

***

It was obvious this conversation was about to become very difficult for Father Arres. Pausing for a sip of water, it was apparent that he did not want to continue. So, I had to ask, "What can you tell me about the Alichan?"

When the time finally came to speak the name of the Rios legend, the clergyman's whole countenance changed as he began to describe the darkness itself . . .

I
THE FIRST TRIAL: EARTHQUAKES

And the light shineth in darkness;
and the darkness comprehended it not.

John 1:5

7

Sprung in 1910 — Durango, Mexico

THE ALICHAN IS NOT like any other animal. In fact, many wonder whether it was ever really an animal at all. Beyond the Galancita, far up in the Sierras of Durango, there is a place so dark that light may never reach it. It is a place beyond reason, beyond consciousness, a place we may only glimpse briefly in our worst nightmares. Below this earth there is a very real netherworld where unlit waters flow. This is where the Alichan lived.

For ages, he ruled this obsidian realm lying in wait, suspected but unknown to the world above and unchallenged by any life below. His domain lacked sounds; his home held no odors or tastes. When you come to the loneliest abyss in your life, you will know this place. Void of all palpable life, this is where the Shadow of Doubt sat crouched in silence, hoping, waiting for a chance to escape and fulfill its purpose.

To Alichan, the first thing that mattered was food, and it all tasted the same—a plant, a mole, a fish, an insect, anything else with the misfortune to come near. Without a thought, without remorse, he lashed out and took in anything to survive. Even an animal this isolated came to the powerful realization that to live you must grow.

It had no family and therefore never received any love, education, or faith. Born into such darkness, it is said that the Alichan must have only one purpose in life: to destroy whatever creator cast him down into this pit.

One evening, his sleep was disturbed by the tremendous impact of a meteorite crashing into the stone façade above. Though the meteorite was only a few feet in length, it caused the thin shell of this hollowed mountain to collapse into a crater later known as the Devil's Cauldron. The next day, the ground rumbled, and the earth swayed violently from side to side. This new break in the surface brought fresh air into the stale pit; for the first time in centuries, light entered this boundless chasm.

On that day, the Alichan decided to end its tenebrous existence one way or another. Grasping a crag with crooked claws, he pulled in a new direction. Struggling against unseen gravity, he arose to a new position, then paused just long enough to enjoy the strange new sensation of blood pumping from one end of its enormous body to another.

At times, he may have recollected life as a beautiful being. But then a ray of light brought his attention back to the talons at the end of grotesque extremities, thick, hard skin, and a low dragging belly. This thing called day must have made it wonder, Who am I? What am I? Where have I been and where am I going? Why me?

Until that day, there never seemed to be any chance of escaping the darkness. Carefully savoring each new position, the fresh air from above taught a new song. A whole new world was about to unfold for this dormant terror. Finally, the time came to strike out.

***

The little whirlwind Apolonio left the Coronels stunned. Frozen in time with their thoughts, each member of the family pondered their unique daily assignments. Everyone had a purpose, a meaning for the day. Once all the children and livestock had been fed, Francisco entered the kitchen for the Morning Prayer. Francisco turned to Luke 10:18 and started to read in his deep, rich voice, "And he said unto them, 'I beheld Satan as lightning fall from heaven.'" A few of the tiny bowed heads peeked up to see if their father was reading or talking about an actual recent event. When they realized that he was reading verbatim, all eyes slammed tight and chins went grinding into their little chests with hands clenched tightly before their heads.

Their father continued, "'Behold I give to you the power to tread on serpents and scorpions and over all the power of the enemy: and nothing shall by any means hurt you.'" Francisco paused at that last phrase for emphasis, then he concluded with verse 20, "'Nevertheless, rejoice not that the spirits are subject unto you; but rather rejoice, because your names are written in heaven.'" Occasionally, Francisco took the liberty of slightly paraphrasing some Bible verses to make the language more understandable for his young ones. The message however was always true to the Word.

The heavy Bible shut with a solid thud that reverberated around the table. Francisco crossed himself and opened his eyes to see the rest of the family now clinching tightly to their rosary beads. The fear in their shivering bodies was evident even to the toughest cattleman in the land. Perhaps he had gone to the wrong words, but the message was clear to him.

"Don't you see mi hijitos, God has given us the power to defeat any enemy and nothing can hurt you.

Little Timoteo could not quite grasp what his father was talking about, but he could see the concern in his siblings' eyes. Paulo and Pedro were somewhat comforted by the strength in their father's tone. The older boys responded positively to what their father was saying, and Rosita really took it to heart.

Dionicia was not so convinced by the power of her husband's God. In her own upbringing, the power of her parents' gods was always more self-evident than any of the so-called miracles of the Catholic Church. She attended mass only to marry Francisco. It was the only church in the land, but the whole litany made no sense to her when God was obviously right outside in the form of nature.

Just as everyone was about to break to his or her assigned duties for the day, the ground began to rumble. Slowly at first, the room swayed from side to side, then more violently. A sudden jolt shook one candle loose from the ofrenda and it crashed to the tile floor. Francisco and Dionicia were familiar with the sound and knew it was time to get all the children beneath the sturdy kitchen table. Taking hold of the stocky wooden legs, Francisco felt the heavy mesa above them rock and roll but it did not bend or break. Its dense wood and weight protected them from plaster and plates falling from shelves nearby.

Fortunately, Francisco had built their home on a massive slab of granite, harder than any other stone he could find in the area. Dionicia cried out "Terremoto! (Earthquake) Terremoto!" as she pulled as many of the smallest children to her sides as she could. Francisco waited for the ride to end and checked calmly into the eyes of his older sons.

Mateo, the oldest, felt the strength in his father's cool stare and held fast. The younger boys had no idea when this would end, so they were more concerned. Rosita was puzzled by the strange ways in which her world was behaving this morning. The younger boys were now in a full range of tears, as they never thought the shaking would end. Yet it did. What lasted less than 30 seconds seemed like forever.

More abruptly than its onset, the shaking ceased. El temblor was over. This temblor was more of a shiver or tremble, perhaps an aftershock or foreshadowing of a greater disturbance to come. Cisco looked around at the structure and beamed to see it all remaining in one piece. He almost began to take some pride in his own construction work, but caught himself and said, "Look at what a strong house the Lord has built for us." Yes. Indeed, there were plates and candles scattered within the thick adobe walls, but the expansive wooden ceilings were all soundly in the same position they were a minute ago.

Dionicia knew that any quake that large would most certainly be followed by several more for the next few days so she started to prepare her smaller children for the next blow. Once the little ones were over the initial shock, they marveled at all the destruction outside.

Trees had fallen, carts full of vegetables were overturned and scattered, yet the chickens and dogs and pigs for some reason were not as excited about this whole new turn of events. In fact, the animals all seemed a bit more chary than usual as the kids scurried about. Just as that strange observation dawned on them, the ground proceeded to rumble again. The pigs squealed once more, as if they were going to slaughter. The boys all dashed inside for the great mesa of comfort, but by the time they got there, the shaking had stopped.

"Whoa," Mateo said, "that wasn't so bad."

Francisco was not able to make it back to the table in time. He was attending to the few hired hands who happened to be outside when they were knocked off their feet. Physically they were fine; spiritually the teenaged helpers were a bit rattled. Cisco took a casual pace back to the kitchen once he realized this was not another big one. Dionicia could hardly waddle back to the doorway in time to see her kids all begin crawling back out from under the table. She happened to be in the outhouse when the second tremor hit. A few minutes later, another aftershock rocked the Galancita, but by then the kids were on to El Diablo's game.

Dionicia looked a bit pale, and as everyone stood looking at her in the doorway she announced quietly, "Here comes another one!" The smaller boys immediately took cover beneath the enormous kitchen table again, but the rest of the family stood puzzled by Dionicia. She stood frozen in the doorway without any intention of saving herself. Then she buckled over in pain and waved them off.

"No, no," she said, "this one is inside my belly." A few moments later her contraction ended, and she was able to wobble back over to her bedroom.

"Cisco, I think it's time for you to call for the midwife."

"Well, it doesn't look like I'm going to be working on the barn today," Francisco responded cheerfully.

Lily was still a bit spooked, but ready to ride. Francisco was not able to get a full damage report before he had to dash off for one of his younger cousins to help with the delivery of his tenth child. Regardless of the possibility that he might lose some of his best cattle to thieves or coyotes, his wife's health was his first priority for that day.

The damage to the hacienda from el terremoto was significant. Nevertheless, most of the repairs could wait until after tending to the herd. In past years, lesser quakes had sent a few of his cattle high into the Sierras and over steep cliffs. The magnitude of this most recent terremoto was great enough to scatter his livelihood even farther afield.

The Coronels put great trust in their hired hands. Although they were able to get the corral shored up right away, most of the horses were out of the barn. Each successive tremor, although decreasing in size, was increasing the scope of the problem.

By the time Francisco returned with his cousin Lydia, it was too late to think about chasing critters. The fences needed mending, but the walls were all up and the sun was down. The only thing to attend to now was Dionicia. Dionicia was pale and trembling when they entered the room. He did not know why, but after offering a few brief comforting words, Francisco boiled some water. Rosita, seeing her mother in such pain, automatically took charge of the little ones as the big boys had to fend for themselves.

Between contractions, Dionicia cried out for her rosary beads. Though she really did not believe in them, the mindless prayers took her away from her pains for a few moments at a time and that was enough to get her through to the next contraction.

The tremors below ground had mostly subsided by the time the real quaking commenced for Dionicia. Half praying and half swearing; she finally threw her rosary across the room and watched as the black and white stones burst upon the opposite wall. One by one, they rattled and rolled across the floor. A few minutes later, Dionicia finally stopped her screaming as another voice started to cry in her place. It was a girl!

She was an incredible sight. From the moment her father laid eyes on her, he knew he would never see another child as beautiful as this.

"The Lord has finally given you victory over all your pain and suffering, Dionicia. We must name this girl Victoria." And so, she was named Victoria.

Even Mateo, who saw his baby sister for the first time the next morning, had to admit, "She's the prettiest baby you ever had mama." Rosita was so amazed by the new child's glory that she did not have time to bother with her older brother's insensitive comment.

"I've always wanted a little sister," Rosita cried.

As each of the boys took turns petting their new sister, Rosita begged to hold her. Surrounded by so much love, Dionicia had almost forgotten the pain of bearing this little pearl. Then as if El Diablo sensed the presence of too much joy, he nudged her bed with an aftershock one more time just for laughs. The children were all terremoto veterans by then and could not be bothered by another little shiver.

Dionicia on the other hand was sorely in need of some rest and recovery. At the ripe old age of 31, all the labors of bearing ten children were finally catching up with her. When Rosita finally got to rock her sister for the first time, Dionicia winced in pain as she rolled to one side and asked, "What happened with the Rioses yesterday? Have they found El Diablo yet?"

All his troubles had melted away during the evening, but now Francisco had to get back to dealing with the harsh realities of another day. Maybe his wife was still delirious from the pain of childbirth or maybe she really did believe El Diablo landed somewhere in their Sierras. At any rate, this was the perfect opportunity to set his whole family straight once and for all.

"El Diablo was cast down long ago and he is nowhere near our Galancita. I thought I told you all yesterday that whatever the Rioses saw was probably just a comet or a falling star, who knows? Even if a meteorite did land somewhere up in the hills, it is just a big piece of rock. No harm is going to come from this."

Lydia brought in a light breakfast for Dionicia. It was time for the baby to rest and the children all needed to eat. Timoteo was no longer the baby of the household, so he walked a little taller to his chair in the kitchen.

When the morning meal was ready, Francisco searched for an appropriate reading from their worn Bible. Knowing that many of his cattle and horses had been lost the day before, this was going to take some thought.

The family was gathered for the morning prayer when a knock came from the front door. Lydia invited the young man into the tiled entry and announced Santiago, one of Don Rios' hired hands. Francisco met him with a firm handshake. With hat in hand, the boy said, "Excuse me, Don Francisco. I'm sorry to disturb your morning meal, but Señor Rios would like to request the assistance of a few of your horses."

The young man was obviously troubled to be making the request; however, it was not unusual for Francisco to provide support to his neighbors and friends in the mining business. Santiago continued, "I know it is rare for us to be moving a boulder this early in the season, but Don Rios found one yesterday, moved by the quakes, and we need to seal the cave before anyone tries to enter."

Francisco could see the dilemma. During this time of year, the Rioses typically did not keep a full staff of riders to work the mines or move large boulders. If an intruder were to enter the caves quietly during the off season, they could easily remove millions of pesos worth of gold and silver before the regular teams returned in the summer. Therefore, what Santiago was really requesting was not only the horses but also the manpower to ride them up to the entrance of a cave and help with the movement of a large boulder.

"Of course, my friend," Francisco replied. "Tell Daniel I will be at his ranch before nine o'clock with four horses and riders." Santiago smiled in relief that he did not have to make the next request for manpower. The young man graciously and quickly made his exit to provide his jefe, his boss, with the good news.

Cisco announced the change of plans for the day, and then every head at the table bowed. Dionicia was too weak to join the rest of the family, but Victoria's newborn cries reached the kitchen. Hearing this, Francisco knew exactly what to pray. He turned to Psalm 100 and read, "Make a joyful noise unto the Lord. Serve the Lord with gladness: come before his presence with singing. Know that the Lord is God: it is he that made us and not we ourselves; we are his people, and the sheep of his pasture. Enter into his gates with thanksgiving, and into his courts with praise; be thankful unto him and bless his name. Amen."

Cisco selected his four best Andalusians and informed the hired hands of a change in plans for the day. Lydia prepared sacks with tamales, fresh fruit, and water for the men. She handed them up to each rider as they sped off towards the Rios ranch.

Riding up to the grand entry of the Rios Hacienda known as El Platanar de Coluta, (the banana plantation of Coluta) Santiago and two other hired hands were packing down their gear and preparing to mount the horses. Daniel Rios was already aboard his prized steed Sparta and sauntering down the long driveway to greet Francisco. Coming up alongside Francisco, Daniel shook his neighbor's hand with great enthusiasm and gratitude. Even in the saddle, Daniel, at over six feet, was notably taller than his broad-shouldered German friend. A picture of Daniel could well appear in a contemporary Spanish dictionary next to the word *machismo*.

After over 300 years of Spanish domination, the Mexican version of machismo developed into an aggressive masculinity which included characteristics such as suspicion, envy, vindictive brutality, and a willingness to kill without hesitation in order to preserve the manly image. Some of the other traits that defined Daniel as a macho man were his indifference to peril and his ability to suffer in silence for long periods of time without any sign of discomfort.

This manliness was at times recognized by a propensity towards untruths and relations with many women outside of marriage. While Don Rios was not specifically described as macho in this respect, there were rumors of certain acts of misconduct that went unquestioned.

Some of the more favored aspects of the machismo image include behaviors designed to protect and sustain the family and instill courtesy and high moral standards in children. For the most part, Daniel's rough exterior was a defense mechanism built up over several generations to seem invincible to those who might bring harm to his family, mines or plantation.

El Platanar was not really a plantation any more. Very few banana trees remained, but people often told Daniel that he was bananas to stick around Mexico after his grandfather Apolonio Rios was killed in 1866 by the guerillas of Benito Juarez.

In 1865 the French emperor Maximilian of Hapsburg took the throne of Mexico by the bayonets of Napoleon III. Within one year, Juarez captured Maximilian and had him executed. Forty-four years later, Daniel's thick black hair, long eyelashes, and tall, thin frame were all that remained of the French influence.

The long ride to the mines gave the men a chance to catch up on events since they last saw each other a few months earlier at Christmas time. The six young men behind them passed rumors surrounding the meteorite and subsequent tremors. On the way up the hillside, an ominous cloud appeared in the sky that reminded Francisco of the old tales Dionicia's grandparents used to tell around the campfires along these same trails.

As the legend was told back then, there once was once a great serpent known as the Alichan that lived deep within the caves of the Espinazo. Some said it was a dragon; others argued it was more like a giant iguana; while still others claimed that it was El Diablo himself. Whatever it was, Francisco had no time for such superstitions. However, since he had no doubt there was a God, there must also be a Satan. In fact, for one brief moment a few days ago as he crouched beneath his kitchen table, he thought that evil might indeed have something to do with all the unusual recent events.

Scattered along the trail, Francisco occasionally spotted a cow or horse with his familiar brand wandering aimlessly. There was some temptation to dash off and round them up, but that task would take too much time and energy. The chore would have to wait for another time. The Don hoped the animals would get hungry or cold and find their way back home eventually.

After about four hours of climbing along the steep trails, winding through forest and scrub brush, the men finally arrived at the entrance to the Rios' cave. Unloading a set of pulleys and thick ropes, the eight men and horses made quick work of the mammoth boulder that partially rolled away from the entrance.

When the stone was firmly in place, the men ate lunch and prepared for the ride home. Just as they were about saddle up again, Santiago wandered around the corner of a massive boulder to relieve himself in a nearby stream. It was there that he noticed some unusual tracks. Notifying the others, they all stared in amazement at the path cut by some gigantic animal.

"What could it be Señor?" Santiago asked of his chief. Gazing in disbelief, Daniel looked somberly over at his old friend Francisco and said, "Well it's too big to be a cow or even a bull. What do you think?" Francisco did not respond immediately because he had never seen a track this large before.

Though he did not want to believe his eyes, he had to admit the tracks were fresh, "I don't know for sure, but I think you must have a pretty good idea." The sun would be setting in a few hours so there was no time to follow the trail—only time to wonder . . .

II
THE SECOND TRIAL: A CYCLONE OF FIRE

With your own eyes you saw those great trials, those signs and great wonders. But to this day the Lord has not given you a mind that understands or eyes that see or ears that hear.

Deuteronomy 29:3–4

8

June 1911 — Durango, Mexico

IN THOSE DAYS, THE creature probably heard the distant thunder of men at work. For some reason, they entered his dominion to remove worthless minerals, metals and ore; nothing of value to a creature of the deep.

It is said that on one fine morning, while prowling about like a lion, the Alichan decided to hide in the tall trees and brush beside a meadow where these slower animals often wandered. When the opportunity finally presented itself the Alichan simply opened its mouth wide and cast its spell. A loud penetrating "VAOUW!" roared from the phantasm and captivated one of Francisco's meandering cattle. The sound had a warm and magnetic, almost vacuum-like, effect on the mindless bovine. The cow was so intrigued that it walked straight into the Alichan's mouth.

A short while later, after enjoying all the nutrients and entrails of the large cow, the Alichan regurgitated the remains and left only the leathery skin and bones to rot in the sun. For an animal used to so little for so long, this was a satisfying victory.

Over the next few days the Alichan's legs grew stronger and carried him further afield in search of more tasty treats. Although the Alichan at times encountered taller animals we know as horses, they were too swift to approach and less susceptible to the Alichan's magic. Smaller animals, such as sheep and goats were just as delicious to the palate as cattle, just not as large.

With larger meals came greater appetite. Light rains seemed to bring more wandering cattle and sheep out into the open meadows and bogs surrounding the Alichan's lair. With greater appetite came physical growth. The Alichan's belly began to grow until surprisingly one day a baby Alichan burst forth, then another; one black and one tan.

Over time, as more livestock disappeared mysteriously, stories developed surrounding the unidentifiable tracks of some large illusion that no one could ever find. Natives believed the creature received power and authority over the skies to increase the rain and thus the number of fish and animals in the streams and meadows around the cave entry.

While the Alichans prospered, the Coronels suffered. In the months immediately after the great temblor of 1910, flash floods hampered Francisco's ability to recover many of his lost cattle. Crevices opened by the major quake and aftershocks seemed to swallow whole groups of the scattered herd. Over the next few years, the herd dwindled until the cost of driving the remaining animals into town each year outweighed their value in the marketplace. Within six years, a majority of the sheep and horses lost after the great quake were either stolen by bandits or lost to some other strange, unexplainable poacher.

Simultaneously the heavy rains and floods washed away any remaining gold and silver that rested within easy reach for the Rios family. Each year they had to dig deeper for smaller finds. The danger grew greater as the miners worked further up into the Espinazo, and many lives were lost.

Although Don Francisco never doubted that the Lord would provide, Dionicia was not so sure. She bore no more children, yet her bones grew weary of the constant struggle to make ends meet. The children were no longer able to wear the latest fashions from Europe to church or on special occasions. They outgrew their play rags faster than their mother could keep up. More troubling to Doña Dionicia Coronel were the astonishing stories that poured in from workers in the fields who more frequently found cattle and sheep mutilated and devoured in a way never seen before in the valley.

Victoria was growing into a delightful young girl. The oldest boy Mateo was now sixteen and Rosita was twelve. Though they steadily grew and enjoyed their youth, Francisco could see that his children always seemed to want something more from life.

Dionicia always wanted to take the kids into the town of Tamazula to visit with her sisters, brothers, and cousins; but Francisco never had the time to make the trip with all his commitments to the Hacienda. Francisco's own brothers and sisters all lived in El Rodeo, not far from Tamazula. There they were teachers and storeowners with children of their own, so the opportunities to get together were few and far between. One day Francisco relented and allowed his family to travel alone by mule train into El Rodeo. He however, had to stay at home and tend to the ranch.

The celebration was magnificent. Fireworks in Tamazula, dancing, Tequila de Maguey. Cowboys fired their pistols into the air and Dionicia was feeling alive once more. It reminded her briefly of her youth before meeting Francisco. She had almost forgotten how in those days she never needed to worry about the overwhelming burdens of parenthood or managing a vast estate. Even more ponderous than managing large assets was the trial of managing large sums of debt with little to show in terms of income.

The years were taking their toll on Dionicia, but then an old flame in Tamazula detected a flicker of her youth. Ismael Bertran invited her and the children to stay at one of his hotels just outside of town where he had a casino with all types of gambling and entertainment. Ismael had many children for the Coronels to play with, but no wife of record. While the children ran and played throughout the casino, the adults caught up on old times and drank long into the evening.

At some point, late that night the children finally ran out of steam and retired to their rooms upstairs. Rosita, as usual, took charge of the little ones while the older boys commandeered their own separate room next to the girls. Dionicia remained downstairs at a card table imbibing with Ismael until she could hardly stand.

Outside the winds began to howl as a storm rolled in and kept little Victoria awake. The boys were exhausted from all the gallivanting of the day, so as soon as their heads felt clean pillows, they were sound asleep. Rosita tried reading to Victoria, but the little girl insisted on having a cup of atole blanco before she would sleep. The atole was a thick tea-like drink made from sweet herbs and corn meal. It was warm and soothing to the head and stomach. The big sister was curious to find out what their mother was still doing downstairs. So as soon as all the boys were soundly sleeping, she decided to sneak down with Victoria to spy on her Mom under the pretense of finding a drink for Victoria.

In the early 20th century, the construction of hotels in Mexico was cozy and attractive, but flimsy at best. The sandy soils around the town of Tamazula were hardly ideal for development, but since there was no such thing as zoning requirements, it didn't really matter. Besides, any time an official questioned Ismael about any of his buildings, there were always incentives for quick approvals.

Although Dionicia by this time could hardly see, somehow, she sensed her young girls watching from near the top of a nearby stairway and summoned them down to her side. Ismael noted the sleepy girls' request and immediately went into full host mode. He took all three of the ladies towards the end of the bar near the door where a warm pot of atole stood by.

Though somewhat embarrassed by appearing in such a condition before her daughters, Dionicia hoped that the cool air coming in the front door might sober her up a bit. As the girls enjoyed their warm atole, the rain poured down and the winds shook the timbers. Left alone, it might have taken Dionicia several more hours to sober up, but just as the girls were ready to return to their room, a particularly vicious gust of wind rocked the building and caused a central column to collapse onto a card table.

The lack of support caused the ceiling to collapse and furniture from the upper levels, complete with beds and customers, came pouring into the casino. Stunned by this turn of events, Dionicia instinctively swept the girls up into her arms as Ismael swiftly shepherded them through the open front door.

A few other women were able to follow them out before the entire second floor came crashing down onto the lower level. All the highly flammable furnishings burst into flames when they came in contact with kerosene lamps, as well as pots and pans on the stove.

Ismael ran for help, but within minutes the entire building was engulfed in fire as the ladies outside screamed for their families inside. The winds quickly fanned the flames into a massive conflagration.

Running around to the side where the Coronel boys were sleeping, Dionicia and the girls shrieked in terror hoping to arouse someone inside to fight through the rubble. At one point, Dionicia tried to rush into the flames to pull the boys free, but another witness immediately pulled her back from the wreckage which was now billowing in smoke and unapproachable.

Even across the street, heat from the flames scorched the little girls' memories forever. The second floor had come down so quickly and the flames erupted so rapidly that no one on the upper level had a chance. By the time the rain finally extinguished the last of the flames at daybreak, not a prayer remained. Dionicia and the girls were huddled in tears, soaked from head to toe in sorrow.

III
THE THIRD TRIAL: SORCERY

*Let no one be found among you who sacrifices their son or daughter
in the fire, who practices divination or sorcery, interprets omens,
engages in witchcraft, or casts spells, or who is a medium or
spiritist or who consults the dead.*

Deuteronomy 18:10–11

9

May 1917 — Tamazula de Victoria, Mexico

ALL SEVEN OF THE boys were buried in the large cemetery just outside Tamazula. Francisco wept fiercely as each blue casket was lowered into the ground. The women all wailed and moaned in agony. Victoria buried her face in Rosita's black dress and prayed that it would all be over soon. The grief was deafening.

Francisco could not forgive himself for letting the family travel alone, "How could I leave my little angels alone to fry in such a wretched place?" Francisco hated the big villages and towns. Whenever he got to Culiacan with a big herd, he couldn't wait to be paid so that he could return to his hacienda and the wide-open spaces of La Galancita.

With Victoria tucked under her right arm, Rosita held her father's right hand and gave it a little squeeze for hope. It was just enough to bring a slight pause in the tears. Seeing the simultaneous sadness and calm in his elder daughter gave Francisco the strength to move forward. Together they had to do something to lift Dionicia from her state of misery.

Although Francisco wanted all the boys interred at La Galancita, Dionicia insisted on being buried someday with her children near Tamazula where she grew up. La Doña was in no condition to be argued with at the time and so it was done. For three days, she wept at the boys' gravesite.

Don Francisco might have been in a bigger hurry to return home if it were not for the fact that the herd had dwindled to a few dozen. His few remaining hands could easily handle them. Only one of the new calves survived birth, and one cow was also lost on that catastrophic morning of May 6, 1917.

Francisco could see that his wife's distress was taking its toll on the girls too. Though he didn't want to leave her in Tamazula alone, her brothers and sisters seemed better equipped to deal with her there than he was. Furthermore, he could not bear to have the girls see their mother in this condition. Ultimately, Francisco and the girls chose to return to La Galancita without Dionicia.

Weeks turned into months, and still Dionicia found no peace. The only solace she found came from the small hand-rolled cigarettes that Ismael provided on a regular basis. The potent weed he grew in secret gardens up in the hills brought Ismael an even greater source of income than his former casino. Eventually with the ill-gotten gains from his "farming," Ismael was able to rebuild an even larger casino and hotel near El Rodeo known as La Luna Morado (purple or bruised moon).

Stronger doses of the weed, along with an increasingly potent hooch called pulque (a fermented alcoholic juice of the maguey plant), savagely tore Dionicia's mind apart from her past. That summer, she moved into the hotel with Ismael and helped him run a brothel within the new hotel.

Rumors of Dionicia's behavior reached La Galancita, but Francisco would not believe them. Even if they were true, he no longer had the luxury of time or money to retrieve his wife. After a long, wet summer, there were barely enough cattle to keep the children fed. Lydia stayed on as a housekeeper, and a few of the cowboys came around to help in the summers but the days of the big roundups and dozens of staff members were long gone.

Don Daniel was suffering some of the same trials at his hacienda up the road. The mines had all but dried up, but his workers still enjoyed spending any or all of their remaining money and time in El Rodeo, where the grand new casino was in full swing every evening.

One day, Daniel sent two of his bravest workers, Santiago and Jacinto, up to the Espinazo to do some prospecting. The Mexican revolutions were in full swing by that time, and few men were brave enough to wander up into the mountains in small groups. Rumor had it that Pancho Villa himself might be hiding somewhere in the area. American troops led by General Pershing had Villa on the run for a while, but by then the famous bandit was most likely regrouping for future revolts.

The remote and isolated peaks and valleys of the Espinazo provided many places for danger to hide. Later that evening late after indulging in some of Ismael's finest smokes around the campfire, Jacinto heard something rustling in the brush just outside their campsite, and it was not the horses. The smoke and agave let them lapse into a carelessness that allowed enemy eyes to fall upon them.

"Did you hear that, Jacinto?" Santiago asked.

The sound grew louder and louder as something fairly large was about to break through the darkness and into their firelight. Even in their severely inebriated state, the men sensed it was time to take up arms. Each prospector always stayed close to a reliable rifle as well as their sidearm.

Santiago already had his rifle drawn and pointing into the darkness when they both heard the roar "VAOUW!" Both men froze in their boots. They had never heard or felt a note like it. Before either could react, their spines were paralyzed.

Jacinto didn't even have time to raise his rifle before the timbre reverberating from this strange thing enraptured him. He couldn't really see what it was other than darkness.

"What is it?" he asked.

The tone had a unique warmth that slowly coaxed him to take one small step towards it.

Then he asked one final question aloud, "Who goes there?"

Snnnaap! The tawny Alichan leapt forward just as Jacinto calmly dove into the gaping jaws of death. Santiago could see what was happening, but couldn't react in time to save his partner. In fact, he could not believe what he had just seen— or, what he thought he saw. Maybe it was just the agave having its way with him, or perhaps he was already asleep and just dreaming. Then abruptly the spell turned towards him and Santiago too felt the warm cozy invitation of permanent rest "VAOUW!"

For some reason, just as he was about to step forward to meet his demise, Santiago's right hand involuntarily made the sign of the cross across his face; and that broke the spell. The dun nightmare was only over for a moment. Whatever just devoured his companion was now hurtling towards him, and so without thought or malice, he pulled the trigger.

Crrraaack! The bullet tore through real flesh and real bone. As the recoil further sobered Santiago, he fired again and again. Whatever it was no longer moved. The horses were startled and just about ready to tear loose from their reins. When Santiago realized he was not dreaming, it was time to go. He did not want to take the chance of turning back and being recaptured by that powerful trance.

There was no chance of saving Jacinto now. Santiago untied both horses and mounted his own. Jacinto's horse followed Santiago home.

The next morning, just as the sun was beginning to rise, Daniel Rios strolled out to his barn when he noticed Santiago riding down from the hills at a full gallop. At first, he wondered why he was coming right towards him in such a big hurry. Then he spotted Jacinto's riderless horse chasing wildly. Something was very wrong. Even in the weak morning light, Don Rios could see the terror in Santiago's face before he brought his horse to a dusty halt.

"What happened Santiago? Are you all right?" Before the young prospector could catch his breath to explain, the blood rushed to his head and he rolled down from his mount to the ground. Daniel rushed to his side and shouted out to the house for help.

The Rios boys were already up and around preparing for their daily chores when they heard the commotion and went running out. Daniel's wife, Natividad, was watching from the kitchen window and sent her girls out with a pitcher of water and towels.

Daniel searched for some signs of injury but found none. When Santiago finally came to, he was completely incoherent and just barely on the edge of consciousness. Apolonio was 14 years old by then and Lazaro was 13. The boys were quite tall and strong for their age, so once Daniel finally helped Santiago to his feet, the boys were able to steer him inside to lie down for a while. The only other ranch hand the Rioses had left, Leopoldo, took care of the horses which seemed almost as traumatized as Santiago.

The Rioses could not afford to lose another worker, so Daniel was anxious to find out where Jacinto was. Though Santiago wasn't able to speak intelligibly for several hours, his malodorous clothes spoke volumes. The stench of weed and agave were heavy in the room where Santiago wiggled and moaned for most of the morning. Daniel could not stand to think of the possibility of losing a strong worker to the evil sorcery of El Rodeo, so he stomped out of the room in anger.

Natividad Rios prepared some soup to calm the young man down, but his hands were shaking so much that she had to spoon feed him. Once he finished eating, he began to pink up a bit, and Doña Rios asked softly, "What happened Santiago? Where is Jacinto?" His face went pale again as a memory returned and he tried to form a word, but it just wouldn't come out. With great effort, he finally sat up and stammered painfully, "Ah–ah–ah, lii–chan."

In the room next door, Daniel wasn't close enough to make out the words exchanged, but he was close enough to hear the bowl fall to the floor from his wife's hands. Could all the stories really be true? For years little children had been telling tales of strange creatures they had spotted from a distance, but no one ever came close enough to an Alichan to tell what it was. As Santiago slowly recovered over the next few days, the Rioses debated whether to discuss their dilemma with anyone else. What if Santiago shot Jacinto for some reason and made up a fanciful tale to cover his tracks? With all the smoke and alcohol in his system that evening, who knows what really happened?

Daniel questioned his trusted vaquero repeatedly, hoping to find some truth in the story, but it just didn't make any sense. Eventually, Santiago could not keep his secret any longer and the news spread like wild fire. The whole village was abuzz with curiosity and agitated reservations. Most assumed Santiago was insane.

It was hard for anyone to take the story too seriously, because whenever someone would ask Santiago, "So, what did it look like?" he couldn't really tell.

"Well I never got a clear look at it," or "it was just too dark to tell," were his standard responses. Those who knew or heard of Santiago's less–than-orderly drinking habits gave even less weight to the cowboy's tale. One fact remained: Jacinto was missing. After a while, people wondered what really happened up in those caves and why the rain suddenly ceased in the middle of the monsoon season.

The Alichan was apparently agitated as well. The loss of one of its two offspring did not bode well for the remaining wandering herd of Don Coronel. Cattle and sheep were wantonly destroyed and scattered throughout the valley even in close proximity to small farms and ranches.

One day when Miguel Rios was about 12 years old, he was out in the cornfield playing with his younger sisters, an unusual shadow off in the distance caught his attention. It was too large to be a cow, yet too low to the ground to be a horse. It appeared to slither like a snake, but it had short, stout legs. When it spun around, he could see a long spiny tail, but the head was not visible. It seemed to be dragging a sheep or no—it was a goat! The goat seemed to be begging for mercy in its own language, but Miguel decided he had seen enough.

He quickly rounded up Florentina and Juanita and they raced back to their house like lightning. When they came in with their reports and shouting, "Alichan! Alichan!" Daniel immediately loaded his rifle and headed off alone into the corn field. The tall horse gave Daniel a great view of the terrain, so it didn't take long before he spotted the figure of one of his goats. Just as a precaution, he fired a shot into the brush to scare off anyone or anything that might still be lurking about.

By the time he reached the goat, it was already dead, but only partially consumed. Whatever caused this damage left a clear path as it fled rapidly into the thick forest nearby. Don Rios followed the trail for a few miles before it disappeared into a river and never came up on the other side. Whatever it was that went into the river must have been a powerful swimmer to disappear upstream in such a hurry. The water was just a bit too deep for his horse and the sun was beginning to get low in the sky. This mystery would have to be solved another day.

By the time Daniel got home, his family was wildly concerned that some other astonishing tragedy occurred, "We heard the shot, Papa! What happened? What happened? What happened?" they all cried in unison. It took a while to calm everyone down but once they realized that all was well, Daniel thought about paying a visit to his friend Francisco soon.

The stories that evolved from that day forward grew more and more frightening. Children were scared to play outside and eventually the news made its way down the hills into El Rodeo where Dionicia was becoming quite the persona in town. She began to be called more often by her nickname of Nicia, and on weekends, she performed some fairly wayward dance routines that drew crowds in by the droves. In fact, the new Purple Moon Saloon was becoming such a popular hangout that even celebrities such as Pancho Villa were inclined to pay a visit when in the vicinity.

On one particular evening in 1918, the renowned bandit wandered into town disguised as a Catholic bishop to avoid any trouble from the federales. Knowing that he could find shelter and pleasures at the Purple Moon, he quickly struck up a warm relationship with Dionicia, who was now going by the last name of Bertran. The hospitality was so much to the liking of Bishop Villa that when Dionicia asked for certain favors in return, the semi-retired cattle thief felt obliged.

Although Dionicia had not seen her daughters now for a long time, she had always wanted them baptized by a Catholic official. Perhaps it was the ridiculous stories coming down from the hills. Perhaps it was the guilt associated with seeing a Catholic robe again. Maybe it was just the weakening effects of the weed and alcohol or the mounting responsibilities of running a large establishment like the Purple Moon. For whatever reason, Dionicia felt led to request a private baptismal for her two daughters in La Galancita.

Dionicia packed a few mules for the bishop and sent him off with directions to her former home in La Galancita, saying, "I'm sure the Don Francisco will take good care of you once you tell him that you have traveled far and wide to baptize his girls." And with that, Dionicia slapped the mule carrying Villa and shouted, "Via con Dios!".

Somehow, the gravity of her behavior brought Dionicia back down to earth. A heavy remorse settled in that could no longer be cured by maguey or marijuana. If anything, the addition of more narcotics just made things worse. Nothing her customers or Ismael could say seemed to make things better. Although she yearned to see La Galancita again, it would be too painful to face her daughters in this inescapable condition.

In the morning, she went to see a local curandera by the name of Celia Aispuro. A curandera is a healer; a medicine woman or shaman of sorts trusted for their worldly wisdom by the natives of Mexico. The curandera detected evil spirits within Dionicia that a modern licensed psychologist might describe as some type of mental illness. The curandera, however, told Dionicia that she was going to have another child soon—a son.

There was no way for Dionicia to know for sure, but her fetus could have been the child of Ismael, or any number of men who frequented the Purple Moon, or perhaps even the Bishop Villa himself.

The cure, as prescribed by the curandera, was to take her baby and travel alone to the Espinazo del Diablo and wait there in a specific place for a number of days.

"And how will I know when my spirit is cured and when can I see my children again?" Dionicia asked.

"Wait until you see a vision. A Great Spirit will tell you what you need to do. Then your spirit and your child's spirit will be free from all evil and you will be able to return to your original family."

When Pancho Villa arrived quietly a few days later in La Galancita, the news leaked out that a bishop was in the village. Several families brought their children around to the Rios hacienda to be baptized along with Rosita and Victoria. Francisco was so excited and honored to have a Catholic bishop visit his ranch that he even offered to build a small church for the community, but the imposter was not interested in calling so much attention to his visit. No one in the area recognized the famous bandit, and Villa was pleased with that. During a brief ceremony held at La Galancita, many members of the community were christened along with Rosita and Victoria.

After indulging himself for a few weeks upon some of the finest remaining livestock, the faux bishop saddled up a few new ponies and resumed his trek across the valley. Wherever he went, the peasants lavished gifts upon him and pointed him towards the next unsuspecting hacienda.

Dionicia took the curandera's message to heart, and eventually she plotted a way to sneak away from El Rodeo to have her child. With ample supplies for a long slog into the caves of Espinazo del Diablo, she didn't realize that she was moving away from the fires of her past and into the Devil's Caldera...

***

With the sudden and unexpected disappearance of Nicia, the Purple Moon lost its star attraction. Truly alone for the first time in her life, Dionicia began to recapture some of the vitality lost as a slave to the world with all its lusts, greed, and pride. Here alone with an innocent child inside of her, she could finally enjoy the peace and tranquility of the quiet forest. It enchanted her. Though her beliefs as a young girl were all based upon the power of nature and its many gods, she never actually had time to spend time alone in the wonder of its majesty.

After several days of travel on foot, Dionicia stopped in Topia for a few supplies and met a curandera by the name of Santita, who agreed to help her with the childbirth when the time came. In a short time, Dionicia got the knack of fishing with a makeshift hook and line. There weren't many streams to fish, but the few she did cross always had a few still, quiet places where the bounty was nourishing.

Though she could not remember ever being on these trails before, they seemed familiar somehow. It was almost as if she had been there long ago and was finally returning home. Where the trail split in two directions, she always seemed to choose one or the other without hesitation, as if she knew exactly where she was going.

After almost two more full days of slow walking and hiking, Dionicia unexpectedly came upon a gaping hole in the mountainside. The crater she spotted had to be at least 50 yards in diameter. Some trees around the mouth were dried up and charred as if there had been a brief fire around this ring of darkness. A few younger green trees pushed their way up from beneath dead bark and grew around the rim. This suggested that whatever burned its way into the mountain had been extinguished more than a few years ago.

Cautiously, Dionicia noted how sharply the entrance to this cave dropped out of site. She cast a large stone into the abyss to test its depth and waited to hear it echo off a stone surface below.

Oddly enough, some parts of the rim appeared damaged more than others, and at one point there was a spot where the stone descended more gradually down into the pit, almost like a circular staircase. A few meters into the hole the ledge widened, and she could safely lead the hesitant mule out from the hot sun above. A little further down into the cavity a gigantic dimple in the wall provided shelter for the evening, so Dionicia lit a candle to prepare an evening meal.

The baby was kicking fiercely now, and it wouldn't be long before she would give birth. This was a concern now, given how steep and deep this new sanctuary was. Nonetheless, the place had a certain cozy appeal that brought warmth, comfort, and eventually sleep. When Dionicia awoke later in the evening, she had a brief craving for the sweet temescal of her former casino home. To make the craving and pains of childbirth pass, she opened a saddlebag and rolled some of her precious weed into a small thin cigarette and started to hallucinate; at least it seemed like a hallucination. Images of dried bones began to form armies of marching skeletons that marched and danced about the inside of her head. The Dia de Los Muertos was coming to life.

Dionicia awoke, startled, and propped her feet up against a wall as she cried out in pain. The contractions came closer and closer together. These strange noises awakened another tenant of this cave—the Alichan. Warm torchlight confused the demon as it made the woman appear cloaked in bright sun while the moon shined upon her from above. His acute senses could discern that she was not alone, but with child.

As the creature crept slowly towards the invader, Dionicia heard something breathing and felt the heavy animal dragging its belly along the cold, black slab. The pain and weed must have overwhelmed her as she stood and turned to face the ominous sound. In the flickering torchlight, she thought she saw an enormous red dragon with several heads crowned in the moonlight. Just then, the hulk spun and lashed out with its tail that slapped her hard against the wall. For an instant, she saw stars and then all went dark.

The red dragon stood in front of the woman for a while so that he could devour her child the moment it was born. Then a loud noise from above caught the Alichan's attention and he climbed up to investigate.

***

Father Arres had us hanging on the edge of our seats when we were all jolted by the most startling sound ever . . .

IV
<u>FRIENDS OR ENEMIES</u>

"You know, maybe we don't need enemies.
Yeah, best friends are about all I can take."

—Bill Watterson

10

Late Tuesday Afternoon — Tamazula de Victoria, Mexico

HEEEE-YAAAHH! WHAT A HORRIFIC sound! At that moment the story was interrupted by Reno braying loudly and kicking at the cool night air. "Yes, Reno! You are right. There is not much time to spare. You must get going now." Father Arres didn't have time to finish my whole family saga. Instead, he gave us an earnest blessing and sprinkled us with holy water, "Once you set out, keep moving. I pray that on this expedition you will find the faith you need to overcome the floods of misgiving rising all around us . . . Amen."

As much as I wanted to hear the rest of the story right then, we had to reach RuMa as quickly as possible, and our initial detour through El Rodeo was the only way in or out of the Espinazo. As long as we held to a steady pace, we could reach the Cauldron within about a day.

Even in the dim moonlight the jungle began to feel less like the old Mexico we had left behind and more like the Rocky Mountain trails back home. Gabriel and I rode the first few miles quietly past El Rodeo then upward. Once we were at a safe distance, Gabriel began to brief me on the trajectory of the upcoming voyage. There was evidently much to learn from this young man, as he had logged so many miles along these paths that he was able to navigate with ease through the pitch.

There were so many questions swirling about my head, but if we were indeed heading into some kind of battle, I had to ask, "Did Grace and RuMa have any kind of weapons to protect themselves in case trouble arrives for them before we do?"

For a moment the air was still, so he was able to assure me quietly that "Yes, they had a few small arms and several places to hide with enough explosives to seal off parts of the cave if necessary."

"What? They don't know anything about firearms or explosives! How did they get a hold of that?" I asked.

"Unfortunately, it was the acquisition of those weapons that got them into this trouble in the first place. You see, in order to blast through a wall where they believe a valuable skeleton and great treasure are hidden, they inquired into the availability of dynamite. It was then in a nearby village that they unknowingly met up with a helpful drug dealer who provided what they were looking for. Regrettably, that purchase has since set off a great deal of interest in their exploration."

It seemed ironic that RuMa and Grace, teetotaling friends who never touched a drop of alcohol or took a narcotic in their lives, were now mixed up with a bunch of thugs due to their hard-core scientific discovery addiction.

My young guide called back from his steady mule, "Stay in the center of the path and you will be blessed!" The animal I rode was cranky, but strong and trustworthy. There was no margin for error on these narrow rocky trails.

"Remember what Father Arres told us about the Pathway of Blessing," he cautioned. "If you stray to either side now, you will be cursed by steep penalties in the darkness far below."

Am I in too deep? I wondered to myself. Have I lost my mind? If so, there was no turning back now. The way forward was about to get more complicated, so I had to stay focused now as my guardian Gabriel continued to tell the Rios tale in greater detail . . .

11

November 1918 — Durango, Mexico

WHEN DIONICIA AWOKE FROM her nightmare, she was surprised to find that she had had given birth to a healthy boy whom she named Manuel or Manuelito (little Manuel). She was too weak to climb out from the lower level of the den where she was lying in great pain. So, when she heard someone above she began to cry out for help.

Fortunately, it was one of the Tarahumara ladies from Topia who was out looking for her. The Rarámuri have an incredible ability to travel and communicate over long distances. This particular lady was named Santita, which means little saint.

"Hello!" Santita called down.

The echoing voice was music to Dionicia's ears.

"Yes! Help us please!" she shouted to the unseen voice above. "God is with us Manuelito," she said to her surprised baby boy, who then began to cry. This sound startled the Alichan and he ran to hide for the rest of that day.

The newborn's cries drew Santita down to them like a magnet. Within a few minutes Santita was introducing herself and hugging the baby tightly.

"We must get you out of here right away. I heard something outside the cave that may be living in here and rain is finally coming."

After preparing a quick meal and attending to the newborn child, Santita coaxed them up towards fresh air.

Dionicia asked her rescuer, "How did you find us?"

"I knew you were in this area, and while looking for you last night I kept hearing your cries. At first, I thought it was *La Llorona* and you frightened me."

There are several variations of the story of La Llorona (the weeping woman) but the legend told among natives has endured. The parable is about a lovely young girl named Maria who felt she was too good for the men of her village. One day a handsome young rancher rode in from the plains who was wealthy and charming. Maria married the ranchero and they had two children who received so much of her husband's attention that one day in a rage of jealousy, she threw them into a river. When she realized what she had done, she tried to rescue the children but ended up drowning along with them. As the story goes, the villagers still hear Maria crying down by the river, "Where are my children?" To this day, children are warned of the danger of pride, and not go out into the dark for fear that La Llorona may snatch them up and never return them.

Santita continues, "Even though it was quite dark, I heard the baby crying and decided to keep looking for you." By then, they had reached the surface where a scroungy mule was waiting patiently.

"Oh, thank God you came for us. We were almost completely out of food, and I'm exhausted. We could have never made it out of here without your help. Thank you so much. How will I ever be able to repay you?"

"No need to worry about that now," Santita said. "You and the baby will ride and rest on my mule, Grácil (graceful)." With a sudden boost of energy, Dionicia was able to get up on Grácil's back with little assistance.

Santita said, "If we maintain a steady pace we can get to my home in Topia before sunset. You can stay there with me at least a few weeks until you are healthy enough to live on your own." On their hike back to Topia, Dionicia learned about another home that Santita kept far away to the north where they could stay indefinitely.

After a few weeks in Topia, Dionicia moved to Santita's vacant home near the village of Dolores, which eventually became a wonderfully safe and cool environment. Away from the heat of long summer days, Dionicia enjoyed exploring her new neighborhood with Manuelito.

A streamlet ran right along the far edge of the curandera's property and provided fresh water. The slow current even provided an occasional fish for a meal. At first the desolation felt a bit dispiriting and mysterious, but after a while it became comforting and peaceful. Though the darkness continued to stalk them, a single glass crucifix hung outside the door seemed to annoy the Alichan enough to make it avoid that part of the world all together.

Santita would visit occasionally and they would all go into the nearby village of El Frijolar together. For a while, Dionicia was happy with her new son in their new dwelling. However, losing all her other boys at once continued to haunt Dionicia. In smoke-induced dreams she could see them screaming and crying for help from the flames. Once the saddlebag was emptied of its weed, the dreams subsided and Dionicia hoped that she would never become so addicted to her bad habits again.

***

Francisco wondered if he would ever see his beautiful wife again. When he first learned that his wife was no longer in Tamazula and that she disappeared into the hills, he could not believe it. In all their years together, he had never seen her behave so erratically and with such disregard for her family.

One day, Rosita interrupted his thoughts with the announcement of their neighbor's arrival from El Platanar. The two men walked out to the site where Francisco was working on the foundation for a new church. The recent visit from the ersatz bishop took his mind off Dionicia for a while and inspired Francisco to take on the challenge of providing a new place of worship for his entire community. It took some time to raise the materials, but finally the time came for action.

"What are you building here Don Francisco?" Daniel asked.

"This is going to be a place where we can finally pay our respects to the Lord in a proper manner. Every other big hacienda has its own chapel, but not ours. With a little more faith, I know we can get through all this."

Daniel could see that the drought and depression had taken its toll on this good friend. Rios looked a bit skeptical, but he had never known his neighbor to falter in the past. After relaying his recent experience to his compadre as best he could, Daniel finally came to the point.

"Francisco, I do not believe the stories myself, but the evidence does suggest there is something odd going on here. I don't know what kind of bandits we are up against, but they do not ride horses and yet they're incredibly swift and brutal."

Francisco always tried to focus on the task at hand, but this news was troubling, and he said, "If this wasn't a human bandit, it must be some kind of coyote at work here, or maybe a jaguar? Of course, they can bring down even a bull in packs but how do they escape without leaving a clear trail?" Francisco could hardly believe his own words, but the details were curious. Trails would typically lead a short distance from the sightings but then disappear into a bog. They thought perhaps a river or cloud of dust swept them away.

Don Rios could not believe that his friend was really going to spend the last of his resources on a building that which would most likely never return a single centavo. It just did not make any sense.

"What do you expect to accomplish by building a church here, my friend?"

"Can't you see, Daniel? All these hardships we keep encountering must be due to us not paying attention to our Lord. All these years we've been chasing our own dreams, looking for El Dorado, but it does not exist."

"You don't believe me, do you?" Rios questioned. "Santiago says he can take us to the place where Jacinto was lost. Then we can see for ourselves whether he was telling the truth or not. I do not want to go up there alone. Won't you please come with me? Then we can both decide if any of these stories are true."

"The truth is those hills are crawling with bandits right now and we don't have the force of our men to protect us anymore. If you must go, I'll go with you; but don't expect to find any monsters. Lord willing, we will find Jacinto's body and bring him home to his poor family."

The next day Rios returned with Santiago and saddlebags full of ammunition for whatever they might encounter along the way. Coronel had his horse fully loaded also, but his hope rested primarily on protection from above. Santiago brought much news to Daniel from the town of El Rodeo that he wanted to share with Francisco, but he did not know exactly how to approach these subjects, so he just got on with it.

"The people in town say that when the Alichan learned one of its children was killed, he stopped the clouds from raining."

The long pause afterwards made him feel silly, but he couldn't keep it in any longer. These men had to know what they were about to face.

Francisco asked, "Santiago, don't you believe in God?" and Santiago nodded sheepishly in the affirmative.

"Then why do you worry so much about a whimsy you can't see? Tomorrow has enough problems of its own."

That reminded Francisco of a verse from his favorite book of the Bible, Matthew 6:26, the book he had named his first son, Mateo, after.

"Look at the birds, Santiago. They are not afraid."

Since La Galancita was too small to have its own priest, the responsibility of ministering to the people who came to the new church would ultimately fall upon Don Francisco. Therefore, he took this opportunity to share the word of God with these obviously troubled men. To the best of his abilities, Francisco tried to recall an appropriate passage from the Sermon on the Mount.

"Behold the birds of the air: for they do not sow, neither do they reap, nor gather into barns; yet your heavenly father feeds them. Are you not much better than they?"

For several minutes there was no response, only contemplation.

Rios was more interested in practical matters, and he knew that eventually everyone in their community would need to count on the granaries of La Galancita to provide for their health and survival. This much everyone understood. The skies had been undeniably dry for too many months.

Finally, Don Rios had to ask, "Many of us have been running low on supplies and we were wondering if your granaries have enough in reserve to get us through the next winter?"

The resignation in Daniel's voice troubled Francisco.

Normally Don Coronel would have assured his neighbor that everything was going to be fine, but given the recent drought and lack of rain in the forecast, perhaps there was some reason for concern. The rice, beans, and corn that once filled his granaries were now down to their lowest levels ever. It would be irresponsible of him to promise something he could not deliver. Without some sort of miracle, the Galancita could indeed be in for a disastrous famine.

"O ye of little faith!" Francisco persisted for his own encouragement as well as that of the others, "Seek first the kingdom and his righteousness and everything you need will be provided."

Santiago, who was riding the lead horse, came to a halt and signaled to his superiors, "This is it. Just around this corner is where we built our campfire that night." The men all dismounted and prepared themselves for whatever they might see next.

Santiago cautiously followed the path to where he had camped not so long ago with his best friend, Jacinto. The fire ring was just as he remembered it, with his boot prints still scattered about the area. Memories of that fateful evening overwhelmed Santiago again and he froze in his own tracks. He could go no further, he could only point towards the spot where the darkness first entered their firelight.

Francisco and Daniel clearly understood now that this was the place. They both stepped around Santiago and moved towards the spot where he was pointing. It was a startling sight. There, exactly where Santiago was pointing, they observed a white, sun-baked skeleton. Don Francisco approached it first in awe. It was not much larger than a small calf, but the legs were much shorter and at one time had a very long tail. The strange thing about it was the head was massive. A single fortunate round from Santiago's rifle had shattered the skull. The mouth was still full of long fangs that were nothing like any cattle he'd ever seen. Daniel paused to catch his breath before stepping forward for a closer look. Inside the ribcage beneath heavy scapulars, he saw the most frightening part of all – Jacinto's belt buckle and boots.

Francisco made the sign of the cross and prayed for protection. Daniel knelt beside the carcass to retrieve the only remains of his former laborer. Not a scrap of cloth or skin remained. Recalling that hellish attack was so intolerable for Santiago's eyes that he burst into tears.

The younger man had seen enough and was ready to leave, but Daniel wanted to look around some more. Francisco stared for a long time in awe at the unusual spines along the animal's backbone. He tried to imagine what it must have been like alive and could only visualize some type of small dragon. How could such a relatively small animal do so much damage?

After conducting a brief search of the perimeter of the campsite for more clues, Daniel concluded, "This is not the animal that was in my corn field."

Feeling a bit more secure with the circumstances, Daniel reached down and grasped one of the front hands of the skeleton.

"Look at these claws," he remarked. "These could easily kill a goat or maybe even a small cow, but these did not make the prints that I tracked at Coluta. This is just a baby."

"So, this is not the animal that you chased?" Francisco asked Daniel.

"Similar, yes. But exact, no." This comment caused all three men to pause and consider the ramifications of more than one animal such as this.

"Well, I guess that if there is a bigger animal around somewhere we should probably be getting home before dark," made very good sense to Santiago.

Don Rios wondered aloud, "Do you think we should try to bring this back with us? No one will ever believe this."

The bones looked heavy, but they were mostly intact and probably light enough for a horse to carry in a sack. Francisco thought about the spiritual consequences of moving such a wretch from its place of rest and thought it best to leave the skeleton alone. Just to prove Santiago's honesty, Daniel insisted that they keep one of the forearms, a few teeth and claws. That would be enough to satisfy those back in the community who might not believe their story. Don Daniel respectfully placed Jacinto's belt buckle and boots in the sack along with a few bones.

As they mounted up and headed for home Santiago muttered to the men, "Even now that I have seen the Alichan alive and dead, I still can't believe it."

***

Seasons passed and the legend of the Alichan grew, but the attacks dwindled. For years people sustained a belief that the draught was caused by the death of Alichan's youngster. Don Coronel did all he could to dispel the myths. He stretched the meat and milk products from his few remaining animals, but the last reserves of feed had to be doled out carefully to angry mobs. By the time a few light rains finally returned to the valley, many children had perished from famine or disease.

Don Francisco eventually completed the construction of his small church, but not many came. The villagers despised him for abandoning them in their hour of need and eventually came to blame all their misfortunes upon Don Coronel and his cruel God.

Rosita and Victoria missed their mother's bedtime stories and delicious cooking. The loss of their brothers and mother all at once forced the girls to grow up quickly. They loved their father immensely and tried to bring him some cheer, but the house just seemed so quiet all the time. The years of poverty were finally taking their toll on the man they saw as invincible.

***

Meanwhile, in the village of El Rodeo, frequenters of the Purple Moon became concerned about their prize belle, Nicia. Ismael was especially displeased over his loss of income for a while. Eventually people in the area became so desperate that their only hope was to somehow strike it rich in the casino. There was obviously no gold or silver left in El Diablo. The Purple Moon was the only place that offered any promise of satisfaction, one way or another. For those who lost their money at the card tables, there were always other distractions offered to soothe the pain.

The ever-compounding stories of Dionicia's adultery, sorcery and disappearance were just further reasons for the community to blame Francisco for all their losses. The regimes in Mexico City proceeded to go through one upheaval after another so that the chances of any support from the government were nonexistent. A few of the bravest laborers packed their bags and headed northward in search of better prospects; but most sought comfort within the confines of Bertran's saloon.

The long painful turn of the tides eventually eroded the confidence of Francisco's last remaining friend, Daniel. Workers frightened by the reports of the Alichan refused to go up into the mines any more. Instead they preferred safer jobs working as dealers or servers in the big casino. If necessary, they would starve or leave the country before ever venturing up into the hills where Jacinto was lost.

Ultimately, the Rios reserves ran out and Daniel had to allow his own sons to work in the casino restaurant to earn enough for the family to survive. Apolonio, now 21, became an accomplished chef and was able to hire on his younger brothers Lazaro, 20, and Miguel, 18, as his assistants. Their younger sisters Florentina, 17 and Juanita, 16 had grown up into beautiful young ladies. Good reason for Daniel to keep them at home and as far away from the Purple Moon as possible.

While Apolonio and Miguel enjoyed their work in the kitchen, Lazaro was more interested in the action at the card tables and wanted to become a dealer. In due time, Lazaro won the confidence of el jefe and was trained to work at the tables. After hours, Lazaro would stay on to drink and gamble late into the morning. Although Lazaro was probably too young to be doing some of the things he was doing, there was no law in El Rodeo that Ismael Bertran couldn't evade or buy.

The Purple Moon was a lot of fun for Lazaro, but Ismael wanted to build something even bigger and grander. The prohibition of alcohol in the United States spawned a new opportunity for Señor Bertran. He sought new ways to displace some of the mental malnutrition suffered from being in one place too long.

The hurdle of making contraband was not the problem. Plenty of maguey could be planted in the isolated hillsides near Coluta.

The only limitations to the production of temescal and agave in town were storage capacity and publicity. Once the shipments of pulque began to make it across the border, the cash flow would buy any law that the people of El Rodeo could possibly invent.

Ismael knew the Rios family had a large and underutilized hacienda in the Coluta hillside. This was one reason he took such good care of Lazaro and the other Rios boys, to win influence and eventually an invitation to visit with their father.

Daniel had no desire to meet with the sleaze baron from down the hill but eventually the vague offers of some fantastic new business opportunity proved too tempting even for a principled man such as Don Rios.

Ismael did not intend to tell Señor Rios what he was really up to. Instead, he hoped to survey the hacienda and see whether it could meet his needs for a maguey plantation and distillery. If it did, perhaps then he could then make an offer to purchase the property under the veiled guise of returning Coluta to its original state as an enormous banana plantation.

When Ismael finally got to meet Don Rios, Lazaro was on hand and went so far as to give his employer a complete tour of several old abandoned mines in the area. The facilities were ideal and greater than Ismael had ever suspected. All the old mining equipment and buildings could easily be converted to use for storing barrels and distilling the maguey. The terrain was ideal not only for its existing vegetation and irrigation, the isolation and protection provided by the fearful Espinazo made this spot absolutely perfect for corruption.

Ismael did not want to seem overly enthusiastic about the property but at the same time, he could see that Don Daniel was barely providing for his wife and daughters. The boys were the only ones making any reliable income at all, yet it was certainly not enough to sustain an entire hacienda. Without Ismael's money, El Platanar would surely collapse quickly under its own weight.

Don Rios realized this too, so when Señor Bertran returned a week later with an offer to purchase, Daniel was willing to listen. Natividad could not bear the thought of leaving her home. Any offer would require that the Rios family be allowed to stay on as managers of the property and to live essentially in the same manner as in the past.

It was hardly an appealing condition, but the dollars and bottles sneaking back and forth across the border would not last forever. At some point, Rios would learn the truth about what was really being grown there and he would balk. No, having Daniel around simply would not do. Even in his poverty, Don Rios still held enough land and influence in the region to cause too many problems. An alternative plan was definitely in order.

Meanwhile, big dollars began to pour into the Mexican border towns. There was no time to waste. A direct attack upon Don Daniel would be too obvious. Ismael believed that he would be discovered as the culprit immediately if anything were to happen to Don Rios, and all the money in the world could do no good if he were behind bars or dead.

No, the best way to get at the Rioses would be to go after his friends or children. Going after innocent children seemed a bit low-down even for Ismael, so he decided instead to focus on El Platanar's current means for subsistence—Don Coronel. After remembering how quickly his first saloon crumbled when one support column was compromised, Ismael figured that if he could bring down La Galancita, Don Rios would have no choice but to sell or starve. Francisco Coronel held the largest remaining hacienda between El Rodeo and Coluta. He was the last source of grain for most of the valley beyond El Rodeo.

With the Rios family out of the way, the people of the valley would have no choice but to turn to Ismael and his new distillery for their survival. A direct attack upon La Galancita would be much easier too because the Coronel hacienda had fewer men and less fortification in the event of an all-out gun battle.

Still there must be a better way to get rid of Don Daniel. Ismael decided to ponder that puzzle over a bottle of cerveza. Ismael heard about the church that Francisco built on his hacienda. So, he decided to pose as a believer and paid a visit to La Galancita.

Upon arriving at the little church in La Galancita, Ismael was amazed at how full the building was. People stood along the walls and even outside the windows and doors. The singing was powerfully moving and even a hardened sinner like Bertran was caught up for a moment in the message of Francisco's words.

Though he had no formal training, Francisco was well versed in the Bible and conveyed its message in a way more powerful than anything the peasants had ever heard before in the Catholic Church. Although Francisco never thought of himself as anything other than a Christian, Ismael could clearly see this was not his father's Christianity. A few of the churchgoers felt they might be sinning by not attending a proper mass, especially when Coronel spoke of salvation through grace alone.

Ismael stood towards the back of the building, hoping not to be seen. Surprisingly, though, when the service was over, Don Francisco spotted him and rushed over to introduce himself to the famous saloon maverick.

In the early summer of 1924, the bishop in Culiacan sent a messenger from his cathedral to inquire as to why the contributions from Tamazula had fallen off so significantly over the last few years. The diocese required that every parish perform favorably for the Lord. Tamazula was the lone outpost in the Sierra and a father named Juan Carlos was the pastor of that parish.

****

The new President Obregon finally brought some signs of stability to the national economy, and the light spring rains were producing at least some hope for the first decent summer yields in years. It didn't make sense to the real bishop of Culiacan that a verdant valley high up in the Sierras with all its wealth of cattle and mines shouldn't be sharing more of its prosperity with the big city mendicants.

Everyone in Tamazula knew that the mines had been fruitless now for almost as long as the plantations. Father Juan Carlos was also aware of all the gossip surrounding the Purple Moon and the Alichan, but he had encountered fanciful tales of drunken laborers before; however, the impact had never been this severe. Contemplating the message from his bishop, Father Juan feared that the real cause of the depression within his diocese was less agricultural or economical and more spiritual.

The villages were also suffering from numerous illnesses and deaths from tuberculosis and silicosis in the miners, as well as pellagra, typhoid fever, and smallpox.

Therefore, the only priest in the area then decided to send himself upon a short mission to El Rodeo from Tamazula to find out why so many of his congregation were no longer attending church. He had heard all the gossip of the Purple Moon and how it was having considerable influence on the valley, but there seemed to be something more than dissipation going on. While it may have been more appropriate for the priest to spend an evening with one of many friendly families in town,

Father Juan Carlos decided instead to spend an evening at the Purple Moon.

There he met Ismael Bertran and was also introduced to the Rios boys. At first, Ismael thought the sight of a Catholic priest could be bad for business, but the Rios boys made a favorable impression upon the vicar and Juan Carlos had a surprisingly liberal view of all the drinking taking place in the casino.

Although the father would not gamble, he was amiable to the idea of having a glass of red wine at a corner table with his host. The atmosphere was lively yet civil, and having a respected figure around helped keep the place from getting too raucous. After observing his new surroundings and exploring Ismael's beliefs for a few minutes, Father Juan Carlos came quickly to his point.

"Señor Bertran, may I ask why you think so many members of our parish no longer attend church on Sundays?"

For a moment Ismael thought a condemnation of his establishment might be about to appear. Then with his devious mind fast at work he saw the question as an opportunity. The door was about to open upon Rios's demise.

"Padre, I think that if you look around you will see a lot of familiar faces." Ismael paused to throw a big Cheshire cat smile at the priest and allow him a few moments to carefully study the many other beaming faces that indeed he once knew from his parish. "Many of the people who come here on Saturday nights used to visit your church every Sunday morning. In fact, I think we create more sinners here for you than anywhere else in the Sierra."

The father had to chortle at that one.

"But the reason that most of these people are not going to your church any more is because they are going to the church that Don Coronel built at La Galancita."

With that, the father's expression changed rather noticeably. He was simultaneously enraged and curious about this new church. The priest fired question after question at Bertran until he could clearly see that the hook was set. It was then time to reel him in.

"Father, with all due respect, I think there are more than a few of us here that worry about what Don Coronel is teaching the people. It's not right. You know that his wife has left him, don't you?"

Father Juan Carlos flipped between outrage and disbelief as Bertran answered one question after another. The priest just could not learn enough about all of Francisco's alleged heresies.

"I personally do not attend his church because he often speaks out against the Holy Father. A few of the people here are also worried that we are being punished for sins that he will not confess to a priest. He claims to be an innocent man, yet the people here have all felt condemnation. The droughts, the famine, the Alichan himself—these are all signs, are they not? Even though I am not a very religious man myself, I know that this punishment is for some reason. Perhaps I should make a confession before you leave." Ismael had lowered his head almost in prayer before the priest and now looked up to see if his audience was buying.

"We should not rush to judgment, but obviously God would not have brought such catastrophe upon Francisco and his household if he weren't guilty of some considerable sin," said the father. "I would be most pleased to hear your confession whenever you are ready. If what you say is true perhaps Don Francisco should be making a confession also."

The evening grew late, so Ismael decided it was time to bring his newfound ally aboard.

"Padre, if you would like, I would be happy to offer you my confession in the morning and take you to La Galancita, so you can see all these things I've told for yourself." Bertran showed the priest to one of his finest rooms for the evening. It was hard then, as now, to distinguish the difference between your true friends and enemies.

V
THE BEASTS

"A beast does not know that he is a beast,
and the nearer a man gets to being a beast,
the less he knows it."

—George Mac Donald

12

Tuesday Evening — Durango, Mexico

"WHERE THE HELL ARE we now?" I called up to Gabriel. The young man's style of storytelling was somewhat different from that of Father Arres, but they both held a reverence for the past that shared a common quality of dignity that chapped my hide.

Sensing my growing irritation, from the darkness ahead he replied, calmly, "We are climbing towards El Espinazo del Diablo where the trail will continue to grow steeper and rockier. When the sun comes up we will take a brief rest before the final ascent towards El Reino del Cielo."

Gabriel's machete occasionally clanking in its scabbard was the loudest sound under the dull moonlight. Every once in a while, he would pull out the blade to clear a low-hanging branch from the trail. The mules seemed to know exactly where they were going as they stepped lightly upward. I tried to relax but had to know more about our mission.

"So, what's so important about this Palabra and Red Dragon that RuMa and Grace are out here somewhere risking their lives over them?" I asked.

"Father Arres believes that the sword you are carrying may contain information that we need to understand the maps and

Scrolls they found. She hopes that perhaps my understanding of the ancient Toltec symbols on La Palabra will help them learn where the Red Dragon rests before anyone else. Do you know what *boustrophedon* means?"

I had no idea.

"Is that some kind of dinosaur?"

Gabriel chuckled lightly before he replied, "No, that is an ancient way of reading and writing that moves from right to left and then backwards from left to right, in the same way that farmers used to plant their fields. I have been studying the Scroll and it seems to be written in this style that is familiar to the Tarahumaras. Tomorrow in the daylight I would like to study the Palabra to see if it has any similar inscriptions."

He was moving so quickly that I really just wanted to catch my breath, so I had to ask, "Your English is excellent. How did your people become so swift and how do you know so much?"

"I was raised in the Rarámuri tradition, so my parents always taught me that before you can be a strong runner, you must be a strong person. Wisdom was revered as a strength above speed or even knowledge. Also, we now have a library in Tamazula with internet and I spend a great deal of time there."

"I haven't studied very much of your native history, but from everything I've heard, the Tarahumara were wily people who were not to be trusted."

This didn't seem to disturb Gabriel at all as he replied calmly, "Well you have to consider that most of our history was written by European Jesuits. If they had considered the Indians to be equally human, perhaps they could have given a more balanced appraisal."

The humble young man obviously had many advantages over me on this dark journey, so I had to finally ask the most important question of all, "What are the odds that RuMa and Grace are still alive?"

"Unfortunately, some drug traders overheard one of the ladies in the nearby hamlet of Canelas talking about some chabochi women looking for the remains of a Red Dragon that protects a priceless sword and perhaps even the riches of El Dorado lost long ago."

Gabriel continued, "I believe that it would be difficult for anyone to find them, but men do have a tendency towards evil where riches are at stake. Even more important than gold may be the clues we need to discern recent signs in the heavens warning of a rapidly approaching end time when the Red Dragon will return for its glorious revenge."

This folklore sounded vaguely familiar, but in my youth, such drivel was never heeded. Gabriel was obviously obsessed with gaining some wisdom and RuMa always sought peace and security in the form of great fame or wealth, so this journey was finally beginning to make some sense. The Red Dragon fairy tales held little interest to me, but I was curious enough to ask, "So who were these hibachi women in Canelas and how much gold are we talking about?"

"No, no—not hibachi—cha-bochi." Gabriel chuckled. "*Chabochi* is simply the word for all non-Rarámuri. The chabochi women in Canelas were Grace and RuMa". He later explained that the Spaniards not only disrupted the native lifestyle with firearms and disease, but also with disturbing facial hair. "Chabochi literally means person with spider webbing across the face."

Pressing further into the jungle, Gabriel continued, "The tales of El Dorado have been told for centuries, but they hold no interest to the natives because their economy is based upon barter, not gold. They view work only as necessary for their survival; it is secondary to their spiritual obligations and the more important matters of their souls." He paused for a moment to point out a cluster of lights above, "See those stars there? The Tarahumara believe that each light in the sky represents the soul of a man or woman whose life has been extinguished."

For someone without any formal education, Gabriel was incredibly astute and aware of many facts and foreign traditions that I had never heard of. In particular, he held a keen knowledge of Hebrew writing. He shared, "The Torah says when you go to war in your own land against an oppressive adversary, you are to sound an alarm with trumpets; then God will save you from enemies."

His spirit was as bright and joyful as the noise that came from his shofar, a musical utensil that he handmade from a ram's horn. As a musician, he carried this instrument with him wherever he went and just before daybreak as we settled down to rest, he brought out his horn to play a great fanfare. He said it was not only to ward off evil spirits but also to welcome the Lord.

"The good news is that a Savior is coming soon," Gabriel cried excitedly; and with a bright flourish he sounded a long blast on his shofar. The note carried up towards the fading stars and far beyond as his campfire story continued to echo endlessly into the valley below . . .

13

July 1924 — Durango, Mexico

ACCORDING TO LEGEND, ONE evening while deep in a dream-like state, the Red Alichan discovered that he could morph into any object or animal he wished to become. Without accountability the leviathan could become a shape-shifter without gender or form.

Dionicia too, after being essentially alone for so long, felt as though she was becoming part of the darkness. They say that one evening, she also had a vision. At least she thought it was a vision; perhaps just a dream, a shadow, or peyote. Then as it drew closer she wondered whether she really was asleep. She could not give credence to her eyes, "My mind must be playing some kind of trick on me," she whispered.

The specter had a powerful form. He was tall, handsome, and nonthreatening, even in this environment seemingly void of all warmth. Now her ears lied to her as well because the apparition spoke . . . softly.

"My name is Apolonio. Are you all right?"

The voice sounded faintly familiar, and so soothing that he certainly brought no harm, whoever this was. Manuelito was sleeping soundly as Dionicia fumbled in the dark for a candle to shed some light upon this enigma.

Indeed, the voice did remind her of Don Rios's oldest son, but what, how, why would he be down in this desolate dwelling in the middle of the night? These were too many questions for a dream. She must have been awake as she held the candle closer to the voice to see what else it might have to say. She was still too stunned to speak.

The young man stepped into the candlelight and repeated his question: "Are you all right?" In the flickering shadows Dionicia could see that this was indeed the grown son of her former neighbor the Don Daniel. Apolonio recognized Dionicia immediately and realized that he must have startled her.

"Don Francisco heard from someone in Canelas that you were seen there, so he sent me to look for you. No one wanted to talk to me, but I was finally able to find Santita and convinced her that I must see you." Still there was no response, so he probed further, "Have you been injured? Do you need any assistance?"

Finally, trusting that she might not be dreaming after all Dionicia replied, "Api is that really you? I am fine, but how did you find me here?" The long silence was over. She was finally communicating with someone from her past life and she was at ease. They embraced each other.

As tears began to well up in Dionicia's eyes Api told her, "Everyone in the valley has been looking for you but I was the only one crazy enough to come this far up into the Sierra. People down below are afraid that some wild animals might be up in this area."

Apolonio didn't want to frighten the lady with any of the stories of the Alichan, but Dionicia was well aware of the legend. She thought about telling Apolonio about her strange dream on the night that Manuelito was born but then thought otherwise.

"I'm not afraid of any animal that your God has ever made."
Then upon further thought all the toil of her life came to mind.
"The only animals that scare me are men. I'm afraid of all the things
that men have made to destroy my life." Visions reappeared of the
kitchen chores, the debts to pay and too many sins to confess.
The homecoming idea suddenly turned sour. "Anyway, my family
must hate me by now. I can never return to La Galancita."

Apolonio soon noticed the sleeping child beside Dionicia
and asked, "Who is this?"

"This is my son Manuelito, isn't he beautiful?"

More reasons not to return home - the explaining, the
painful memories, the shame, and the regrets. There was so much
she could have done; should have done. Going home would only
compound the misery. The darkness at least hid the pain from
others, if not from herself.

"Why yes, but . . . when, I mean. . . how? I mean, yes of
course he is beautiful. We should celebrate!"

That was an unexpected response to her unforeseen news,
but as soon as she stood up beside the attractive young man she
could not resist his clumsy request, "We should sing and dance,
would you like to dance?"

Of course she would. Even in her darkest hours, Dionicia
always longed to dance. "Quietly, though. We don't want to wake
him up." As they began to murmur sweet songs and dance silently,
the moon watched from above.

When the morning light crept into the lodging, Manuelito
stirred. He was a bit puzzled by the extra body in their home but
not particularly concerned. If it was all right with his mother, it
was fine with him.

Once everyone was awake, Dionicia introduced Apolonio to
Manuelito. Api had a bag with a pan, some eggs, and a flint to start

a fire. Manuelito helped gather some dry brush and twigs so that in no time they were enjoying a delicious breakfast complete with tortillas, tomatoes, and avocado. That was something Dionicia and Manuelito hadn't seen in quite a while. The smoke felt good on their face even as the realities of the outside world began to sink in.

Apolonio knew he would have to get back home soon or his father would send a search party.

"Dionicia, I promised to find you and bring you home. You must be ready to leave this place?" Her expression turned sad again at the realization that he may be right.

"If not for yourself, you must realize that Manuelito is going to be a young man soon. He can't live alone in here with you forever." That was exactly the right nerve to hit.

"I can never just enjoy life for myself! It's always for this child or that man or this animal or some *thing*. Why can't I just be left alone to die in peace?" Her quiet desperation no longer stifled, "My husband probably has enough trouble trying to feed the two girls he already has. How can he possibly want two more mouths to feed?"

No, she was definitely not going back, "This place might be cold at night, but I have everything I need right here." Dionicia pulled her legs up into her body and tried not to notice the dismay crawling all over her son's face. It was no problem for her to think about spending her eternity in this remote abode, but it was also beneath her to consider forcing the same fate upon her only living son. Api wanted to help, and she could see that.

"Well, if you don't want to leave, I can't force you," he lied. "If you are afraid of what people might say, I'm sure there are families that can care for your son. He will need to see if he can become a man someday and he'll never find that out here."

"Api, you must promise me one very important thing."

"Sure, whatever you need, just ask."

"You must promise you will never, ever, ever tell anyone where we are or about my son. Please, can you do that for me?" She pleaded her case firmly with both hands clasped tightly before her heart. Her tragedy-stricken face wore no mask.

Every pain she had suffered in the past: the agony of ten childbirths, the death of seven sons, the loss of her marriage, the lost hacienda, all the evaporated material wealth. It all came back in that moment as Apolonio retreated into the daylight.

Apolonio could see the pain in her face and his last words to her before he turned to ride away were, "Don't worry Dionicia, I will return soon to bring you some fresh food and supplies." True to his word, Api returned as soon as he could sneak back with provisions and a promise to never tell anyone of her whereabouts.

"My family will be worried if I'm not home soon," Api said. "But don't worry, I will return after a while to make sure that you and Manuelito are still doing well."

"No, no, NO!" she pleaded. We are doing quite well here, and it is best if you never return. Please promise me once again that you will never tell anyone that I'm here."

It was a difficult thing to say, but in order to leave he had to say, "Yes, okay, I promise." And he did his best to keep that promise as long as he could . . .

***

Daniel Rios was relieved to see his son back safely from his expedition into the Espinazo. Though he trusted his son's skills and strength, he never felt easy about what might be still lurking about there.

VI
THE BEAUTIES

*Whose adorning let it not be that outward adorning of plaiting the
hair, and of wearing of gold, or of putting on of apparel;
But let it be the hidden man of the heart, in that which is not
corruptible, even the ornament of a meek and quiet spirit, which is
in the sight of God of great price.*

1 Peter 3:3-4

14

Wednesday Morning — Durango, Mexico

AFTER A FEW BRIEF hours of rest, Gabriel woke me to begin our last push up to the bowl through some of the most breathtaking jungle scenery I had ever seen. Spectacular waterfalls and majestic rock formations appeared at every turn.

As our mules settled into a gentle rhythm, Gabriel and I grew closer. He wanted to know more about how I met my wife, so I told him, "She was the most pure and lovely girl I had ever encountered, but it took me a long time to recognize her true beauty." There was only adequate time to share a brief glimpse of our previous joyful life, yet it was enough for Gabriel to understand my great sense of loss, "So why do you and RuMa no longer travel together?"

That was a difficult question to answer, because over time we tend to only hold onto the brighter moments in life. However, this young man seemed sincerely concerned and capable of receiving my best perceptions, so I searched deeply for some credible reason.

"That is difficult for me to explain in any language, but I suppose it was the gradual rise and fall of our own unreasonable expectations for one another. When I lost my job and father not long ago, my self-image and confidence decayed to a point where nothing seemed to matter anymore. I think that without any family nearby or shared hobbies, there was no meaningful purpose for life once our children grew up and moved on. After losing our home to overwhelming debts, the relationship never really recovered."

Gabriel did not interrupt with anything other than, "Yes, I can see that you are in great pain. Please tell me more. How do you deal with so much suffering?" So, I continued to process this dilemma of life for him out loud. "Well, back home I ride my bike on lonely trails like this to help heal some of the wounds, but as RuMa rode further in her own direction, we lost each other. The beauty in my life is gone and the only hope worth holding onto seems to come from this crazy idea that maybe she is looking for me too. In the meantime, I distract myself with work and a few small accomplishments on the bike to get me through each day. Happiness is out there somewhere Gabriel, but she just always seems beyond my reach."

Fortunately, my regular physical training gave me the strength to continue along the pathway as it steadily became steeper and steeper. At one point the stony trail became too difficult for the animals to negotiate with our weight, so we had to dismount and scramble up an unyielding wall of loose boulders.

Later in the light of that day, the road leveled out for a bit and the young man paused to look at the engravings on La Palabra. He was obviously taken by some beauty that I could not see in the petrified relic. "This sword was named after the Word of God, and it is written, 'Man shall not live by bread alone, but by every word that proceedeth out of the mouth of God.' I am not certain," he said. "but it looks as though this writing confirms my greatest fears. There is a great battle ahead of us and it is coming soon."

Approaching the peaks that would test my faith, something astounding happened, I began to face my doubts. Beyond the message of La Palabra, what more could I take to RuMa that might change our future together? I was also beginning to appreciate how much my great grandfather must have longed for the return of his dancing Dionicia.

As Gabriel picked up the story again of my family history I was amazed by how much detail he retained from hearing these words from Father Arres. It was almost as if the priest was still with us telling the story through his own observations . . .

15

September 1924 — La Galancita, Mexico

ROSITA WAS NOW A radiant woman of twenty years. Her apron was frayed at the edges, yet still whiter than the snow that she could only see upon the distant peaks of El Reino del Cielo. Her little sister had grown into a gorgeous young lady by the age of fifteen, yet whenever she passed a mirror, she only noticed every slight flaw. On a typical late afternoon, Victoria swept dust from the patio and swatted a few chickens away from the front door before entering. The younger girl tucked the broom into its corner and prepared the table for dinner.

The elder sister stared out the back window while rinsing out a large olla (pot) in the basin.

"What are you dreaming about now?" Victoria asked as the sun set slowly upon another day for the few hearty peasant ranchers of this isolated ranch land.

Francisco gathered his tools and saddles from his favorite horse, Lily, after a long day in the high grassland. Isolated from the rest of the world by high mountains and dry valleys bordering steep cliffs, two wide rivers full of fish rushed around the perimeter of El Rodeo. The lack of engineering or bridges protected La

Galancita from most visitors for most of the year. Only during these driest summer months would the rivers recede enough for mule trains to course a crude stone pathway just below the surface.

Only experienced riders on horseback or sure-footed mules could cross El Rio Tamazula and a tributary of the Humaya named El Rio Fuerte (the strong river). Isolated by time and culture, this place might have seemed to the casual observer as close to Shangri-La as any place in the world.

The next morning Rosita was up before the roosters to prepare coffee and gorditas (fat little corn cakes usually topped with meat, vegetables, cheese or butter) for her father's long ride ahead. The walls of their home were badly cracked, but with a little earth, water, and hay, the great seismic events of 1910 were mostly a memory.

Although there were only about ten horses and a dozen cattle left in the corrals, there was still much work to do outdoors. The new church that Francisco built took the majority of his time. Since most of the inhabitants of the valley no longer traveled into Tamazula to attend church, Francisco had, in addition to supplying the last reserves of grain, become the unofficial pastor for all the local campesinos (peasant farmers).

Apolonio had a few days off from his work at the Purple Moon, so he decided to pay a visit to his neighbors to the west. The young man occasionally used to offer his services as a wrangler in the fall but mostly he offered his services to Don Coronel as an excuse to visit Rosita.

Victoria was enamored of Apolonio and was excited to greet him when he arrived at their front door.

"Good morning Victoria, I came to see if your father needed any assistance today."

She loved his long eyelashes and thick black hair. But just as Rosita had no interest in the men of their Valley, Api still saw Victoria as just another immature child of the Galancita. Though her youthful allure was hard to ignore, he found himself peeking over her shoulder and around corners to see if he might spot Rosita by chance.

Rosita's dreams of romance lived beyond the jagged peaks of the Sierra Espinazo. One of the few great pleasures in her life was reading the books, magazines, and newspapers that her father brought up from Culiacan. She understood the rapidly changing world lying far to the north, a place where real dreams could come true. Not cowboy dreams or farmer dreams or dreams of El Dorado, but a place where the possibilities of real discoveries could be made. The Twenties were roaring in America, but not here.

Victoria struggled to hold Apolonio's attention as she walked him along the long entry corridor towards the barns at the back of the home where her father was saddling his horse. Apolonio's cooking skills and the fact that he had a real job working as a chef impressed the young Rios.

"What will you be preparing at the Purple Moon this week Apolonio?" she asked.

Apolonio could talk about food all day. It was his favorite subject. Victoria knew which keys opened the man's heart. Food was always a favorite topic of conversation for Apolonio and as he approached the kitchen he could smell breakfast on the stove. Aware that Rosita would be preparing the morning meal, he saw the opportunity to visit with her.

"What are you having for breakfast this morning?" he asked.

Knowing where this was headed and frustrated by his lack of attention, Victoria replied indignantly, "Aye, I am so sick of huevos rancheros I could just gag."

That opened the door for Apolonio to suggest, "Maybe there's something I can do to help?"

"Oh, no," Victoria became a little girl again, shrugging her shoulders and rolling her eyes, "I don't think there's anything anyone can do to make huevos rancheros appealing any more, but thanks for offering."

Just then they passed by the kitchen entry and there she was. Rosita was setting two plates on the table and she caught Apolonio's eyes. He had to pause if only for a moment, "Good morning Señorita Coronel." She only acknowledged his existence with a simple nod. Api was about to continue down the wide hallway with his escort when he decided to try one more greeting, "Your cooking smells wonderful as always."

Still not a remark she was looking for. The aroma was rich, but Apolonio knew there was something missing.

"May I bring you some fresh onions from our garden next time for the rancheros?" Now he was beginning to chap her hide. Her non-response allowed Victoria the opportunity to take Api's left arm and nudge him onward again towards the barn. The silence from the kitchen seemed a bit harsh to the young man.

Every rose has its thorn, but Rosita could be incredibly cool and distant in a way that frightened all but those who knew her well. Master Rios knew Rosita well, but not well enough. The warmth and light he once saw in her eyes disappeared along with her mother and brothers.

Though Api was a full year older than Rosita, she still saw him as a little boy chasing pigs and goats. Whatever skills he may have learned at the Purple Moon were of no use here where the food stock was at the basic subsistence level.

Rosita might have let the boy flounder and retreat on down the hall, but the idea of fresh onions was enticing. Api had barely passed out of sight when Rosita called out, "That would be nice Apolonio, thank you."

Victoria knew when to leave well enough alone and once again quickly steered the young man on towards the barn. As he appreciated the artwork on the walls along the long corridor Apolonio could not wait to return later. His escort was looking forward to seeing him again if only for a few moments, then a thought occurred to her.

"Would you like to join us for dinner this evening Apolonio?"

"Why yes, but shouldn't we ask your sister and your father first?"

"I'm sure they would enjoy your company.

Victoria opened the barn door gracefully to announce Api to her father. When Francisco saw the tall young man with his riding boots on and a saddlebag across his shoulder, he knew automatically why the boy was standing before him.

"Apolonio you are a welcome surprise. I was just about ready to round up a few of the cattle that have been wandering a bit far up the Sierra lately."

"Well they can't be too far yet. I saw a few of them on the other side of the valley on my way down." The men made immediate preparations for their horses and saddles when Victoria interrupted with her idea.

"Papa, Master Rios is going to bring us some fresh onions, and I was thinking maybe we should invite him to dinner this evening."

Francisco smiled at his young daughter, knowing how infatuated she was with Api—and all the other boys in the valley for that matter. Then another thought crossed his mind.

"You know, that is a good idea. In fact, your father has been meaning to speak with me lately about something and I haven't had the chance. Would you please invite him also?"

"Of course, Señor Coronel, I'm sure he would be pleased to accept."

"And be sure to bring your brothers and sisters too."

This invitation become a well-remembered fiesta, "Thank you, but I'm afraid that my brothers will be working tonight. Though I'm certain Florentina and Juanita would enjoy a chance to get away from El Platanar for a while."

Victoria was not really interested in seeing the Rios girls again. They were a few years older and she always thought that they were a bit too haughty for her simple tastes. The girls would just distract her from her real interest, but he was obviously more interested in Rosita anyway.

"Oh well, I better get back to the kitchen and tell Rosita to get ready for company."

Victoria sighed heavily and walked away.

"Tell Rosita that if we can find the fatted calf we will have a feast tonight."

"Oh no, Señor Coronel, you shouldn't go through all that for us. We have plenty of chickens that we can bring over and fresh vegetables too."

Francisco insisted, "No, as long as I have your strong hands here to help me butcher a calf we should celebrate. It has been too long since we've had a good reason to celebrate. Tonight, we will celebrate . . . I don't know. We will celebrate something. Let's ride!"

The men had already eaten their breakfasts and hit the trail hard. It didn't take long for them to reach the swamp area known as La Cienega. There they found a few cattle wandering along the dryer hillsides. The fattest calf somehow managed to trap itself up on a ledge where it could not get down and stood mooing in fright. Apolonio spotted him first and pointed him out to Don Francisco with a sharp whistle.

"Yes! There's our dinner Api."

A few of the other cattle had moved off in a different direction so Francisco decided to go after them.

"You're a better climber Api. You go after the little one and I'll turn these old leather bags around."

"Ok!" Api shouted as he climbed down from his mount. Francisco rode swiftly out of sight and in the few minutes that it took for Apolonio to cross a small ravine and climb up to the calf, the animal became eerily silent. A dust devil appeared in the distance and approached from the east. Picking up more dirt and shrubs, it grew larger and caliginous as it came closer. It was beautiful in a way, but troublesome if it were to knock the little calf from its precarious perch.

The calf was within a few feet of Apolonio's reach when the earth began to rumble. It was a familiar but disconcerting sound to hear with the calf just a few steps above his head. The rock face started to sway, and the rolling motion grew more forceful. Suddenly a crease in the ground appeared in the dry soil below.

The ground came to a halt as a figure appeared from out of the subsiding dust cloud. It was a man in black.

"Who are you?" Apolonio called to the man across the ravine. The man seemed to be wearing a black cape and hat, so his face was shielded.

"You have not been tested yet." It was as if the man in black could clearly hear the question but ignored it and persisted.

"Tell your father to give up El Platanar. I still have work for you to do."

The words made no sense, but the voice seemed to know him. Somehow the man seemed familiar to Apolonio also, but how could he know this person?

"You have not been tested yet!" The chimera repeated its initial statement then became silent as a dust cloud rose up behind him again.

Apolonio cried out to the phantom a second time to ask what it was talking about.

"Who are you?" he shouted louder as the ground shook once more. Whether the man in black could hear him or not, Api would never know. The dark cloud swept him up and dropped him into the ravine.

The earth moved once more, and the crease was gone. As quickly as the ground had opened up it closed again, swallowing the voice along with it.

The calf was quiet now. Apolonio stood stunned for a moment in silence. Then, he scrambled down from the rocks to see if the mysterious man in black could be saved. When Francisco felt the temblor, he rushed back to check on the closest person to a son he had left. He was surprised to find the calf still perched on its ledge with Api scratching around in the dust below.

Francisco asked, "What happened Api, are you all right?"

"I think so. I mean, there was a man here, but he fell into this crevice." The fissure was all but gone now, so Francisco could not understand what the young man was talking about.

"What are you talking about Api, there's no ravine here."

"There was a minute ago. This man came out of nowhere and started talking to me then the ground shook and . . ." Api was frantic now kicking and scraping at the ground with a loose stone, "He was right here!"

Francisco could see that Api was nearly crazed by whatever he had just seen.

"Ok, hold on a second let's see if we can hear anything."

Francisco halted the frenzy for a moment to listen to the ground. They both held their breath and pressed their ears to the soil but there was no sound. Both brought out small shovels and tried to find some signs of life but there were none. The little calf watched curiously for a while before giving out a short moo to remind them it was time to go home.

Apolonio climbed up and carried the calf down on his shoulders to a more level surface. Francisco gathered the other cattle and the calf ran to join them. Just as they were about to leave, they both noticed an interesting white rock just above the ledge where the little calf was stranded.

"Doesn't that look like a dove to you Apolonio?" Don Francisco asked. Api looked up and saw a very well defined white bird shape naturally sculpted into the stone.

"It sure does. I've never seen anything like that before. It looks almost as if someone painted it by hand."

On the long drive home, Api tried to explain what he had heard but it just didn't make sense, "I have no idea what that man was talking about. What do you suppose he was trying to tell me, Don Coronel?"

The older and wiser man pondered the question for a while before answering, "I'm not sure, but I know these things we see with our eyes are not always what they seem."

"What do you mean by that?" Apolonio wondered aloud.

"Well, in the Bible there are many stories about battles between good and evil. Perhaps this was part of a spiritual battle going on right here all around us. We can't always see it, but sometimes we can feel it. Think of all the tumult that our valley has seen in the last few years. This must be the evil one at work. He's trying make us doubt God's word, don't you think so?" Francisco paused to give Api time to think through the question.

Apolonio didn't read the Bible or attend church at La Galancita. In fact, just hearing the name of God made his skin crawl. Api finally had to admit, "I'm not sure what to believe any more Don Francisco. What kind of God would allow the type of death and destruction we have seen lately?"

"You need to come to church on Sundays and listen to the Word of God. All the answers to your questions are there if you are willing to listen." Don Francisco thought about pursuing the point further but instead just left it at that.

The riders were approaching the Platanar and Api needed to stop in to tell his family about their dinner invitation. There was no time to tell his father all about the events of the day. After a few minutes Api returned with a bag full of clean clothes and fresh fruit then they hit the trail again. The cattle were getting restless and knew their way home from El Platanar.

When Francisco arrived at his hacienda, he was surprised to find two horses outside his front entry. Inside, Rosita and Victoria were keeping two unexpected guests company. Ismael Bertran was awaiting their arrival with a special visitor from Tamazula, a Father Juan Carlos.

Although Francisco was not comfortable seeing the notorious Señor Bertran at home with his daughters, at least he was in good company. Don Coronel knew the father well from his travels through Tamazula, but Ismael introduced the two men anyway as if some special fellowship existed between them.

"Father Juan Carlos has come to visit your new church and bring blessings upon your household."

No matter how hard he tried, Ismael just couldn't help but say ridiculous things. The priest and hacendado shook hands and smiled at each other knowingly.

"I insist that you spend the evening here with us. We were planning to kill a fatted calf tonight. Now you have given us a reason to celebrate."

Francisco led his guests into the grand sitting room where his daughters entertained them until dinnertime.

Apolonio helped Francisco butcher the calf and together they prepared a meal fit for kings. It was the first time in many years they had seen such festivity. Lydia and a few other campesinos from the area came in to help serve the meal. In return, they knew they would each receive a healthy portion of beef and side dishes to take home to their own families.

Once everyone was seated, Don Coronel asked Father Juan Carlos to pray over the meal. All around the massive dinner table the conversation was lively. Don Francisco sat at the head of the table closest to the massive fireplace. Father Juan Carlos and Ismael sat on either side of their host.

Don Rios sat at the opposite end of the table with his daughters Juanita and Florentina at each side. Miguel was seated opposite the table from his brother between Florentina and Victoria Coronel.

Api made sure he was seated next to Rosita that evening, so he might have the opportunity to discover what troubled her so. It should have been obvious to anyone, but men are not so sensitive to matters of the heart. Rosita missed her mother.

"I would love to leave this valley someday and see the world on the other side of all these mountains. It would be so much easier to leave if I knew where my mother was and that she was safe."

This troubled Apolonio, because he knew exactly where her mother was, and he also wanted to leave the valley with Rosita for his own calling.

"Did you know that I have always wanted to own my own vineyard?" This drew no response, so he added, "Whenever I go out looking for land I always ask people about your mother." He noticed how quickly his last comment drew her attention closer.

***

Father Juan Carlos spent most of the evening interrogating Francisco on issues of theology and questioning his loyalty to the church.

"So, Don Coronel, since you have appointed yourself as the vicar of this community tell me, where do you receive your authority to command such a flock? Has the bishop or perhaps some cardinal been in contact with you regarding the care of Christians within his diocese?"

The priest knew full well that the bishop had not authorized the building of a church in the middle of La Galancita, but he thought he might be able to catch the rancher in a false statement.

The host's answered directly, "My authority comes from the same source as yours—Jesus Christ. It is written that He has been given all authority in heaven and earth."

Father Juan Carlos knew of the Coronel's German heritage and was aware of the many Protestant traditions the Europeans brought with them in conflict with the Roman Catholic Church.

"But what about our creed? Do you not believe in one Holy Catholic and Apostolic Church?"

"Of course," Francisco replied, "but should that prevent us from sharing the good news however possible?"

Ismael was hardly interested in issues of the church and theology, but he was interested in the Coronel's property. If Don Daniel was not interested in giving up his hacienda, this place would do just as nicely. La Galancita was closer to El Rodeo, so he could keep a close eye out on the Purple Moon from here. Bertran thought about making Francisco an offer then and there but decided to hold his tongue until Don Rios made his decision.

Since Apolonio seemed more interested in her older sister, Victoria decided to turn her attention to the younger Rios, Miguel. Closer to her in age, he seemed more obtainable than the lanky Apolonio and more suited to her wild temperament. She was surprised how much they had in common and by the end of the evening they found themselves strolling alone together under the warm starlight.

Juanita and Florentina increased the distance between Ismael and their father who was not ready to talk about business until he had a chance to discuss the offer with his wise neighbor Francisco first. It would be best to discuss the matter tomorrow after church when Bertran and the priest left.

At the church service, the following morning Father Juan Carlos was given a seat of prominence at the front along with Señor Bertran. When the campesinos of the hamlet learned that a real priest was in town, they flocked from all over the hills to have their children baptized and confirmed. As a token of his appreciation, Don Francisco sent all the collections of that day home with the father.

Maybe the villagers were being more generous than usual, but for whatever reason the collection was particularly bountiful that morning. This disturbed the father even more and made

Ismael wonder if perhaps the mines were producing profitably again. For a short while, there was hope that the beauty of La Galancita would return and the riches of El Dorado would soon be discovered.

VII
THE QUESTS BEGIN

"Over the Mountains
Of the Moon,
Down the Valley of the Shadow,
Ride, boldly ride,"
The shade replied, -
"If you seek for El Dorado!"

—Edgar Allan Poe

16

Wednesday Afternoon — Durango, Mexico

THE SUN BEGAN TO fade behind the mountains behind us as we continued to ride away from a valley of growing shadows. While we sought urgently after Grace and RuMa, they were on their own quest for some greater truth in their excavation work. Some discovery was out there driving them to risk everything in these remote drug-infested mountains. The Sierra's beauty and promise were alluring, but the dangers - immense.

"Keep moving!" Gabriel called. "God willing, we will be there later tonight." He seemed intensely focused now on the trail as he pointed towards a narrow approach towards the highest peak called 'El Reino'.

Perhaps the message of the sword unsettling Gabriel had some significant value that could provide the safety, security or greater spiritual reward we were all looking for.

"So Gabriel," I asked. "What makes you believe that some higher power wants to bless us for staying on this pathway?"

"What makes you think there isn't?" he fired back. Before I could think of a decent answer he had an unexpectedly easier question for me. "Do you know what permutations and combinations are?"

"Sure" I said hesitantly. Statistics was one of my favorite subjects in business school. The details from classes taken so long ago were a bit fuzzy, but where the heck was he going with this conversation?

"Then what do you think the probability is that we are all out here by chance?" For a long time, anger drove me to believe the worst of everything. This had nothing to do with mathematics, science, or any empirical evidence.

"This is not about luck or chance Gabriel. My question is about the intentions of some unseen creator and why he would have any concern over whether we live or die out here."

Gabriel paused to consider my response, but not for long.

"My questions are not about chance or intentions, Mr. Martin. They are about seeking truth. I believe there is much truth to be gained from the word of God. The Bible says that 'All Scripture is God-breathed and is useful for teaching, rebuking, correcting and training in righteousness.' Do you believe the Bible to be the true word of God?"

"I think the Bible was written by several very sincere men who were all created by the same laws of nature and probability as every other creature in the universe. It's a great collection of interesting stories, but they all seem to share some common delusion of immortality that I cannot understand. I've got too many questions that need answers RIGHT NOW, not in some future life."

Obviously, Gabriel spent more time worrying about these matters than I did, because it didn't take long before he had a pretty sharp response:

"I see, then you must believe that the message of the gospel came about through insanity, a series of lies or just some random coincidence of time and space." That seemed to cover just about every possibility I could think of from the saddle of my sore ass. But before I could respond, Gabriel continued.

"If that is the case, then all of the prophecies leading up to the appearance of Jesus would also have to be false. Did you know that the probability of all the correct predictions in the Bible occurring by chance is less than one in 1.5 times 10 to the power of 239?"

Where did he get such crazy data from? Certainly, that had to be a rhetorical question. Those numbers were zillions of times beyond my ability of comprehension. Perhaps with some stronger reasoning I might be able to consider the possibility of a compassionate being.

"Then what is the probability that we are on the pathway of blessing today?"

Surely, I thought he would have a quick answer for such a simple query, but just then he paused and hopped down from Reno to take a closer look at something on the trail disconcerting him more than my question.

"There is a large group of horses moving towards Topia. We will have to take another route to El Reino. It will be more difficult but more direct, and we can still get there before all of these other riders."

"How many?" I asked.

"Looks like about twenty; militia and local police together. They will probably stay on this new road, which is wider and a longer distance, but they are moving more quickly than our animals. We must hurry."

Gabriel mounted up and we quickly turned northward along a narrower, steeper trail. The more important questions in life would have to wait for now. Gabriel seemed to know the territory well enough to get us to our immediate destination before the horde. He had mentioned earlier that the Tarahumara are some of the last remaining naguals (master students) of the Toltec people but I didn't pay attention. Tarahumara also means 'where the night is the day of the moon'. Apparently, some are still able to translate the ancient language spoken silently by this land.

"I'm paying attention now," I called forward. It was in that moment a realization fluttered by that confidence is more fragile than a butterfly's wings. RuMa must have been pretty frightened by what she learned to call on me for help. While there was still some breath left in me, I had to ask one more big question.

"Gabriel, what am I doing here?"

"At first," Gabriel said, "Grace did not want to share her latest discoveries with anyone. But RuMa convinced her that you were the only one who could be trusted. I can tell you more later, but please, we must keep moving."

The value of this history rose greatly as the tale continued and more important answers grew closer. We rode boldly onward …

17

November 1924 — Dolores

TRUE TO HIS WORD, Apolonio returned to visit Dionicia with fresh food and a mare named Alas (Wings). Inside one of the horse's saddlebags, Apolonio packed a bar of gold that would provide Dionicia with enough money to buy food and supplies for quite a while. All she needed to do was shave off a few flakes of gold from the bar, then ride into the nearby village of El Frijolar whenever she needed to satisfy any critical needs.

However, as soon as Api left, Dionicia began to worry that he would tell someone where she was. She often thought of going back to Ismael or La Caldera, but the trek would be too cold and dangerous for Manuelito in the winter. Since she felt as though she had failed her other children, she did not want to risk the chance of losing Manuelito.

The one thing she no longer needed was attention. She was satisfied to spend time alone with Manuelito. There was plenty of tall grass and shrubs for Alas to munch on. Occasionally, a group of Tarahumara Indians from as far away as Topia or Canelas would come along to spend time visiting with Dionicia. She enjoyed sharing stories with them and hearing again of their legends and beliefs.

They told her their religion was a mosaic of indigenous customs and Roman Catholicism. When Jesuits were expelled in 1767, the Rarámuri were left alone to modify and create their own symbols and practices without outside intervention. These morphed into various ideas, including a belief that Riablo (the word for their devil) sometimes collaborates with God to arrange appropriate punishments that can only be appeased through great sacrifice. Therefore, Riablo was not considered to be wholly evil, only tainted by its ties with the Chabochi (non-Rarámuri). In some cases, it was even thought that Riablo could be persuaded to act as a benevolent entity.

The native Mesoamerican people also believed in serpent deities since Olmec times (c. 1500 BC) The Quetzalcoatl deity was often depicted as part resplendent trogon (a brightly feathered bird) and part serpent. When lightning strikes sand, it can form undulating strands of glass similar to the curves of the snake. Before she met Francisco, her Indigenous parents taught Dionicia their beliefs. Now after losing her entire family, she wasn't sure what to believe. She only knew that the few remaining Tarahumara provided her with beans, squash and pinole to nourish herself and Manuelito. They also shared a veneration with other Uto-Aztecan tribes for a divine messenger known as peyote.

As she gained confidence in her Topian friend, she decided to entrust Santita with a relic that she came across years earlier while exploring the Cauldron. It was a deteriorating old sword with some sort of symbols near the handle. While she could not understand it's meaning, the Curandera of Topia, seemed fascinated by the object and promised to protect it from any harm.

18

November 1924 — Durango

BACK ON THE RANCH, Don Rios finally had a chance to speak with Francisco in confidence about the offer he had received from Ismael for El Platanar.

"I'm thinking that maybe we should give Ismael a chance to put some more crops into the fields and see if he has any better luck with this place than we have."

Francisco could see the fatigue and desperation in his neighbor's face.

"But you have had this land in your family since Maximilian. What does Ismael know about growing anything legal? He told you he wants to grow sugar cane here? This soil has been drying for too long, it will take him years to grow cane here. Pretty soon he'll have his people up here drinking, carousing, and stealing our good women. Once he is in charge, you will never get him to leave. Don't you think there is at least some chance that some gold or silver might be left somewhere up in those mines?"

"Cisco, we have turned over every stone from here to Canelas and there is not a trace of any color. I suppose that someday with better equipment or more help we may find something, but this land has worn me out."

"Rios, you sound like an old man to me. How old are you now forty? Forty-two?"

"I turned forty-three this year," Daniel admitted quietly.

"You are a young man. There is still much life left in this land. Things are going to get better; just be patient and give God a chance to do some work here."

Daniel could argue with Francisco all day, but he could not argue with God.

"All right amigo. I will wait on the Lord," Daniel said.

And with that the gentlemen shared a manly abrazo and parted company.

The following day, Daniel sent Lazaro into El Rodeo with an important message for Ismael that the offer was not acceptable. and that El Platanar would remain in the Rios family. Lazaro was glad to be trusted with such an important assignment and even further honored to be invited into Señor Bertran's private office.

When Ismael heard the news, he became so enraged that he pulled out his favorite pearl-handled pistol from a desk drawer and shot Lazaro right between two very frightened eyes. The young man never even had time to react. By the time he realized what was happening, it was too late. Lazaro was dead.

With all the noise and calamity taking place in the casino down the hall, only the tall, slump-shouldered guard with a long handlebar bigote (moustache), sitting right outside the door noticed the sound of a single fatal bullet. Ismael's right-hand man came rushing in with his revolver drawn, but when he saw the boy slumped in the chair he holstered his weapon and quickly closed the door behind him.

"What happened?" The droopy-eyed toady named Mario asked.

"Never mind," Ismael snapped. "Just get rid of him—and fast!"

This was not an unusual assignment for Mario. People who disagreed with Ismael often disappeared in similar fashion. When the hall was clear, Mario disposed of the body in one of his many secret burial grounds around town. Mario was not a prized thinker, but he was a sharp shooter and that made him one of Bertran's most valuable donkeys.

Now most criminals might think about laying low or perhaps even leaving town; but Ismael had become so brazen and above the law, that the thought of leaving never entered his mind.

Word got out that Don Rios was openly accusing Ismael of killing his son. After a week of persistent questions and inquiries from the Rios boys as to their brother's whereabouts, Bertran rode up to El Platanar with his entourage of about a dozen heavily armed horsemen. He knew that both of Daniel's sons were working the casino that day, so the house was quiet when they arrived in broad daylight. Marching right up to the front door, Ismael kicked it open and headed straight for the dining room.

Don Daniel happened to be having his midday meal with his wife and daughters. Before he could even think about reaching for his pistol, Bertran came bursting into the room with one barrel pointing right at the Don and another towards his wife.

"Daniel!" He erupted, "I believe that I have been more than generous with my offer to purchase this miserable wreck from you and now you have the nerve to accuse me of murder?"

A few of Bertran's men now fanned out along the adobe walls inside the dining room and took aim at the girls. When the young ladies heard a trigger cock they cowered behind their father as he stood in a rage.

Daniel knew he could never prove that Bertran killed his son, but he also knew in his heart that somehow Ismael was guilty. Unfortunately, in that moment justice was not in his favor. Whatever bargaining power he once held was gone. All his land and property were worthless if he could not somehow save his family in this moment.

Mario moved in slowly behind Daniel and reached for the closest girl to him, which happened to be Juanita. She screamed and struggled for a moment, but there was nothing she could do once he had her in his powerful grasp and shoved the barrel of a Colt 45 into the side of her head. Daniel thought about lunging towards the man with the long bigote, but froze instead when he quickly considered the potential loss.

"Bertran, you will lose everything you ever owned if anything happens to one of these girls! What are you doing here?" Daniel demanded an answer as forcefully as he could under the circumstances.

"Well, well, well, it's funny you should ask Señor Rios."

Bertran grinned as he holstered his weapons and pulled an envelope from the inside breast pocket of his riding coat. Having two fewer barrels pointed at him did nothing to improve Daniel's odds. There were still five other men in the room taking aim at his three ladies, plus seven more guns that he couldn't see outside and in the hallway.

Bertran slapped the envelope down on the table and tossed a writing pen over towards Daniel.

"I took the liberty of bringing over a copy of my purchase offer so that you might reconsider. Unfortunately, I can see now that you are harboring some hard feelings, so this contract no longer provides any opportunity for you to stay here with your family. Once you sign these papers, you will have five days to take all your personal belongings and leave. If I ever see you anywhere near this property again, my men here will be happy to escort you away permanently."

As the other men in the room snickered, Daniel collapsed into his chair and grabbed the top of his head with both hands in agony. With his elbows resting on the table and tears welling up in his eyes he asked slowly, "What have you done to my son?" He really didn't want to know.

The ladies were all crying now and through the fog in his eyes Daniel could see the numbers on the contract before him.

"This offer is criminal, Bertran. This is not the amount we agreed to, and you know it. You know where my son is, too, and before I sign anything I want to know exactly where Lazaro is."

"Well I'm afraid I really don't know the answer to that question, but I must be getting back to the casino now so if you wouldn't mind signing these papers . . . I would hate for one of my boys here to mess up your daughter's hair."

Mario clicked back the trigger on his revolver one more notch just for effect and Juanita shivered. Although Bertran and his men were all cold-blooded murderers, they still held some value and respect for families. If the community every learned definitively that Bertran killed Daniel or any of his family members, they would all turn upon him and no one would be left to work the mines he was ultimately there for. Of course, in that moment Daniel couldn't know that for sure.

"So, this is how you do business?" Daniel gathered his remaining composure and sat up squarely in his chair. He was prepared to face whatever fate had in store.

"Señor Rios, I'm afraid my patience is growing weary of these negotiations. This offer is about to expire, understand?" Bertran placed his right hand slowly back upon the pistol in its holster.

Daniel had no choice. He was out of words, out of ideas, out of action. The only thing left to do now was sign the papers quickly and hope this despicable nightmare of a man would leave quickly.

Natividad and Florentina whimpered and moaned with their hands upon Daniel's shoulders as he signed several documents in haste. There was no time or reason to read the fine print. Señor Rios folded the appropriately signed documents and put them back into the envelope along with the pen. Bertran smiled as he tucked the envelope back into his coat pocket.

"Now Señor, if you would kindly hand over your pistola, we will be on our way."

Carefully, Daniel removed his sidearm from its holster and slid it across the table. Mario shoved Juanita back over towards her family and the men slowly backed out of the room.

"It was a pleasure doing business with you Señor Rios. So sorry we can't do this again some other time."

And with that, the filthy dozen mounted up and led their dastardly leader away in a cloud of dust. It was over.

Daniel and his wife didn't have much time to grieve over their loss. The following morning, Rios had to ride down to La Galancita to ask his neighbor once again for a favor. This time the favor was greater than any before.

"Don't worry Don Rios, we are like brothers now and a brother is born for adversity. From now on your children should consider me as their uncle."

"Don Coronel, I am most appreciative of that, but whatever it takes, my sole purpose in life now is to destroy Ismael."

Francisco was shocked to hear what his neighbor was suggesting.

"He has taken everything I own and probably my son as well. We cannot let this injustice stand." He knew well the grief of losing a son—times seven—still, the idea of taking another man's life and violating one of God's most sacred commandments. . . Francisco spun the idea around in his mind but just could not reconcile that concept.

"You may be right, Daniel, but we cannot take the law into our own hands. I know your heart is broken and we must do something, but let's think this through. Let's get you out of your house first. Tomorrow I will bring all the men I can round up and we will move you in here with us until we can figure out what to do next."

Within a few days the Coronels helped move all the Rios's belongings into their barn for safe storage. By the time the Bertran regime moved in on the fifth day, not a trace was left of the Rios's personal effects.

Shortly after the Rioses moved in, Don Francisco came down with a painful case of boils. The sores first appeared on the soles of his feet and then all over his legs. The sores soon covered his entire body and became so painful that he could not get out of bed.

Days turned into weeks and weeks became months, but Daniel's rage did not subside. Francisco hoped that given time the former Don Rios would find a more reasonable way to bring Bertran to justice than murder. Obviously, the Rios boys could no longer work in the presence of such an evil man, so they had no choice but to hang around with their father and grow angrier each day as well.

The Rioses were grateful to have such a devoted family caring for them but at the same time the charity felt oppressive. While Francisco was able to cope with his grief through faith, Daniel felt no such consolation. The rage endured within the Rios boys until it drove them to the brink of insanity. The more Daniel heard Don Coronel's preaching and praising, the more he became outraged with a Savior that could allow such evil to exist. One day the madness boiled over, and Daniel began to rant in front of his two remaining sons, Apolonio and Miguel.

"Obviously Don Coronel must have sinned in some way to bring so much suffering upon all of us. And now just look at the disease that he is suffering. Soon we will probably all become infected with his sickness and die a painful death. What can we do?"

Apolonio suggested, "Maybe we should ride into town and see if we can get Father Juan Carlos to help us out."

Miguel said, "I was thinking maybe we should bring a doctor."

"You are both right. I'm so glad that you are both thinking more clearly than your old father now. You must ride to Tamazula first thing tomorrow morning and bring that curandera lady with you too."

Within a few days, the boys rode back with all three healers— Celia the curandera, a doctor named Salvador Zavala, and Father Juan Carlos. After only brief conversations with Don Francisco, all three condemned him as a sinner and each refused to treat him.

It was hard to find one good thing about losing his brother and home, but Apolonio did finally get to know Rosita better after living in the same household for a few months. While she remained somewhat distant, their common experience of adversity slowly melded them together. Victoria and Miguel also became closer in the same way.

Knowing that it was the only thing that might bring a smile to her face, Apolonio really wanted to tell Rosita that he knew exactly where her mother was. Still he could not betray his promise to Dionicia . . . or could he?

Despite all the counseling and care provided by his wife, his daughters, the curandera, the doctor, the priest, Daniel fell deeper and deeper into despair.

"Maybe I should have sold Ismael the property right off. Lazaro would still be alive; we would still be living at El Platanar. I should have never listened to Francisco."

Many years had passed since Don Coronel lost his sons and he began to wither away. Francisco begged for mercy from his Lord, while Daniel cursed his own gods for all the suffering, loss, and regrets. The ladies of the household ran the hacienda to the best of their abilities, but the Rios boys, along with the few remaining campesinos, could not keep up with the mounting debts. At least when Francisco was well the church had provided some income, but now most of the inhabitants in and around La Galancita traveled into Tamazula again for church. The people of the valley all blamed Francisco for their ills and cursed his name.

One day, after a trip into town, Apolonio went in to Don Francisco's home office to talk about business concerns.

"We are not selling enough produce any more to meet our obligations for the upcoming taxes. I've been hearing that whatever Ismael is growing on his farm is doing relatively well and he's interested in acquiring your property now too."

This was neither pleasing nor unexpected. For years Francisco knew that if his fields did not produce enough to spawn more growth in the herd he would have to sell the limited remaining cattle. Now without more than a few bulls and only one cow for milk and cheese, the day was coming soon when he, too, would have to make a deal with Ismael just to keep his family alive.

"Api, I wish the Alichan would come down from his cave and just devour me right now! I know I shouldn't complain, but this pain is just too much to bear. And what have I done wrong? Tell me Api, what have I done in this life to deserve so much suffering?"

He paused for a response, but though his own father now cursed the Coronel name on a regular basis, Api could not think of a single thing Don Francisco had ever done wrong. He was truly blameless.

"You know, if only my wife Dionicia were here. She could at least cook us a marvelous meal. Then I could die a happy man. If I could just see her smiling face one more time . . . ohhh," he sighed, "or to watch her dance. I would jump right out of this bed in a second if she would walk through that door right now. I pray she is safe and happy wherever she is."

Cisco looked up and smiled towards the doorway as if it might possibly happen; yet Api knew it could not.

Carelessly, Api replied with the first sentence that formed in his mouth, "I'm sure she's doing just fine and . . ."

He stopped speaking abruptly to make sure he didn't say the wrong thing, but it was too late. It wasn't his words so much as their weight that gave them away.

"And what Api?" Francisco quickly spotted the change in Api's body language and knew he had something more to tell.

"Do you know what happened to Dionicia? Did he take her life as he did your brother's?"

Apolonio's shock and silence convicted. What horrible thoughts haunted this poor old man. Api tried not to look directly into Francisco's eyes, but he was sitting up now at the edge of his bed and facing him in his chair. Trying to peek up under Api's hanging head, Francisco started to reach out to place his hands upon Api's just inches away from his own. Then he pulled them back quickly remembering the appalling sores all over his hands and arms.

Folding his arms across his chest, Francisco leaned back and let the silence work upon his prey for a few more moments. "Api . . . if you know where Dionicia is, you must tell me. Please . . . I'm begging you now. You cannot wait another minute to tell me. She may be the only person left in this world who can save us from all this turmoil."

Francisco wanted to go on, but he couldn't. He burst into tears and sobbed into his gown. Dismayed that he somehow betrayed Dionicia's trust, Api had to ask, "How Francisco, how? How can she save us from all this chaos? What good would it do for her to come back and see us all suffering like this?"

Francisco wiped his eyes and slowly a trace of hope appeared in his face again.

"Api, she can help me find my heart."

That's it. That's all he needed. This strange power of love had such an overwhelming affect upon his adopted uncle, what might it do for Rosita to hear that her mother was alive?

"But if you know where she is, how come you didn't tell us before?"

Api had made a solemn promise, but that just didn't seem like a very good excuse. The best explanation he could come up with was, "Well, I'm not exactly sure where she is but I know where she might be."

It wasn't a completely honest answer, but it wasn't really a lie either. For all he knew, Dionicia could have moved on or moved back to her cave. He dared not think of what else could have happened to her since he left her.

"Oh Api, you have no idea how much better it would feel to just have my heart back. If you have any idea where she might be, you must go to her at once. You can have anything I own if you will just bring her back to me . . . safely, swiftly."

The idea of riding all the way to the foothills of Mohinora during the monsoon season did not seem particularly appealing or within the realm of anything safe . . . or swift.

Rosita overheard the excitement in her father's voice and came in to find out what possibly could have caused him to speak with such vigor. Entering the room, she was surprised to see her father sitting up and, could it be?

"Is that a sonrisa (smile) I see on your face father?"

His new countenance even got Rosita to lighten up a bit and she asked, "What mischief are you up to in here?"

"Your friend Api here thinks he might know where your mother is," Francisco could not contain his enthusiasm.

"What kind of game are you playing with us?" Rosita asked skeptically.

Tears welled up in Rosita's eyes and she put her hands squarely upon the young man's shoulders, "Apolonio Rios, if you know anything about my mother's whereabouts you must tell me right this instant!" She shook him gently at first, but her amusement quickly turned to fury. When the shaking didn't get the proper response, she slapped him resolutely across the left cheek. SMACK! "Where is she?" Rosita shouted.

In that moment, a spark of joy and excitement that had been buried under years of frustration, appeared briefly from Don Francisco as he cried out, "Oooh Hoo! Now you're talking. Ask him again."

"No, no. Please let me . . . " Api caught Rosita's right hand just before it was about to repeat the question. He held it tight because he wanted to respond but just needed another moment to let the blood flow back into his tongue.

"How dare you come into our home and live off our land and . . . and, you knew where my mother is this whole time?!" She yanked her hand free and was about to reload when Api finally got his voice back.

"Please . . . " this was not exactly the response he was expecting to get for divulging her mother's secret, but perhaps he could find a way back into her good graces. "Rosita, your mother made me swear to never tell anyone where she is. I couldn't betray her trust. It was for her own safety. She thinks that if Ismael ever finds her again he will kill her."

Again, though not totally truthful, he thought it might save a few teeth.

"Well, for your own safety, you had better tell us where she is, because if you don't go after her right now, I will. I don't believe that she is afraid of any man and I'm certainly not afraid of Ismael Bertran."

Whoa! Api had never seen such passion in Rosita before. It was a bit frightening, but he liked it.

"Well I hope you are ready to ride for about ten days because that's how far away she is."

Api had never known Rosita to be much for horses, so that little piece of information should have stopped her right in her tracks, but it didn't.

Rosita stomped right out of the room. She only paused long enough to turn and announce undeniably that, "I will tell Victoria we are leaving early tomorrow morning and if Miguel wants to come along, that's fine. Natividad will have to look after you while I'm gone Papa." She was about to take off again when Api jumped out of his chair calling out to her.

"Rosita, you don't need to go with us. Miguel and my father, we can bring your mother back in no time. It's no trouble . . . really."

"Trouble! You think I'm worried about trouble? If you show up and my mother doesn't want to come home, that's trouble for you. If I show up and she doesn't want to come home—she . . . . she . . . " panting now and pausing just long enough to recall where her iron will came from, Rosita continued, "That will be trouble for her. I will make her come home!"

And that was that. Off she went. The Don had never seen such conviction before in his daughter. This was her moment, her time and opportunity to finally ride out of El Valle and into life's great adventures.

"Oh boy, Api," Francisco sighed happily, "You are in big trouble now. Victoria doesn't have a clue about horses. You know if there was any way I could go with you I would. Better have your father get these girls and horses up to speed, because without his help, you are never going to get Dionicia back here."

Api knew there was much to do in preparation for such a long trek. He stood and prepared to make his exit, but first had to wish his uncle well.

"I hope you are feeling better soon. Dionicia won't want to dance with you if you're still covered in sores by the time we get back."

Francisco stood and stretched, "I feel better already mi hijo. I'll be here praying for you. Ride safely—and may God be with you."

"God bless you too, uncle."

It took Api a while to find his father. He had been out in one of the remote storage sheds cleaning up a few of his old guns and rifles. When Daniel came back into their rooms of the hacienda Api asked, "Where have you been?"

"Oh, I was just out trying to find a few old things. Where have you been?"

"I think we better sit down, because I have a lot of pretty important questions to ask."

The problem was, Api did not know where to begin. Eventually he was able to explain the whole dilemma thoroughly, it was just that Daniel had a different agenda in mind for this week.

"Well, that's great news Api. I'm happy for you. But I'm afraid that I have made some other important plans for this week and I just can't make this trip with you."

"Couldn't this business wait until we get back?" Api hoped.

"I think not."

Daniel saw this as the perfect opportunity to finally settle a score and take care of business without the risk or worry of having his sons in harm's way.

"The ride to Dolores is an easy one for you. We made that trip together lots of times. You know the way. And the girls . . . they can ride too. I've seen them chasing sheep around. They'll be fine. Just make sure you all take ponchos, because there will most likely be some rain on the way."

Apolonio was curious about what venture his father had that was so important. Regardless, Rosita was riding tomorrow at daybreak whether Don Rios came along or not.

At daybreak, it finally dawned upon Rosita that she was about to travel farther from home than she had ever been before. Yet that made no difference to her as she made sure everyone on this mission was up before the roosters, packed and ready to ride. Victoria, at age 15, had never been on such a journey before either, but she was excited to be traveling along with Miguel, who was now 18. Natividad and Daniel were up early to see their sons off. Florentina and Juanita even got up to say so long, but they were certainly not planning to be any part of this expedition. Someone had to stay home to take care of the hacienda – or what was left of it.

As soon as there was enough light to spot the trail, Rosita gave her colt Sapo a little nudge and they were off. Before the sun poked its head over the top of El Diablo, the four friends were on their way to recover their hearts. Don Coronel waved goodbye tearfully as the four horses trotted off into the sunrise.

***

Daniel also had big plans for the day. After grieving for too long, he decided that day to finally take matters into his own hands and find out exactly what happened to Lazaro. If there was any chance his son was somehow still alive, he had to know.

It didn't take Daniel long to make his way down to El Rodeo. Now the former Don, Daniel walked into the saloon noting all the unfriendly faces. This made him realize that he really didn't have a plan for finding Lazaro. At the far end of the casino, near the stage and a piano player, Ismael sat smugly at a card game with a few catty looking women hanging on each arm.

He couldn't just walk right up to Ismael and demand to see his son's body. Neither could he just walk right up and blast him in broad daylight. Bertran owned just about every police officer and official in the state of Durango, so trying to get help from them would be about as smart as shooting himself in the foot.

Old Bertran was beaming right at him by then, so he couldn't just walk away either. Daniel adjusted his belt and stepped forward. One step at a time, he approached his enemy as armed men throughout the building took notice and congregated all around him.

Mario was standing directly behind Bertran, watching every move Daniel made from the moment he entered the saloon. It took a while for Rios to make his way through all the smoke and chatter but by the time he finally got to within speaking distance of Ismael, all 12 of the filthy, uninvited visitors to his former hacienda were assembled all around him. They were all easy targets, but if he were lucky Daniel might be able to hit one or two before getting shot himself.

"I know I'm not welcome in Coluta any longer, but you never said anything about coming around here."

Daniel paused to make sure he was still breathing.

Ismael took a puff from the huge cigar hanging at the corner of his mouth, "Well you must have forgotten to read the fine print, because it doesn't look like you're very welcome around here either."

Everyone in the vicinity laughed at Bertran's fine joke—except Daniel.

The piano player paused, and every conversation stopped for a moment while Bertran quickly stood from his chair and motioned Mr. Rios over to an open seat at his table, "Please, sit down and have a drink. It's on your house." The laughter returned, and the piano began to play again.

Rios failed to see the humor in Ismael's game, but he could go for a cold beer after that long ride; he didn't really have anywhere else to go today.

"Sure, why not?"

"So, I hope you saved some of that money I gave you. You ready to play some cards?" The beer came quickly, and the small talk went nowhere.

"I didn't come here to play games with you today, Ismael. I want to know where my son is!" A few of the filthy dozen had begun to move away from the area and back to their own games when that question got their attention.

"Well, if you're not here to play cards, then maybe we should step upstairs to my office and let these other fine folks enjoy their game, hmm?"

That wasn't exactly the invitation Daniel was looking for, but once again he wasn't holding any decent cards in this game with Bertran. Without another word, Bertran extinguished his cigar and walked towards the stairs. Killing a man in his own office wouldn't be so bad if you knew for sure that he murdered your own flesh and blood. But the guards at the bottom of the stairway had their own ideas about that.

Daniel started to follow Ismael up the staircase when his host turned and admonished, "Ah, ah, ahh, sorry Señor Rios. No guns allowed upstairs."

Bertran escorted Daniel directly to his office, where he offered him the same seat where his son Lazaro sat upright for the last time. Bertran closed the door and Mario took his post just outside.

The cards were stacked against him again. Now what? Why me? All the pointless, hopeless voices swirled around Daniel's mind again. Maybe he really was insane for coming to this place after all.

Looking around at the opulence of Bertran's office, Daniel thought he might have put himself in an inescapable position once again. Ismael thought about reaching into his desk drawer and replaying Lazaro's final moments. What kind of a fool would walk right into a lion's den and expect to leave alive?

Rios was not particularly well educated or as learned as his neighbor Francisco, but he always knew how to find his way out of a dark cavern. Ismael's blatant financial success and the accompanying pride were his weakness, a light at the end of Daniel's tunnel.

"You know Bertran, I've been thinking about your original offer to stay on as a plantation manager and the reason that never appealed to me is that I'm really more of a natural born prospector." Daniel could see that he had his host's attention now.

The stout man leaned forward to open his humidor. Ismael pulled out two fine Cuban cigars and offered one to Rios.

"Oh really? Tell me more about this 'natural birth' of yours."

"My grandfather came into this country with Maximilian in search of El Dorado." Rios paused to clip the end of his cigar. Ismael leaned over to light a match for him.

"It was only by necessity that my father closed the mines and turned Coluta into a banana plantation. You see when Maximilian was executed in 1866, Benito Juarez wanted to confiscate all the lands of Maximilian and his financial supporters. Juarez never found out where old Max was getting his gold, because by the time he sent his troops to come looking up here, Coluta was nothing but El Platanar. And now you are growing bananas again?"

"Oh, sure Señor Rios, you would not believe how many people in America are going bananas these days." Ismael was the only one left to chuckle at his own jokes now. "Bananas, tortillas, manzanas (apples), guavas, you name it, we grow it up there." Bertran failed to mention the marijuana and opium.

"The crops are coming in so well, I don't know why you wasted so much of your life looking for legends that don't exist."

The simple truth in that comment stung a bit, but at least the tobacco was rich and there weren't any gun barrels pointing in his direction . . . yet.

Daniel could see that Ismael was quickly losing interest in this conversation, so he had to get to the point. What was that point again?

"Oh yes, that's wonderful. We know that soil is fertile, but there is some truth in every legend. I can tell you that at the time we sealed the mines a few years ago, there were still many caves and many avenues within those caves that we never pursued. The only reason we never finished exploring certain areas is because the drought came, and we ran out of money. The workers didn't want to go into the caves anymore because of that ridiculous legend of the Alichan."

"Hmmm," Ismael seemed puzzled. "But I always heard that you actually saw the Alichan with your own eyes. That is one myth that I was beginning to believe in. Don't tell me there is no Santa Claus either. What about the bones Apolonio was telling me that you brought back from the Sierra?" Bertran kicked his heels up onto his desktop and waited to hear more of this tall tale.

"That was all just a story we dreamed up to keep the Indios and bandits from raiding the mines when we couldn't defend them any longer," Daniel lied. "Those were just some old cattle bones we found and carved up to make them look a little more threatening."

Daniel truly believed there really was a great fortune buried somewhere deep within his mines and he had a pretty good idea of where to find it. Up until now, he never had the means or opportunity to retrieve it. The ace card up his sleeve was a map with directions to a golden sword and quite possibly the fabulous treasures of El Dorado. It was a map that he inherited from his ancient Toltec relatives, but never had the means or equipment to pursue at such depths.

Rios knew that Bertran had enough money to bring in as many experienced prospectors and as much equipment to carve El Diablo into Swiss cheese if he wanted to; however, there was one more important piece of bait that he still needed to dangle.

"There are lots of scientists traveling around with new methods of extracting ore from every last inch of this planet, but no one knows the inside of the Espinazo like I do. My sons and me, we can find any vein left in that old behemoth. If there is any gold left, and I think there is, then I'm probably the only one who can find it."

Ismael didn't seem to be buying to the story, so Daniel threw in one last trump card, "Do you really think I'd be sitting here risking my life if there wasn't enough color in there for both of us?"

Now that made some sense to Ismael—but not much. Through all the smoke and legends, he had almost completely forgotten about the ivory-handled pistol in his desk drawer. Mining gold and silver could be a lot more lucrative than growing fruits and vegetables. The stakes would be a lot higher, but the downside certainly couldn't be much riskier than, say, getting caught with a boatload of contraband and losing his entire empire.

"So, what's in this for you Daniel?" Bertran knew that for every offer there must be a counteroffer.

"I'm just tired of living off my neighbor's land. We only need a small percentage of whatever we find for you up there. Then with the generous price you paid for Coluta, we can buy another ranch somewhere else, maybe in Sonora or Chihuahua. Who knows, maybe even California?"

"And just how small of a percentage are we talking about?"

"Fifty percent of course," Daniel chuckled, trying to seem cool.

"Now you do have a sense of humor, don't you? Five percent."

"Twenty-five. Remember we are leaving as soon as we find the mother lode for you." That was for certain, Ismael must have thought to himself; or sooner if there was an accident.

"I will need to spend a lot of money on equipment. Ten," Bertran countered.

"Fifteen." Still a lot more money than Daniel was thinking of.

"Twelve." The number didn't really matter, Ismael knew Daniel wouldn't be around long.

"Done," Rios said. "When can we begin?"

"Just tell me what you need, and we'll get to work right away."

As Ismael handed Daniel a writing tablet and pen he wondered how to keep the Rios boys from finding out about all his secret crops growing upon the shady hillsides of Coluta. Then he sat back in his chair and relaxed, realizing that lead is much cheaper than gold.

VIII
BRIEF REUNIONS

The hand of the Lord was upon me,
and carried me out in the spirit of the Lord,
and set me down in the midst of the valley which was full of bones,
And caused me to pass by them round about:
and, behold, there were very many in the open valley;
and, lo, they were very dry.

Ezekiel 37:1–2

19

Wednesday Evening — La Caldera, Mexico

As we passed slowly through a valley of dry bones, I wasn't sure exactly what to say to RuMa when I found her. Would she be angry to see me, relieved? Happy? Confused? The trail allowed plenty of time to search for ways to bring our relationship back to life, but no answers appeared.

According to Gabriel, opposing factions of Federales and drug lords were preparing to go to war with each other over the massive crops of poppies for opium growing rampantly in the surrounding hills and hidden valleys. RuMa was caught somewhere in the middle and apparently had access to something else they all wanted very dearly: gold.

"Please pay attention, keep right, and keep moving. The last few miles in the dark will be the most difficult," Gabriel briefed me quietly on the situation as the rising flood levels of surrounding rivers posed the potential to trap Grace and RuMa in the middle of a violent collision between paragons, bandits, and nature.

"The last time I saw RuMa, she said funding from scientists at the university where Grace came from dried up instantly when they were unable to produce immediate results from their excavations." He went on to explain how "Their research team abandoned them without any means of escape."

He didn't have to articulate that without any successful discoveries, there would be no hope for future support either. Somehow, from the depths of La Caldera, RuMa and Grace were able to send a plea to Father Arres via the Rarámuri natives. The request reached El Padre with enough urgency to spark a call to my cousin Jose. along with this ensuing search-and-rescue mission. The speed of their communications in this rugged terrain was astonishing.

"Tell me more about your people."

Gabriel said, "The Tarahumara are your people, we are guardians of the little remaining Mixtec wisdom and traditions. We hold onto an attitude of serenity and silence which gives great value to humility, hope and joy. In addition to a strong belief in heavenly symbols, we are also deeply interested in the traditions of Jesus and Mary along with the use of the holy rosary and crucifix."

So, when a fair-skinned Christian lady first appeared in their midst, Gabriel must have been eager to learn all he could about her culture. I was just eager to see her alive again. In order to have any chance at a resolution for my relationship with RuMa, there were still many hurdles to clear. Though Gabriel seemed to have a pretty good idea of where she was hiding, would she be willing to share company with me again and work toward a more harmonious future?

Despite all my knowledge of statistics and probabilities, there was no mathematical formula to predict what was about to happen next. Standing upon the brink of a chasm known as La Caldera, I had to wonder whether my bride was ready for this rescue attempt.

Although the entrance to the gaping maw of the cave seemed harmless enough, Gabriel still tied himself to a nearby tree and anchored me firmly to his own body before lowering us gradually into the void.

At the time, I didn't know that far below, RuMa was preparing a light meal for Grace when she began to hear the rumbling above but could not be sure if it was friend or foe. For that reason, my young Sherpa came prepared with his shofar, and beneath the slender crescent of a new moon, he let loose a loud fanfare to announce his coming in glory. The echoes of every note reverberated deep into the crater until they sounded like an army of rescuers. It was a feast of trumpets.

Finally, the time had come to pack up camp and move on. RuMa quickly gathered her personal belongings and scrambled up the familiar slopes of the cavern. She climbed directly towards the bold aural proclamation and a dim lantern light that she thought would happily usher in the Jewish New Year with a victory over the long bout of darkness in her life.

"Shana Tova!" (Happy New Year) she cried as she spotted Gabriel and rushed to his arms. At first, she didn't notice me in the shadows where I watched them embrace for an uncomfortably long time. Her grip on the young man seemed to last forever and finally ended with a passionate kiss that was too painful to watch.

What kind of fool was I?

At that point I had to turn my head and really didn't want to hear Gabriel tell the rest of the story, but we had to move onward. It was finally time for me to step forward out of the shadows and discover the truth...

20

December 1924 — The Road to Dolores

THE TRUE TERROR OF the Espinazo was still scouring the land trying to track down the woman who invaded his cave years ago. To Alichan, her child represented the image of the same being that created him. In the heat of day, he tried to stay out of site as much as possible while in the evenings he wandered back and forth looking for something to devour. According to the lore, the Alichan was given authority over the sky; so, whenever he couldn't find food or water, he could call forth lightning to strike down animals too swift for him to chase and the rain would provide fresh water to drink.

On one particular evening, he was out and about and spotted a wild pig that looked appealing. With a brief entreaty to the powers above, a thunderbolt struck the ground beside the pig and sent it running for cover. Before the pig could reach a nearby cluster of shrubs a second bolt fell and cooked the pig instantly. The swine made for a tasty meal. A light rain began to fall and soon filled a small trough in the sand where the first fulguration landed. In that very spot, the heat from the lightning melted the sand into a serpent-shaped piece of glass.

The dragon was satisfied with its meal but still craved the taste of any two-legged animal resembling the creature that took its son.

***

As soon as his children hit the road, Don Francisco fell to his knees and spent long hours at the ofrenda praying for their safety, "Dear God, please protect Daniel also. Give him the wisdom and strength to face whatever tasks you may set before him today and give him peace. And although I don't understand all your ways, please know that I still trust in you and will not lean upon my own understandings. However, the safe return of my wife and children would make a great Christmas gift. In the name of the Father, Son and the Holy Ghost." Francisco lit another candle and went to bed.

***

Meanwhile, Daniel's sons were well on their way up the trail with the ladies by midday. Api was surprised at how comfortably Rosita rode along at such a brisk pace. Victoria on the other had struggled with every change of terrain and Miguel had to work a bit harder to keep her close to the lead pair.

The fresh air and wide-open spaces did the girls some good. They had been confined to their dusty hacienda for too many years now. It pleased Apolonio to see the girls with some color in their faces when they stopped for a quick lunch beside a stream.

"I'm so tired," Victoria sighed. "Can we stay here just a little bit longer. I need to soak my feet in the water. These boots are killing me." She pulled the long pointed-toe boots from her feet and laid back in the cool shade to catch her breath.

"We have a long way to go sister, so don't get too comfortable," Rosita said. "How long ago did you say it was since you saw our mother?"

Api thought for a while and counted the seasons in his head, "Three weeks, maybe three and a half. I'm not sure." The cold stream did sound like a good idea, but he needed to stay focused on Rosita's question for another moment.

"She was in good spirits, though. I gave her two very nice colts, and she looked happy. She had plenty of tools and supplies to get her through whatever she might find along the trails. Oh, and I put a gold bar in one of her packs, so she has plenty of money."

"What? Where did you get a gold bar from?" Rosita asked. She was more than a bit surprised at Api's hidden wealth and generosity.

"Oh, I've been saving for a rainy day. You never know, she may need that money someday."

"And I hope when you say tools and supplies that mean you provided her with protection of some kind."

"Of course. She has enough ammunition to win back the Alamo if she wants to. But I think she already had a pistol of her own; so now she has two."

Rosita knew that her mother was pretty handy with a firearm, so that gave her some comfort. Still, the sun would not burn forever. Time to pull her tall boots back on and hop aboard Sapo again.

Miguel was massaging Victoria's feet and she didn't want to leave, "Oh, no," she groaned. "Do we have to get back on those animals so soon?"

Rosita just glared at her sister in a way that required no further response. It was time to move on.

The expedition to Dolores was proceeding nicely as the first daylight waned. Apolonio was hoping they might make it to Canelas by the first evening but given the sketchy riding skills of Victoria and all the extra supplies their horses were carrying they were doing well.

A few miles beyond Cebollas Grandes (big onions) and a few miles short of Canelas, Api spotted a reasonable spot for the ensemble to camp. Victoria had never camped outdoors. She was amazed at how close all the stars seemed up here in the Sierra. Of course she had seen stars before, but they just seemed much warmer now by the campfire beside Miguel. She decided to rest her head on his shoulder for a while to see whether he might have some feelings towards her other than just those of a trail partner.

Gazing into the firelight Miguel recalled seeing Victoria's bare legs that afternoon as she pulled her boots on and off beneath her riding skirt. Her long slender thighs reminded him that Victoria wasn't a little girl any more. Her hair was soft and jet black. Even after a full day in the saddle, she still smelled sweet.

Rosita took note of her little sister's behavior and thought they would make a nice pair. Miguel was a handsome young man, competent as a rancher and well mannered. Most valley girls Victoria's age would be married with children by now. So, if she was just about to embark upon a serious relationship with someone, Miguel was as good a man as any, and better than most.

Apolonio however, was not really her cup of tea. Though she could not deny he was the tallest, and possibly the most attractive single man in the valley, his false swagger lacked a certain sensitivity that she could see in Miguel. Api was more interested in mining and science that being outdoors. He spent a lot of time reading and knew quite a bit about chemistry; he just didn't know how to create it with a woman.

While Api admired his younger brother's ability to laugh carelessly and enjoy the beauty in every moment, he could tell Rosita kept a safe distance from him. She didn't want him to get the wrong idea about her intentions. But Api was patient and willing to wait for her. This was going to be a long ride and he would give Rosita plenty of opportunities to warm up to him. Eventually she would come to see the beauty of his methods. After all, he was going to return her mother to her.

Even though there were no roosters around, Rosita was up and ready to ride before the sun. After refreshing herself with a quick drink from a nearby stream she prepared a light breakfast of pan dulce (sweet bread) and coffee. She wanted to make sure they ate the more fragile pastries first since they wouldn't keep as long in the saddlebags.

Trying to get Victoria up at home before the Rioses came to live with them was always a chore, but now she wanted to look fresh and attractive before the boys were up. Api and Miguel weren't too particular about their own appearances in the morning, but they did appreciate the splendor of a good cup of coffee and sweet bread. Victoria didn't enjoy riding much when she was younger; when she got her first real horse, she said the only thing it would ever be good for was soap. For that reason, she named her horse Javon, soap.

The four amigos arrived in Canelas a bit early for lunch, so they were able to eat quickly and got back on the trail without encountering too many questioning eyes. Victoria wanted to stay longer and visit some of the small boutiques, but this was not a shopping expedition. Rosita pushed the pace. Somehow, she felt reborn now that she was on a more urgent quest. The days were long, but the evenings cool as just before bedtime one evening a light rain began to fall.

As the gallant quartet came to within a few hours from Dolores, Apolonio struggled with the pain of how to explain to Dionicia why he went back on his word. Not only that, but he even brought along the daughters he promised never to tell. Oh, and then there would be a baby to explain. Francisco and Rosita never even gave him a chance to talk about the baby. Should he try to prepare the girls and his brother for that shock or just let Dionicia tell the story. What if Dionicia had already left Dolores?

Rosita was always good at reading people, but she had grown even more in tune with her riding partner over the last few days, "What's wrong Api?" she asked.

The last time he tried to withhold information from Rosita he got slapped so hard he figured it might be easier to just shoot straight, "I was just wondering how your mother will be and all that. Hopefully she won't be too mad at me."

"She was always mad. But she won't be upset with you, she will be very, very angry with me."

"Well," Api was about to explain, "there is something else she might be mad about. One of the reasons she . . ."

"Hey!" Victoria shouted out from the back of the pack, "Hold up for a minute!" The sun was hot, and the front three riders were in no mood for another delay.

"What is it Victoria?" Rosita shouted back. "We need to hurry up!"

Victoria was already down scratching around the edges of something stuck in the sand. Miguel pulled his horse back alongside her, "What is it?"

A shiny serpentine object caught Victoria's attention and she just had to have it.

"I don't know. It looks like a snake don't you think?" Victoria held up the long undulating piece of glass so that everyone could see it. It was the glass created by the Alichan's thunderbolt.

"That's nice, Victoria. Now put it down and let's go!" Rosita hollered once more.

"No way, I'm keeping this." Victoria packed the glass carefully into her saddlebag and climbed back upon her horse, Javon.

21

December 1924 — El Rodeo

THOUGH ISMAEL OFFERED DANIEL a room for the night, Rios still didn't feel safe in the strange town of El Rodeo. As much as any two men could hate each other, these two men needed each other. Daniel decided to stay in Tamazula with family and to visit with Father Juan Carlos to see if he might find wiser counsel for the matters at hand.

Daniel informed Ismael kindly, "Thank you very much, but I have already made arrangements to spend the evening in Tamazula with some relatives. We should be able to get started within about two weeks. My sons are on an outing for a while." He didn't want Ismael to know anything about Dionicia.

"But if I may pay a visit to El Platanar soon, I'd like to begin making plans to excavate right away. There are many promising veins that we haven't had a chance to fully explore. I'm hoping to be welcome upon your property in the future." Daniel still wasn't so sure he was going to make it out of town alive, but he definitely seemed to have something that Ismael wanted and that would protect him for now.

"Be sure to let your friends downstairs know that we are in business together again."

Daniel extinguished his cigar in an elegant ashtray and shook hands with his new business partner. How could he be making a deal with the devil? Desperate times called for desperate measures and Rios hoped to someday avenge whatever happened to his son Lazaro. It was still a bit too soon to ask that sore question again, but the time would come. Perhaps he was beginning to believe that Ismael wasn't such a bad sort after all.

***

By the next day, Rios was beginning to act a bit like a Don again. When his relatives in town heard that he was going to work the El Platanar mine again they were very impressed. Many offered to provide their services once the excavations began. A few knew what Bertran was really growing up in those hills but didn't want to divulge any secrets lest they disappear in the same manner as Lazaro.

Daniel spent a few days in town visiting old friends and relatives. He also made time to call on Father Juan Carlos and they had a nice brunch together at the church. Still severely damaged by the earthquakes of 1910, the parish obviously suffered from the same economic problems as the rest of the valley. Rios had almost forgotten about his own financial hardships when he decided to ask the question that spawned this visit.

"Father Juan Carlos, I don't know if you are aware of this or not but my decision to sell El Platanar was not voluntary." Daniel looked for some response from the priest but there was none.

"Well anyway, the reason we had to sell our homestead is because Ismael Bertran came to Coluta one evening with his men and threatened to kill one of my daughters." The memory troubled Daniel enough that he had to pause before continuing.

"In fact, I believe that he was prepared to kill all of us, my wife, daughters and me. My sons were working in El Rodeo that day but the question that drove him to rage was regarding my son Lazaro."

Finally, the priest's face registered some response to the message, "Yes, I knew your son Lazaro. He was a messenger for Señor Bertran and a very well-mannered boy. Has anyone ever discovered what happened to him?"

"Oh, no that was the reason I came to you, to find out if you might know or have heard of someone who may know something, anything of his disappearance. Is it possible that he is still alive somewhere?" The anxiety was always in his voice when he had to ask this question, but the hopelessness was beginning to sink in deeply.

"Well, I can only tell you what I've heard on the streets that he was either kidnapped or may have run away from home; but no one knows for certain." And, even if he did know his bonds of silence may not have allowed him to divulge any further information.

"Father I must tell you something in confidence that you can never repeat to anyone else, ever," Daniel paused to receive confirmation and acceptance to these terms.

"Of course, I'm very good at keeping all kinds of secrets."

That troubled Daniel somewhat but he continued anyway with, "Well, I suspect that Ismael may have had something to do with Lazaro's murder." Again, no response came.

"I refused an offer to sell my property to Señor Bertran. It was on that day, the day that I sent a rejection letter to Ismael; from then on I never heard from my son again." Daniel's speech was so troubled that the father had a hard time understanding what he was trying to say.

"Do you really believe that Ismael is capable of such a heinous crime as murder?" the father asked.

"I didn't want to believe it, Father, but I must tell you that when he came bursting into our home that day, there was no question in my mind that he was prepared to kill every member of my family. I had no choice, I had to sell. And even now I have no choice.

You're the only person I can trust with these suspicions because if I go to the police they will only ignore me. In fact, I have been to the police officials here in Tamazula and they know me so well now that they just turn and slight me whenever they see me coming. My whole existence has been a tragedy since that day we lost our son. I still fear every day for the life of my wife and children. Father, I don't know where else to turn. Can you please help me, please?"

This was obviously the plea of a desperate man. The father tapped the second knuckle of his left hand to his lips and stared at the top of his desk wondering what he might be able to tell this poor man to calm his spirit. There were many secrets that he knew and many he just could not reveal. The salvation of a man's soul was not something he could compromise. What was lost was lost and what was saved was saved.

"Señor Rios, I'm sorry that I cannot tell you anything more about the whereabouts of your son. When people come to me to confess their sins they leave with a soul that is washed clean as the driven snow. Though we have all sinned, we are forgiven here through the power of Christ and whatever men do beyond these walls is beyond my control."

"Yes, but not beyond your knowledge!" Daniel had to interject because he could see that the priest was concealing something urgent and quite likely criminal. "If you know of some illegal activity you must have some obligation to report this to the authorities."

"My authority comes to me from our holy father in Rome, and if a thief confesses a crime to me in private, when he leaves here he is no longer a thief. Forgiveness is a powerful gift, my son. You must look within your heart and forgive in order to be forgiven yourself. Is there perhaps some sin in your life that you wish to confess to me?"

Daniel was dumbfounded. He came to this priest seeking assistance and now he was the one being accused of something? "Father I have no sins to confess to you other than my constant rage and anger against this invisible enemy that haunts me night and day. Someone has taken my son away and I want to see some justice done. Here. Now! In this lifetime."

"Certainly, there must be some sin you are sorry for Señor Rios? Why do you suppose all these tragedies have befallen your family and the Coronels?"

Ah hah! That's where the father was heading with all this: guilty by association. The father was obviously disturbed by the success that Francisco's small church was achieving in the valley and now Daniel must be punished for his neighbors' sins.

"So, is that what this is all about? Because of my neighbor's church I am being punished? I don't understand what you have against Don Francisco's tiny chapel. What fault did you find with his teachings? You were there, you heard him speak, he shows nothing but reverence and faith for his God and Savior! Tell me what harm is there in that? Did you find any fault at all in that man while you were in his presence?"

"Please, please Señor Rios, this is not an attack upon Don Coronel or his church. It's just that you see we have a responsibility to serve in unity through our one holy Catholic Church and without the proper training and respect for our traditions, souls may be lost." The father could see that his response was confusing, inadequate and needed more explanation.

"Although I'm sure Don Coronel was on his best behavior when I was visiting him, there are stories of heathen natives in the valley of Espinazo still worshipping their ancient Mayan and Aztec traditions."

Daniel was beyond words, so he let out a sigh and allowed the father to proceed.

"We have an obligation to bring the gospel to those who are lost so they may find salvation through our Holy Trinity. There is so much work to do here. In fact, Mr. Bertran has even been considering making a sizable contribution to the renovation of our church here in Tamazula and in my dealings with him, he has only been a respectful business man.

We really do appreciate what Don Francisco is trying to accomplish but I would just like to know what that is. Is he providing religious services for the benefit of his followers or merely providing an income to substitute for his agricultural losses? If the Coronels were willing to work with us more closely, we could better learn what the people of the valley really need."

Well, Daniel was obviously not speaking with someone planning to help him in any meaningful way. For a while he thought their conversation was over but then to his amazement Father Juan Carlos continued...

"We cannot accept the heathen customs or traditions as part of our mass and we will not support a pastor who refuses to accept the authority of our holy father in Rome. Is it true, Señor Rios, that you have some artifacts from the Alichan, bones perhaps, that are used in a ritualistic manner?"

Now the vicar just seemed to be spewing out nonsense. This had to be stopped.

"Yes! That is absolutely true, I eat with them. We brought some bones home from an animal and my son Lazaro carved them into spoons and we eat with them. There's nothing in the catechism that provides guidelines on eating utensils is there?"

"I'm sorry Señor Rios, I am not accusing you of anything, trust me; but if you or any members of your family have been in contact with that fiend you may be in greater danger than you know."

"Okay now Father, let's just slow down here for a moment. With all due respect, you are beginning to sound a bit like you truly believe in these heathen legends."

"Well, did you not just say that you have seen the Alichan?"

Father Juan Carlos was on the edge of his seat now, and Daniel felt as though he was about to go through some intense interrogation. He had no reason to lie to the priest, so he clarified himself, "What I just said is that we found some bones of an animal. I have no idea what it was."

"So, you have never seen a living Alichan?"

Daniel was almost ready to confess but that wasn't completely true, "No, not alive; but I have seen some rare tracks around our cornfields and our children once said they saw something strange when they were young. Who is to say what it was?"

Father Juan Carlos was agitated and hardly let Daniel finish his response before he asked, "Was there anyone else with you when you came across the bones that you found?"

"Why yes, Don Coronel was there and one of my farm hands named Santiago. The reason we were there though is because Santiago claims that the animal killed his friend Jacinto."

The father seemed genuinely alarmed now.

"I have to admit that I was once skeptical too. I have heard these types of stories before, but never considered them to be true."

The Father gathered a bag full of his personal belongings, "We must leave to check upon Don Coronel at once." He picked up a cross and holy water and placed it inside his bag, along with a Bible.

Seeing what the priest was up to Rios asked, "How did you know that Don Francisco is still sick?"

"I didn't know. Yet I'm afraid that he will grow even more ill if there are demons possessing him."

"Do you think we should warn Santiago about this? He lives here in Tamazula doesn't he?" asked Daniel.

"He used to live here. They say he committed suicide shortly after that trip to see the bones."

***

After a brief stop in El Rodeo, Father Juan Carlos and Daniel rode hard for most of the day to make it to La Galancita before sundown. Ismael Bertran was surprised to see Juan Carlos and Rios traveling together, but he didn't worry about it too much. With several businesses now, they required most of his attention whenever he wasn't playing around with cards or women.

Before Daniel left El Rodeo, Bertran told him, "I have some new maps that I would like to go over with you. We don't need to wait for your sons to return, just come up to meet me at Coluta in a few days."

Daniel now feared that a friendly relationship with Ismael was developing, the man he still wanted to destroy.

When the men rode into La Galancita, Natividad took the horses and noticed how tired they looked. Francisco was happy to see his best friend returning with Father Juan Carlos. Although the priest seemed a bit combative at their last dinner meeting, they were allies in Christ now, and Father Juan Carlos seemed to be sincerely concerned about Francisco's health.

"Don Coronel, how have you been feeling lately?"

"Oh, I'm feeling much better now that my sores have started to subside. They seem to come in waves."

"That's good news, but how about your spiritual health? Have you had any dreams or visions lately?"

Daniel thought that was a strange question to ask of someone out of the clear blue sky, but Don Francisco didn't seem bothered by it. If anything, he looked amused.

"Why yes, I have. Some have been dark and disturbing, but most are just dreams of people lost in sin, attacking my church. People, dogs, cows, even that menace the Alichan," Francisco laughed. Father Juan Carlos was not laughing.

"Don't you find that amusing father?"

"No, not really. Don't you see what is happening here?"

"Of course, we have yet to be tested, we are about to fight a great battle. The people I have seen in the darkness, must be saved."

The priest was surprised at how well the man was taking this all in. His entire little kingdom was about to collapse around him, and yet he seemed unconcerned, almost glad. Perhaps the fever from his illness had done some permanent brain damage? Daniel had to take a seat because he couldn't keep up with this lunacy.

"Can you tell me anything about the Alichan? Have you ever seen it here before?"

"No, we only saw the bones together with Santiago. How is he, by the way?"

Daniel and the priest looked at each other gloomily and father Juan Carlos had to tell him, "We heard that he committed suicide only a short time after he came in contact with the bones of Alichan."

Daniel couldn't stand this confusion any more, "Well, I have work to do," he said without thinking and walked out of the room to plan his next move.

Father Juan Carlos and Don Coronel prayed together for the next several hours but in the morning the priest had to return to his flock. As the father departed, Daniel entrusted his map to Don Coronel and waved so long to prepare for a battle of his own.

***

Señor Rios could not wait to get back up to see his old Coluta home. It had been too long. The fields were full and green but there seemed to be a lot of new underbrush up toward the hillsides. The filthy dozen had become the spotless dozens. All the workers were neatly dressed. Their servants were anticipating Daniel's arrival, so they led him to Lazaro's old bedroom where Ismael was standing over a set of maps.

"Welcome, welcome Señor Rios, what can we get you to drink?"

Daniel was amazed. Looking around the renovated room it now opened up into Miguel's old room that was being used as a big office space. He noticed a pitcher of guava juice and helped himself to a glass, "Let's see what you have here Señor Bertran."

Daniel spent several hours marking up the maps and pointing out all the areas that he planned to explore. It was all very exciting.

Rios could almost see himself back in control of his own ranch once more. What a great opportunity to get his children involved again. Everything seemed to be going so well, until after a few hours when they finally finished mapping out the entire plan.

Daniel took a seat with his guava juice and started to take a long, cold drink. It was his last. Just then Ismael pulled out his favorite pistol and shot Daniel once in the chest. As shock took control over the Don's final moments, the last words he heard were, "Thank you very much for your assistance, Señor Rios, but we won't be needing your services here any longer."

When Mario came in to clean up this mess, Ismael had special instructions. This time instead of the usual burial grounds outside of El Rodeo, Bertran wanted to send a message. Perhaps the people at this end of the valley were not aware of the consequences of challenging the lord of Purple Moon.

"I want you to take this body and leave it at the doorstep of Don Francisco. He needs to know that this is what happens to people who break their agreements with Ismael Bertran."

Mario took three of Bertran's men with him in order to make a lasting impression. But nothing could have made a bigger impression upon Natividad when she answered the front door that morning and found the dead body of her husband lying at her feet.

Francisco came to the door when he heard Natividad run away screaming to her room. Seeing the body and four horsemen, Don Coronel demanded an explanation and he got one.

"This is your last chance to leave the Valley," Mario conveyed the message quickly and rode off into a pack of dust with his cohorts.

The grief for the next several days around La Galancita was overwhelming. Francisco could no longer bear the angst of all his losses. The girls wailed and moaned incessantly. Don Coronel no longer could bear the suffering without some justification. He marched into his chapel and got down on his knees before the Lord.

"Why me?" Francisco cried, "Lord, I have been faithful to your commandments. When have I ever betrayed you? I demand that you tell me what it is that I have done wrong! I have never doubted you; never disobeyed you! Why? Why? Why? Test me and know my anxious thoughts. See if there is any offensive way in me."

News of Daniel's death spread quickly. As soon as the word reached Tamazula, Father Juan Carlos rode like the wind to La Galancita. Thunderstorms and lightning began to break out all around as he arrived. There he found Don Francisco grieving and repenting of every sin he could remember, but still finding no reasonable explanation for his grief. Francisco demanded an audience with the Lord to prove himself. When Father Juan Carlos heard this, he could see that Francisco's spirit would not be easily consoled.

"Don Coronel, there are many things our Lord does that we cannot understand or control. God's ways are not our ways," Juan Carlos explained. "I hope that you are not challenging God's authority over his own universe, over his people?" he asked.

Turning to the Old Testament the priest quickly asked these questions: "Don Francisco, were you here when God laid the earth's foundation? Have you ever given orders to the sun or shown the dawn its place? Does the eagle soar at your command?"

Francisco paused for a moment, searching for something meaningful in that question, "No, you are right Padre. Ever since these boils began to appear, I have felt like Job and now realize I have no right to challenge our Lord."

The Word of God spoke to Francisco and this encouraged Father Juan Carlos to turn to another passage within that same book of the Old Testament. There he found a truth in the scripture that he needed to share with Don Coronel in that moment. It was a quote they both knew well, "Brace yourself like a man; I will question you and you shall answer me. Would you discredit my justice? Would you condemn me to justify yourself?"

Then another verse caught the attention of father Juan Carlos, so he skipped ahead several lines to chapter 41 in the book of Job, "Don Coronel, please tell me if this sounds anything like the vision of your dreams, 'The mere sight of him is overpowering.'"

The priest paused for a moment to look for any reaction before continuing . . .

"His teeth are terrible round about. His scales are his pride, shut up together as with a close seal. One is so near to another, that no air can come between them. They are joined one to another, they stick together, that they cannot be sundered. By his neesings a light doth shine, and his eyes are like the eyelids of the morning. Out of his mouth go burning lamps, and sparks of fire leap out. Out of his nostrils goeth smoke, as out of a seething pot or caldron. His breath kindleth coals, and a flame goeth out of his mouth. In his neck remaineth strength, and sorrow is turned into joy before him. The flakes of his flesh are joined together: they are firm in themselves; they cannot be moved. His heart is as firm as a stone; yea, as hard as a piece of the nether millstone."

Father Juan Carlos had to pause because the Don was weeping heavily by then. The description of this creature was so disturbing that it even took the priest's breath away to see the words in print.

'He beholdeth all high things: he is a king over all the children of pride.' Don Francisco, I'm sure you must remember how this story ends? Job repented in dust and ash; then the Lord restored him and made him prosperous."

Francisco slowly lifted his head to confess, "Yes, yes he did, didn't he?"

With that realization, he rose to his feet and ran outside to throw himself down in the dust and ash that became mud and muck. When he was finally able to rise to his feet once more, Francisco walked back into his home covered in wet earth. He looked dreadful but must have somehow felt reunited with his savior.

***

Far away in the high sierras of central Mexico, four young seekers approached Dolores with great anticipation. After being interrupted by Victoria's glass discovery, Apolonio never found the appropriate moment again to tell Rosita or the others about Dionicia's baby. The truth would have to speak for itself. Still, knowing Rosita's great expectations for this reunion, he felt obligated to at least prepare her (as well as himself) for a potential disappointment.

"Rosita, I know that we all look forward to seeing your mother again, but it has been many years since you have seen her. You may not recognize her anymore and you have changed so much, for the better of course, since you were last together." She listened carefully but had already prepared herself for many possibilities.

Api continued, "There's also the probability that she will not want to return home with us, or we may not find her at all." The latter possibility was not one that Rosita cared to consider.

"Api, if she is not exactly where you said she would be, we will ride immediately into the nearest village and question every man, woman, and child until we find out precisely where she is."

Apolonio dared not bring up the possibility that Dionicia might no longer be living at all, but the thought crossed Rosita's mind at the same time, and they both looked at each other somberly yet hopefully.

It was just before midday when they approached the slope to where the secret cabin was tucked away in the pines. The trail was exactly as Api had remembered it from his travels there before. The location was isolated and obscure, but with some effort they were able to find it.

From a distance Api pointed the place out, "There it is."

The girls squinted and shaded their eyes from the sun to see what he was pointing at. Miguel had a better idea of where to look and spotted it next, "Oh yes, I see it."

When they came within about 200 meters from the camouflaged cabin, Rosita's eyes finally picked it out and her pace quickened, "Yes, there it is, let's hurry." There were pots and sticks scattered around the front of the cottage like toys. It certainly looked lived in. Api just prayed that it was Dionicia and not someone else living there now.

Rosita took the lead. The other three horses were nearly at a full gallop trying to keep up. Her horse barely came to a complete stop at the entry and she could hardly contain herself from bursting in unannounced. Instead she pounded on the door with her fist. Gently at first then louder as she cried out, "Mama!" thud, thud, thud, "Mama, open the door, it's me, Rosita!"

The other three horses finally caught up and came skidding to a halt along with their panting riders. Just then Rosita heard movement inside.

A tiny faced poked an eye out from behind the curtain of one small window in front of the dwelling, "Who is it?" A vaguely distinguishable voice asked from inside.

Noticing Manuelito at the window Dionicia shooed him back away to the far corner of their single room, "Shhh, get away from there!" Holding her favorite firearm at her side she called out once more, "What do you want?"

Rosita had no doubt now. It was worn and splintered but it was certainly her mother's voice. She was just about to rush through the door when it opened just a crack.

Victoria barely recognized the tattered old woman as the shell of her own mother. She stepped forward from behind her sister to greet the lady, but the door slammed shut forcefully. Inside they could hear a heavy board settling into place.

Dionicia put the gun down then pressed her back against the door trying to comprehend what she had just witnessed. The young ladies outside were beautiful beyond belief. She barely recognized them as her own. How could they have grown so magnificently? She felt so decrepit. Holding her face in her hands she stepped forward feebly towards a looking glass on the opposite wall. Staring in disbelief at the dilapidated old woman looking back, she began to weep.

"Who is it Mama?" Manuelito asked while pulling upon his mother's apron.

Dionicia felt all the shame of her life tugging forcefully at her side.

"It's us Mama; Rosita, and Victoria!"

The pounding at the door grew louder. Apolonio and Miguel held the horses and watched anxiously as four fists now started to pound on the heavy wooden door.

"We know you're in there Mama, we will not leave until you let us in!" Victoria shouted. That truth was painfully obvious to the lamenting woman inside. What seemed like an eternity in fact lasted only about a minute. Whether she waited an hour or a year, Dionicia knew she would have to open the door to her heart again eventually. She could not hold off the past any longer.

The young ladies' fists were just beginning to bleed when they heard a sound from inside. It was the wooden plank unbarring the door. A smaller latch clicked open and the door parted.

Rosita and Victoria pushed their way into their mother's arms so quickly they almost knocked little Manuelito over. They were not expecting to see a little one nearby. The three ladies hugged and cried for several minutes. It was a rapid transition for Dionicia from the grueling shame of her past to the pure joy of holding her daughters once more. Little Manuelito stood back in awe of the powerful emotions traded.

Apolonio and Miguel took off their hats and eventually crept inside the tiny room where they stood beside Manuelito waiting for the fires to cool. Dionicia finally noticed them and came over to give them big abrazos (hugs) too.

First Miguel, then Apolonio. Dionicia held the taller brother at arm's length and smiled, "Thank you so much for bringing my daughters back to me," she beamed. Then in the next instant— SLAP!

A familiar sting penetrated Api's skull as Dionicia stepped back and said, "That's for breaking your promise! You are forgiven now."

"Aye," Api shook his head and rubbed his left cheek as the girls whipped themselves into a frenzy of inquiry and answers.

There were so many stories to tell; the first and most important question was, "Who is this handsome young man?" Victoria asked first of Manuelito.

The little boy blushed and hid behind his mother.

"This is my son, Manuelito," Dionicia confessed. In that moment, all the guilt associated with the young boy vanished and a touch of self-satisfaction appeared. Raising the boy on her own was quite an accomplishment.

The boy dared to peek out from behind his curtain and Rosita asked him, "What is your last name precious?"

Manuelito had no idea what the young lady was talking about, so he looked up at his mother with a curious gaze, waiting for an answer. This was the moment that Dionicia had feared for so long. Somehow though, she knew that all the doors had to be opened now and the truth would set her free, "The truth is we really don't know."

Dionicia's head hung in shame one more time. Perhaps her daughters would reject her or their half-brother now and leave. Perhaps Ismael would find out and take the child or her life. Whatever was going to happen needed to happen. "Can you ever forgive me?" Dionicia begged.

The little boy could not understand the sorrow over a simple name. Dionicia's ocean of humiliation and disgrace were all still there waiting for the next tide to roll back into her heart. The waves were about to break and come crashing down on top of her when Rosita pulled her to shore.

"Mama, this is a wonderful brother you have given us. We do not need to know where he came from. Your safety and happiness are all we have prayed for," said Rosita.

"You raised this boy all by yourself?" Victoria asked.

"Of course. I will never trust another man as long as I live," Dionicia replied with some disdain as her chest swelled again with self-satisfaction.

"Surely you do not consider Papa as just another man?" Rosita inquired, "He misses you so much and can't wait to see you again. He would be here right now if it weren't for his infirmity."

Dionicia finally had to let go of all her own pride when she heard that Francisco was ill. The afternoon sped by rapidly as they all traded story after story. Manuelito showed some of his toys to Api and Miguel as the ladies prepared an evening meal.

Victoria shared her account of the thunderstorm and the serpentine glass she found shortly afterwards. The object brought to mind a similar memento that Dionicia once owned.

"Yes, I have seen these things before," she said. "The Indians collect them and make crosses. They say they are made out of lightening. You see, if you put two of them together, you can form a crucifix like this—see?" She held her left hand vertically while placing the undulating glass horizontally across it for demonstration.

"Sometimes if they only have one they will just tie a stick across near the top. I used to have one myself."

"How interesting," Rosita said. "What happened to yours?"

"I left it behind to watch over the cave where I used to live before we came here. Someday I thought after Manuelito grows up we would like to go back there to live again."

Dionicia shared her stories of La Caldera far into the evening. Long after Manuelito retired to his blanket and just as the fire was about to burn out, Rosita moved on to the final topic of the evening, "Well Mama, when will you be ready to return with us to La Galancita?"

It wasn't a matter of if; the question was when? Seeing the beauty of their homeland in Rosita and Victoria's eyes made Dionicia eager to see the hacienda again.

"Unfortunately, I'm afraid your father might not be as happy to meet Manuelito as you were. I don't think I'll ever be able to face your father again. He might hate me forever."

The thought had crossed their minds, but the girls assured Dionicia that father would certainly forgive her for whatever sins she may have committed.

"No, no Mama," Victoria cried, "Papa misses you so much. It will break his heart if we return without you."

"Well that may be so, but it would break my heart if he could not forgive me; and I wouldn't blame him if he does not," Dionicia hung her head once more in the sad realization that she might never see La Galancita again.

"But what about Manuelito, Mama?" Rosita asked. "He can't live here forever. He needs to go to school and learn to be a man. You must return with us, you must."

"Perhaps, perhaps," Dionicia conceded. "Manuelito would be better off there and he should attend a good school in Tamazula, but we could never return to the ranch. I would not care to cause your father such embarrassment and pain as I've suffered."

For a moment is seemed as though the unstoppable forces had finally met an immovable object. This is where Apolonio's keen mind stepped in, "Well, if you will not ride back with us then perhaps the girls would like to move in here with you?" Api's idea got their attention. It seemed a bit odd, but they were willing to listen.

"Miguel and I can bring you supplies on a regular basis, and if you like we can find a decent school for Manuelito to attend in Tamazula."

Apolonio knew the idea of leaving the girls behind would never sit well with their mother, but he also knew that Francisco would never allow his wife to live alone without forgiveness. Rosita saw the genius in his plan and found a new appreciation for his understanding of the situation.

Victoria howled at the idea first, "Nooo, we cannot let our mother live out here in this filthy forest full of bats and snakes!"

This helped the idea along because even though Rosita had been away from her mother for several years, she couldn't believe any mother should allow her daughters to pay the penalty for her transgressions.

Miguel listened from the sidelines. He was still a bit too young to fully appreciate the chess match going on. Rosita decided to chime in behind her sister just for effect, but Apolonio already had the Doña in check.

"No Mama, Victoria is right, you must come straight home with us."

"Never!" Dionicia declared. Then came a long silence . . . until finally she resumed, "I deserve to sit here in this lonely forest for the rest of my life, but I can never return to La Galancita." It seemed like a stalemate.

Rosita tried not to shudder at the thought of losing her mother again. Victoria looked troubled while Apolonio's poker face told all else.

"Well then," he said to Dionicia, "We need to get some rest. Let's sleep on this and maybe in the morning you will change your mind, but we cannot stay long. There is a strong storm approaching."

Rosita adored the added sense of urgency that Apolonio provided. Just to be certain, she added one final note that would get her mother moving for sure.

"Mama if you are not going to return to La Galancita, then I will stay here with you. Victoria, Api, and Miguel can take Manuelito back to the ranch if you like."

Victoria thought about staying for a moment, then she caught a glance from Miguel's big brown eyes and thought otherwise. She could not imagine living in this wilderness for the rest of her life. Still, she had to support her sister and mother and was beginning to catch on to the game too. She responded with a sheepish but insincere offer, "Well, if Rosita stays then I will have to stay too."

The trap was set. Rosita could rest easily now. She knew her mother would never separate them from their father. She could also see that Dionicia sensed the passion growing between Victoria and Miguel. To separate her daughters from their futures would be far worse than living with bats and snakes forever. Miguel just watched and learned.

Before the sun appeared, Dionicia made a decision. As breakfast was cleared and the young men packed their bags, she made her pronouncement.

"I hope Francisco can forgive me, but if not, I will be happy to return to this cozy cottage for the rest of my days," said Dionicia.

They were all thrilled by the news. Manuelito at age six, was too young to fear the future or his past. Leaving home in the mountains to live on a ranch was just another chance for discovery. The activity of four new people brought excitement and change. Adding another horse to the caravan would slow the pace a bit, but life was finally moving forward and that made Manuelito happy.

***

Not far away, the Alichan sensed movement and knew it was time to take up the hunt again. The beast spotted them early that day, just as they all prepared to leave the house. Though he wanted to pounce upon them all at once, he realized there were too many to overcome alone. The woman and her child were near the back of the pack followed only by some young girls he had never seen before.

The fiend thought he might be able to devour one or two at best, but they were all carrying those same deadly weapons that destroyed flesh in a manner that ruined its first prodigy. This attack was going to take some precise planning.

Dionicia had felt something evil tracking her since they left Dolores behind. For some time, she just thought it was all her guilt. Perhaps it was her lost sons haunting her for leaving them alone years ago in that hotel room. Could it be the demons of all the maguey and marijuana? She just couldn't tell for sure. Perhaps she was beginning to believe that El Riablo wasn't such a bad sort after all.

IX
INTO THE CAULDRON

My brethren, count it all joy when ye fall into divers temptations;
Knowing this, that the trying of your faith worketh patience.

James 1:2–3

22

Thursday Morning —
La Caldera del Diablo

SEEING RUMA IN GABRIEL'S arms made me realize what a fool I was to believe we could ever be together again. Though the flood waters had not reached Tamazula yet, there was apparently too much water under our bridges now to ever return to anything resembling our once Edenic lifestyle.

When she finally noticed me in the shadows behind my human shield, surprisingly, RuMa ran over to give me the warmest embrace ever. It was almost enough to melt me then and there. Little did I realize that this gripping reunion was about to be rudely interrupted. Just as quickly as she fondly acknowledged my presence, she shoved me away to full arm's length. Still clinging tightly to my shoulders, I clearly saw her visage transform rapidly from concern to tangible fear.

"Alan I'm so happy to see you, but we need to find Grace and get out of here RIGHT NOW!"

It was plain to see that she was highly motivated to exit this chasm as quickly as possible. There was no time to ask how she knew, "There's a whole army of Federales and drug dealers heading in this direction and if we don't get really far away from here, we are going to get caught in the crossfire. No one is going to stop to check passports here. Gabriel, I'm afraid we won't have time to get hooked up to those fancy ropes of yours. We need to get back to Tamazula."

Before she could complete that sentence, she paused as we all listened in horror to a blood curdling scream rising desperately from below. "Help! It's got me trapped!" Grace shrieked.

"Oh my God," RuMa muttered. Racing to the precipice of a tremendous void in the center of this bowl, she threw herself down and called downward, "Grace! Hold on I'm sending a rope down." In a flash, she could see the terror in Grace's eyes, but after a few brief moments of deafening roars, cracking bones and cries of agony, there was no sound at all. Then as the funnel began to crumble around her, she slipped and began falling into the sink.

"RuMa!" I shouted haplessly as she began to disappear. Somehow, I managed to dive quickly enough to catch an ankle. "Hold on! I'm not going to let you go." No, not this time. No way.

It was just then that I began to feel gravity dragging us both slowly into the abyss. It was an instant that seemed to last forever; yet after just a few seconds of terror, there came a breathtaking pressure that strangled my torso. Gabriel rapidly secured a line around my waist and ably pulled us both up to safety. As soon as we were securely upon the solid rim, we all began shining flashlights and calling for Grace—still no response came. We were too late to save Grace. My wife rolled herself back towards the ledge and began to heave into the crevasse from all fours.

For some reason I rushed up to hold her hair back as she continued to convulse violently. When she finally caught her breath, she looked up at me completely ashen and sobbed, "She's gone!"

Using my arms to pull herself up quickly, we both heard a rasping growl and claws clacking their way slowly towards us. In that moment she said, "We have to get out of here NOW!"

RuMa was almost completely out of the Cauldron when she turned to say, "I can explain later, but right now we need to seal this entrance so no one else EVER gets back in there. And more importantly, nothing ever gets out!"

In short order, we were all outside the cave and I was only somewhat surprised to see RuMa pull a large mass of Composition C plastic explosives from her backpack. In expert fashion, she quickly had the device wired and ready to detonate.

Mounting our reliable mules, we got them moving at a pace I had not seen before. Somehow, Gabriel was able to convey enough urgency to these animals that even their dull senses snapped to attention as the improvised bomb went off at a safe distance behind us.

23

December 1924 — El Espinazo del Diablo

SINCE THE BEAST COULD not attack his prey directly, he kept the rain coming down at a steady pace, filling rivers ahead of them to block their path. On the third day of their travels the pack of six could not believe the sudden deluge that overtook them in the middle of the afternoon. They were just about to leave Sinaloa and enter the state of Durango and the range of mountains known as the Espinazo del Diablo, when the rivers around them started to swell. The Rio Colorado to the north rose rapidly and forced them further to the south and west. There they followed a trail dangerously close to a tributary of the Sinaloa.

Lightning sparked and crackled all around them. They saw one bolt bounce off a rock nearby, but they had to press onward. Api knew they would have at least one small stream to cross soon in order to get to the safety of higher plains ahead. However, by the time they reached the small stream, that was barely a trickle when they crossed it on the way, it had now grown to at least three feet deep and three times as wide; still not an insurmountable obstacle for six loyal horses. Api led them in and came out safely on the other side.

The Alichan had been following closely and saw this as his perfect opportunity. Rosita came out of the water on the south side of the stream and so did Miguel. Dionicia was within a few meters of shore when a bolt of lightning startled her horse and made it rear up. She was almost thrown but managed to stay in the saddle. The horse however had spun around and started running back towards the opposite shore.

Then there came a sound that at first they thought was thunder. But this rumble lasted too long to be thunder. The ground quivered and a terrifying sight caught their collective attentions. The stream swelled quickly and in the distance a wall of brown water came crashing towards them at tremendous speed.

Within the brown wall of thunder, they could see bushes, trees, foam, and fury. Victoria's horse, Javon, saw Dionicia's horse, Alas, coming towards him and together they began to spin around in circles. Miguel managed to grab the reins of Manuelito's horse and pulled Alas quickly to the evaporating shoreline.

Without another thought, Apolonio charged his horse into the new river and pulled Dionicia from her saddle and onto his own. With another quick pivot, he was able to steer his horse, Rayo (which means thunderbolt), into position beside Javon and grabbed on to his bridle. Victoria was terrified and could only shield her eyes from the nightmare she saw bearing down upon them.

Rayo was almost swimming by the time he reached the south shore. Dionicia's horse, Alas, dazed by the debris now pelting her at shoulder level, spotted the other horses on shore and swam towards them. But it was too late. The brown wall swept her up and threw her down into the tumbling rush of sticks and stones. In seconds, she was swept out of sight.

There was no time to mourn the loss of Alas because the river was still widening and racing towards them faster and faster as they could not climb the slight grade ahead of them fast enough. The water rose around them again as Miguel fell back to coach Javon forward as quickly as possible. Rayo struggled to get back up to the front of the pack, but the water was already up to Apolonio's boots when they all heard another familiar roar. The trees around them swayed and the horses staggered forward as the deep rumble drowned out the brown wall.

The bass rose to a crescendo as the ground behind them began to fall away. "Terremoto!" Dionicia screamed.

The grade was not severe, but the remaining horses had to pull harder than they ever had before just to keep moving forward as the raging water receded. Behind them a crevice in the earth opened wide and swallowed the rising mud and debris.

It was the most incredible event Rosita had ever witnessed. Two powerful forces of nature battling to challenge their life in one instant and then saving it in the next. The horses reached higher ground and dry soil, but their riders were too frightened to hesitate. Manuelito was incredibly calm in all the chaos. As long as Miguel held the reins of his horse, he knew that all he had to do was hang on and enjoy the show. Api pushed the horses onward as far as he thought they could get from the river without completely exhausting their transportation.

The Alichan saw the six soggy ones escape to the south, but fissures created by the quake trapped him in a cavity so deep that he could not pursue them. Dionicia was saddened by the loss of her horse but Manuelito's horse was appropriately named and skillfully accommodated two riders as well as their supplies. At a safe distance from the mud monster, they all climbed down to comfort each other and only rested for a short while to clean the mud from their faces. Night would be approaching soon, and they still had a fair distance to travel to some shelter from the rain. Api knew of a cave where they could stay dry within a few miles.

***

The six brave riders didn't realize it at the time, but the flash flood was a blessing in disguise. The loss of one horse and the fatigue inflicted forced them to travel at a slower pace. Their destination to the west of Galancita also added a few more days to their expedition. This gave the bishop in Culiacan just enough time to devise his critical plan.

By the time the Alichan was finally able to find a grade gentle enough for him to emerge from the quake's fault, he was disoriented and unable to track his quarry for a while. Eventually he was able to discern their direction and picked up the hunt in earnest.

There were several more streams and rivers to cross over the next few days and though the horses were skittish at first, they slowly regained their confidence as the rains subsided and the rivers flowed more gently. Rosita never realized how many rivers there were in this part of the country. Now each time the posse came to water, the memory of the brown booming fright made them cross all the more quickly.

Miguel unwittingly commented that he would never again ride so far from home during the rainy season.

Rosita took offense with his perspective and let Dionicia know, "Mama, I would have ridden through a dozen cyclones to bring you home."

"I'm so sorry that you had to come all this way for me," Dionicia said. "I will never make you ride so far from home again."

Rosita asked Api, "How far do you suppose this great crater is from La Galancita?"

"It is only about a half day's ride, but the trails to get there are very steep and treacherous. We will all need to be very careful on the way down from that spot." He paused for a moment to decide whether he needed to provide any further details, but the ride was long so there was plenty of time for tales and reminiscing.

"You know, there are some who believe that the crater where Dionicia was staying is the place where that meteorite fell when we were young. Do you remember that day?"

"That was the first time I ever remember feeling an earthquake," Rosita smiled and said. "And Victoria was born the very next day. Do you remember it Victoria?"

Looking at her big sister sideways as if she might have lost her mind, Victoria wondered out loud, "Is Rosita possibly developing a sense of humor?"

Victoria was so sore from riding now that she had almost forgotten how attractive her personal guide Miguel was. Even covered in dirt and mud, he still held a boyish charm that kept her moving forward.

Little Manuelito was completely enthralled by the adventure and couldn't wait to saddle up each day to ride with his mother. Finally, the trail started to climb again as they approached the steep climb up the Espinazo Del Diablo.

Rosita had only seen these jagged peaks from the safe distance of her kitchen window. Now she was riding right into the teeth of the monster. It was still a bit early in the season for snow, but after two full days of climbing the temperature dropped considerably and even in their warmest blankets the conditions were harsh. In a few more weeks it would probably begin to snow at these altitudes.

The last time Dionicia was at this altitude it was in the middle of summer and she never imagined how cold it could get out here away from a warm fire. As they approached 2,400 meters (approximately 7,874 feet) above sea level, Dionicia realized this would be a harsh environment to appreciate for more than a few days of winter.

Not far behind, the Alichan realized where his targets were heading, and he picked up the pace. It seemed as though he was gaining ground as the six riders climbed more slowly.

Still, the group led by Apolonio had a favorable lead on the ogre as they kept a steady pace along the narrow winding paths. At one point the trail became so steep and narrow that the riders had to dismount and lead their horses by the reins. Small roots and protruding rocks from the sides of the cliff made this portion of the journey especially treacherous.

Victoria was bringing up the rear again, huffing and puffing from the lack of oxygen. Suffering from extreme altitude sickness she stumbled to her left and almost slipped over the side of a steep embankment. Javon, following her lead also hit a soft spot in the trail and stumbled not so gracefully. The weight of the horse on a weak stone caused a series of rocks to slide, and before Victoria could scream, Javon went tumbling off the cliff in a cloud of debris. The trail disappeared behind Victoria, and she only had enough time to dive forward and prevent herself from falling down behind her ride.

The impact of the horse on the jagged rocks several hundred feet below made a horrifying thud. As much as she had once hated that horse, Victoria now could not stop weeping uncontrollably. The rocks crumbled and left a gaping hole in the hillside behind them. Since the possibility of an even larger rockslide was now imminent, there was no time to mourn the loss of another good friend.

Before this adventure, Victoria and Rosita had always seen horses as just big pieces of ranch equipment that needed to be fed and brushed every day. Now as they glimpsed the wreckage of another lost equine from above, she understood how men became so attached to their horses. These were more than just machinery or even companions, Victoria had lost a part of herself.

Apolonio could still hear the soft hillside crumbling and trickling slowly away behind them. This was their cue to pick up the pace and remain focused on their destination. As they came around the next corner, the trail widened, and Miguel was able to lift Victoria up onto his horse, Tronido (thunder), for a while.

A short time later Api brought the group to a halt to point out their goal. Far above them, the gaping hole left by the meteorite of 1910 was clearly visible even at a distance of several miles.

"If the Lord is willing, we should be able to reach the crater in one more day," Apolonio said encouragingly.

Api knew that there were not many wider sections in the trail left between them and their destination. When a sturdy looking spot appeared that was just a few feet wider than the rest of the pathway, he decided to call it a day with the sun still well above the horizon. There was no room to build a fire and no fuel around even if they could.

Victoria was feverish and looking worn from the climb but fortunately, Dionicia had preserved a small container of atole blanco in one of her saddlebags. The sweet corn meal drink reminded her of her youth and soon the fog lifted from her eyes. As the sun set and the stars began to rise, Miguel crept in closer to keep her warm beneath his blanket and she knew all was going to be well.

The temperature dropped so fiercely that evening that Rosita almost considered sharing a blanket with Apolonio but opted instead for making a Manuelito sandwich with her mother. Apolonio was left alone at the head of the pile to keep an eye on the horses during the evening just to be sure they didn't accidentally stumble over the edge. With six riders and only four horses remaining, they could not afford to lose another, if they hoped to make a quick trip down from the crater to La Galancita.

Api could hardly sleep anymore, because every time one of the horses would sway or take a step in one direction or another it startled him, and he had to calm himself once again to rest. When daylight finally came, he could not wait to get going again. They were so close.

Api knew that this procession needed plenty of rest, so he let them all enjoy each other's warmth as long as possible. Eventually they all woke from their hibernation and came to the startling realization that they were over a mile and a half above their beloved Galancita.

The Alichan sensed that he was now very close to his game, but as he rounded a narrow bend, the trail disappeared suddenly before him. There was no way to go forward or around the gaping hole in the path. It was just about to provide him access to his weary objectives, but now he had to wait for another idea, and it did not come quickly. The cold was wearing upon the cold-blooded monster as stasis slowed his pace.

There was no choice for the weary travelers; they had to move on. In order to gain greater rest later on, they would have to make one final push for the crater while the sun was just warm enough.

"Once we get inside the cave we can build a nice warm fire," Api coaxed.

Those were the words that finally got everyone moving again. After a few big stretches and yawns, a brief and unceremonious snack was produced from the saddlebags to break their fast. As the sun rose, their bones warmed, and the pace quickened. The atole blanco had cleared Victoria's head and she was now moving along at a comfortable pace. With each switchback, the crater grew larger and larger.

Finally, just before the sun set behind the steep terrain, the trail descended into a wide swath of widely scattered pines and the spent pilgrims reached their objective. From a distance, the crater was just a two-dimensional blemish on the side of a rocky peak. Now up close, the depth of El Diablo's gaping throat startled the newcomers.

Victoria took one peek inside and said, "I'm not going in there!"

"Sure you are," Miguel said reassuringly. "You want to share a campfire with me, don't you? Tomorrow we will be back in La Galancita and this adventure will be all over." Or so he hoped.

Dionicia did not fear the darkness, and after lighting a torch she took the lead with Rosita close behind. Apolonio brought up the rear this time to make sure Victoria didn't change her mind at the last minute. Little Manuelito followed closely behind his mother, and although he couldn't really remember being in the crater before, he seemed unusually at ease there. Once they reached the bottom of the main chamber and had a chance to walk around for a bit, Victoria could clearly see that there was nothing too threatening about the place.

"Are you sure there are no bats or snakes in here?" Victoria asked Miguel again.

"I don't think so," he said. No sooner had he completed his sentence that a wave of flapping wings came flashing from one obscure passage to rush towards the moonlight above.

Victoria shrieked, and Manuelito cringed, but upon seeing that the cloud of winged rats was departing quickly, they were almost fascinated by the orderly and rapid exit.

"You see Victoria, they don't want to be in the same cave with us, they are moving out." Miguel put his arm around Victoria and led her over to the spot where Api was preparing a warm fire.

As the embers of the campfire began to glow, shadows rustled along the walls. Dionicia felt like celebrating. She was home again and if the shadows were dancing she wanted to dance also...

24

December 1924 – Attack on the Church of La Galancita

Meanwhile, back in the burgeoning settlement of Coluta, Ismael Bertran was planning his next move and assembling troops for battle. With Rios out of the way and directions to all the best mining prospects in the caves, he was ready to begin increasing the size of his labor pool. The only potential handicap to hiring would be Don Coronel's pesky little church. Most families in the area belonged to Francisco's congregation and would not likely be willing worship with the man who killed their good friend.

Now that Father Juan Carlos would no longer be able to stand in his corner, Bertran knew that a back-door attack was no longer plausible. Don Francisco's church would need to be attacked directly—with fury and fire.

Bertran's men poured into La Galancita in the middle of the night and quietly doused the tiny chapel with kerosene throughout. To set it all off, a bottle with a lit rag was tossed through a window. It didn't take long for the tiny wood building to burst into flames.

A short while later, heavy rains came and washed away almost every trace of the humble temple of Galancita. Only the foundation remained. Francisco was devastated once again. He couldn't understand it. He thought suffering was finally over, but he was still being tested. So, he did the only thing he could think of—he prayed.

***

Natividad was despondent over the loss of her husband and retreated to her room where the girls, Florentina and Juanita, attended to her night and day.

Don Francisco knew now that he could no longer fight this battle alone. He needed to call on his maker for strength and mercy. When Francisco thought about having to tell the boys that their father was gone, he knew they would never forgive Ismael. If someone didn't take care of Ismael before the boys arrived, they would probably try something rash and face the same fate as Don Rios.

Cisco sought counsel from Father Juan Carlos, who vowed to remain by his side.

"Father we can't let this injustice stand; but what can we do to stop this monster?"

If only Coronel knew how apt that description was. Ismael was indeed possessed by his own lusts, greed, and pride, and at that very moment he was plotting to attack the Galancita one more time.

The priest was running out of ideas, but knew that the bishop in Culiacan could possibly provide some support. After much thought and prayer, the priest crafted a powerful letter to his prelate in the great cathedral of Sinaloa. The next morning, Francisco summonsed his quickest messenger and asked him to ride like never before.

The boys could possibly arrive within a few more days, so the response from his holiness needed to be swift and overwhelming. Father Juan Carlos did his best to emphasize that the evil they were dealing with would never succumb to anything less than devastating force. The law was too late to save them now.

***

The power of the church in Culiacan was not completely tainted by corrupt government officials. This is not to say that many corruptible government officials did not exist within the diocese, this is only to say that the Vicar of Sinaloa had other forces at his disposal besides local and federal police forces. A few of the more powerful judges and governors were still beholden to the bishop and could be counted on to provide a fair trial for the scourge of the Espinazo Valley.

The local law of El Rodeo or Tamazula would be of no value in the solution to this predicament. The wise bishop carefully selected a powerful militia leader to quickly, quietly, and, he hoped, peacefully attend to the plague known as Ismael Bertran.

The bishop requested the audience of a brave man by the name of Antonio Rincon. Señor Rincon was humbled to stand before his holy father and bowed deeply with great respect.

"Señor Rincon, now that you have been briefed on your mission, I wish to give you my blessings as you must depart at once." The bishop laid his hands on Rincon's head and prayed briefly for him before sending him on his way. Under the cover of darkness, Rincon quickly organized a posse of twenty-four strong and faithful riders. Armed only with their faith in Christ, the men were instructed that they would have to race stealthily around Tamazula and the village of El Rodeo in order to approach Coluta without being spotted. The bishop insisted that the men visit La Galancita first to receive their final instructions from Father Juan Carlos and his host, Don Coronel.

X
THE ADVENTURE OF A LIFETIME

Finally, my brethren, be strong in the Lord,
and in the power of his might.
Put on the whole armour of God,
that ye may be able to stand against the wiles of the devil.

Ephesians 6:10–11

25

Thursday Afternoon — Somewhere in Durango, Mexico

BOOM! AS THE EXPLOSION thundered through the valleys below, we made haste towards our base near the place of toads. At a safe distance from the epicenter of our aftermath, it seemed appropriate to quietly inquire into the meaning of all the commotion back there.

Despite the adrenaline still flowing through our bodies, we agreed it was a reasonable time for a short break. Consequently, we all paused to take in a quick meal and process at least some of what just happened.

Up until then I was speechless but had to respond. Pausing only briefly to consider what to ask, the first obvious thoughts that came to mind came clunking out,

"What is going on with you and Gabriel?"

"Well, that's too long of a story for right now, but it's probably not what you think," she blurted through a half-eaten sandwich.

"Got any easier questions?"

"You know that whatever we've been through in the past, you can always count on me to be here for you when it really matters; but you have to help me understand what is going on here."

"Alan, I'm so sorry that you had to come all the way out here for me, but this trip just turned into way more chaos than we ever expected."

Rue did not owe me any apologies at this point, we were almost safe and sound.

"Well," she said, "Gabriel helped us to figure out from some of your great-grandfather's old maps, that there's a secret mine shaft in that old cave that probably leads to a whole lot of gold coins." What I really wanted to know was about her relationship with Gabriel, but she was on a roll, so I let her go with it...

"There's probably so much gold in there that I haven't even had a chance to estimate the value of it all." She continued, "Unfortunately, there's also a whole lot of bad actors right now that would really like to get their hands on some of that, and if they find us out here all alone without any real firepower . . . I don't even want to think about how they might torture us into taking them back to it. And, if the authorities find us first, well, they won't treat us any better than the banditos."

Perhaps what I heard next was the distant echo of plastic explosives still ringing in my ears, or maybe it was the rumble of many horses moving in our direction. At any rate, further questions would have to take place on mule back as Gabriel noted the same clatter and quickly got us all mounted up and heading in the direction of a distant lagoon.

"There's a big storm of angry building up back there," RuMa said. "Oh, and did I forget to mention that the caldera we were in used to be a volcano and it's acting up again."

Watching her ride at a brisk pace ahead of me, I had almost forgotten how strong and lovely Rue was. Notwithstanding the favorable distance we were putting between ourselves and El Diablo, the gentle rumble did not fade. Was it horses or was it thunder? I had many doubts. For example, was that a light drizzle on my face or just rain inside my head? Forget all the things I should have said.

Even though RuMa apologized for bringing this ordeal upon us, I still had much to apologize for myself in terms of my own past hurtful and angry behavior. As a gentle rain began, it felt as though we were heading towards an even bigger battle.

When I finally caught up to RuMa at a full gallop, she leaned over and shouted loudly enough for Gabriel to hear, "Gentlemen, as bad as that storm is behind us, if we don't beat those horses to Tamazula, life is going to get a whole lot worse for us and the rest of the world because they will never know what's coming."

For some reason, even under these extreme circumstances, Gabriel felt compelled to continue telling his story and I did not feel compelled to punch him in the mouth...

26

December 1924 — La Caldera

As THE BATS RETURNED to their cave for the day, Victoria was startled and shook Miguel to wake him for protection. He didn't seem too concerned, nor did anyone else. Manuelito was sleeping soundly beside his mother while Apolonio and Rosita were already up and packing.

"I can't wait to get back home to see my father again and tell him the good news," Rosita told Api.

"Yes, and I can't wait to see my father again to tell him about all the color I've been seeing on our way here. I'm sure those floods will expose even more veins for us to explore in these hills and . . . "

Just then another wave of bats flew in, shocking Victoria so much that she began to scream and flail her arms about hysterically. This in turn caused her to lose her balance on some wet stones and she fell several feet to the rocky terrace below. Writhing in pain, she grabbed her left calf, which was bleeding and swollen from the awkward landing.

"Aye, Dios Mio!" she hollered.

By the time Miguel was able to scramble down to her it was evident that the leg was broken. She would not be able to ride into La Galancita any time soon.

Rosita didn't want to think about the potential for any further tragedy at that time. However, she also realized that if Victoria did not receive proper treatment soon, she could lose the use of her leg forever. Her father was about to regain his lost love and that would certainly make him a healthy man again. For a while Rosita thought about riding ahead with Apolonio because she did not want to miss seeing her father's face when he found out that Dionicia was alive and safe.

Of course, once they stabilized Victoria's leg and cured the pain with Dionicia's secret remedies, they all had to agree that Api should ride quickly home with Miguel to return with another horse and travois for Victoria. Considering the steeper and more rugged terrain between the caldera and hacienda, they might also need some extra manpower. Knowing that the boys could return sooner without her helped Rosita pack a little quicker.

"C'mon, Victoria. It's time for Api and Miguel to go. Say so long for now. They will be back soon!"

Manuelito was sorry to see his new friends leave, but they told him he had to take care of his mother and help keep the bats away from Rosita and Victoria with the torch at night.

"Time to ride!" Apolonio announced. It was all downhill from there. The horses seemed to understand that they were almost home, and their hooves flew over sand and stone through their own familiar forest and grasslands. When the Galancita finally came within view at the end of the day, the horses raced for the barn.

Staring out the window, Natividad was still too paralyzed from her loss to leave her bed when she spotted a cloud of dust and cried out, "The boys are back!".

Api and Miguel were surprised to find so many healthy-looking horses in the barn. They quickly searched for their father but only found piles of sleeping men everywhere. Juanita and Florentina came running down the main corridor and were the first to reach their brothers in tears. These were not tears of joy, something was wrong.

Seeing their brothers again made the Rios sisters wail so loudly that they could not speak. It wasn't until Don Coronel appeared to greet the Rios boys that they finally realized the most terrible news possible.

Rosita and Victoria were not there to help the Rioses deal with their loss, but they were in considerable pain themselves. Victoria could not wait to tell her father all about the sad deaths of Alas and Javon. Unfortunately, Don Coronel had even sadder news awaiting them.

Don Daniel had been more than a neighbor; he was like an uncle to them; and their father was now left without a friend in the world, except . . .

"Where is my Dionicia? How is she? Where are the girls?" Francisco desperately needed to hear some good tidings at that moment. He could not bear another loss.

Miguel recovered enough to join in with the announcement, "She is fine! We found her! The love of your life is well!"

Grief no longer squelched the joy and enthusiasm in his voice. The next question Francisco had was, "Does she still love me?"

"Of course, she does!" Apolonio said. Hoping to delay the news of Manuelito and Victoria's injury just a while longer, he continued with a half-truth, "The only reason she did not come straight down here with us is because she is afraid."

"Afraid of what?" he asked.

"Afraid that you may not love her anymore."

"Oh, if I had any strength left in me I would ride to her now. I'll barely be able to make it to Coluta. She must be feeling the weight of a thousand elephants on her back. If these men were not all here, you know I would go straight away to my sweet Dionicia; but we only have this one chance to remove Ismael."

Don Coronel had learned from his sources that Bertran was planning to send for several new recruits within a matter of days. If he fills El Platanar with his delinquent cronies, there would be no chance of ever approaching the hacienda again safely. Today, many of his men left to their homes for the weekend or to play cards at the Purple Moon. Another evening might be too late.

"Well, if you can't go I'm sure Miguel can bring them back safely. He is a very fine rider now. You should see him fly."

The idea of spending another evening in the bat cave was not an attractive one for the youngest Rios boy, but he was eager to have Victoria home again.

"Yes, I will go. It's an easy ride from here. We can be home before you return from your errands."

Miguel was actually hoping to join the men on their ride to Coluta, but the idea of traveling again with Victoria sounded more inviting. Soon they would have to break the news of his daughter's broken leg and Dionicia's son, Manuelito.

Apolonio, too, needed to be free from all his sudden heartache. He hugged Don Francisco tightly before finally releasing him to share the other part of the news. It must have been painful for him to hear about Manuelito and Victoria, but he never grumbled.

***

Dionicia's first evening back in the cave was just fine with her daughters there to comfort her. She felt warmed by the fire and the boys had brought in plenty of firewood before they left. Once daylight came, Rosita felt so refreshed and renewed that she could hardly wait another day to rescue her mother from this wretched place.

"Won't it be wonderful to sleep in your own bed again, Victoria?"

"Yes," Victoria replied. "That's funny, I was just thinking the same thing. You know my leg feels much better and we don't need to pack much. I wish Sapo could take us all home right now."

***

The Alichan was closing in on a thought. The gap in the trail was too wide to leap across. The rocks were too steep and slick to climb up. Downward was not an option, the walls were simply too precipitous. The only choice was to retreat and find an alternate route. It was a long way back to the next trail that put the villain back on course. The substitute path ran longer, but not as steep or treacherous. Alichan could now make good time. This new route had many caves along the way. Perhaps it could find a way to climb from the inside up to the crater?

Slinking along the inside of the Espinazo, Alichan found a familiar passage. From this point on it knew exactly how to make his way up to the crater. There, the lady and her child would be in the total blackness. Finally, the Alichan would be able to fulfill its purpose and destroy the child made in the image of its creator. Whether she had any companions with her would not matter, because in the dark, everyone is alone.

27

December 1924 —
El Platanar del Coluta

TWENTY-FOUR STRONG RIDERS rode like lightning towards La Galancita from the south. Their pace slowed only briefly on the second evening when they took a detour to avoid being spotted in the one narrow valley where they would not be able to hide from watching eyes during the day.

Rincon knew that Bertran's centurions would watch carefully from the cliffs above at all hours, especially this one steep narrow passage into the valley. The bishop's men had to be particularly quiet, so they covered their horse's hooves in leather boots and led them silently through the narrow canyon. When daylight came, the men rested and took a slightly more lengthy and roundabout way into La Galancita just to be sure there was no possibility of being spotted by any of Bertran's scouts.

***

The riders arrived furtively at La Galancita that evening. In the distance, they could see clouds of bats falling into the valley from the hillsides to hunt for their evening meals. Once all the horses were stored in the barns, the men were fed well, and plans were made to visit Coluta once more.

Don Coronel was pleased to see the men were unarmed, because he knew El Platanar well enough to know its vulnerabilities.

"Our goal is to capture one man and one man only," he reassured the posse. "Once we have Bertran, the rest of the snake will die."

"Yes, that's for sure," Father Juan Carlos agreed. "The company he keeps is a violent and ruthless crowd, but they cannot think for themselves. Once we have Bertran, his slaves will have no choice but to regain their freedom. I really don't think we will receive much resistance once the source of their evil is removed."

Don Francisco's health had returned, and he was ready to charge into the fray with the rest of the men, but Father Juan Carlos advised against it. Instead, the plan called for them to direct the operation from a safe distance.

"Very well," Francisco conceded for the moment, "let's take a look at this map that I have drawn to show you the best paths to make your approach. Once we get to this point here we will need to dismount and continue on foot."

Francisco pointed out all the best hiding places and structures where guards and lookouts would most likely be stationed. Once the initial plan was completely laid out, the men were asked if they had any questions. Everyone seemed comfortable with his assignment and eager to carry out his instructions.

A few of the men had worked for Don Rios in the past and were looking forward to bringing down the depraved tyrant of the Purple Moon.

"You will never know how much your being here means to all of us," Francisco told the men. "I want you to all get a good night's rest. Tomorrow you should sleep late, and then we will have a healthy meal together before heading off around sunset. In the late afternoon before we set off, we will review our plans once more to be sure that we all know exactly what every other man will be doing. We have seen too much bloodshed here over the last few years and we do not want to see anyone injured. Father, I hope you will be praying for us tomorrow evening while we are on our mission."

"Of course," Father Juan Carlos assured the men. "You will all be well armored in God's word and prayers before you leave and throughout your mission tomorrow."

***

In another cave not so far away, Bertran prepared to hire a new team of explorers. He tried to follow a few of the tunnels mapped out by Rios before his unfortunate demise. A few of his men thought they knew something about mining, but they didn't. This was going to be a costly venture, but where gold was involved, Ismael proved he would stop at nothing.

Now as the sun began to set, a plan was prepared at the Galancita as well. This design was not for gold; this plan was for family. If there was any chance that Lazaro could still be alive, Apolonio wanted in on this invasion.

"Api, you have already been riding all day, you need to go with Miguel and take care of Dionicia and the girls when they arrive. We can take care of this business," said Francisco.

It was not going to work.

"Ismael took something from me and now he needs to pay for it," Api insisted.

Miguel, too, was ready to go to war with the fiend that stole their brother and father.

"I would like to go also!" he said.

Api informed the men, "I know those mines better than anyone else in the world other than my father. I can save you a lot of trouble and get you close enough to the house before anyone knows we are there."

Francisco could see that he was not going to be able to talk Apolonio out of coming along on their mission, but he had a more important assignment for Miguel.

"Miguel, can you do me a favor and ride for the girls to be sure they stay safe on the trails? I will allow you to carry your firearms because you will be alone."

In a more subdued voice, Francisco pulled Miguel aside and whispered to him privately, "There is also one other great weapon that you may need in your travels. Your father left behind a map in my care to give only to his sons in a time of need. In a time such as this."

Turning to Api, he continued, "If you are going to be one of my soldiers then you will need to promise to take orders. Can you do that much for me Apolonio?"

"I suppose so," said Api.

"And how about you Miguel?"

"Yes sir."

And with that, he sent Miguel off with a blessing and the inherited secret map to prepare for an early morning ride.

"We have our last-minute plans to take care of, but I want you to be well rested so that you can bring Dionicia and the girls home to me safely."

As Miguel left the room, Don Francisco unrolled his maps to review the plans one more time for Apolonio. In conclusion Francisco announced, "Once we have Ismael in custody we will all ride quickly into Culiacan where he can be tried fairly for the murders of Lazaro and Daniel."

Father Juan Carlos needed to make one point clear, "There is to be absolutely no bloodshed on this outing if at all possible. We must all promise to leave our weapons here. If you have any weapons with you, please hand them over now." No one came forward.

"Very well then, we will go in with our bare hands, our ropes, and the full force of our Savior. Now, before leaving we must all pray for safety and success." And with that, the priest stepped forward in his dark cloak and collar to bless each of the unarmed warriors.

After Father Juan Carlos laid hands on each man, Francisco stood at the head of the table in the dining room where they had gathered. Opening his Bible to Ephesians 6:13 he began to read, "Wherefore take unto you the whole armour of God, that ye may be able to withstand in the evil day, and having done all, to stand."

It was time to move out. Miguel and the ladies all waved goodbye as 26 horses stepped lightly onto the trail. Since the men would not be home for several days, Miguel wanted to rest well before departing for the Espinazo again.

The dim moonlight barely provided enough light for the men to see the trail before them. This was an advantage for them, because the horses knew where they were going and the sentinels of Coluta would have a tough time spotting their caravan. Apolonio felt perfectly at ease spending days at a time within the pitch-black mines of Coluta. The dim moonlight was a bright beacon for him. The idea of bringing his father's, and his brother's, killer to justice gave him great strength. He quickly forgot that he had already been riding a full day.

XI
<u>BATTLES TO FIGHT</u>

For our struggle is not against flesh and blood,
but against the rulers, against the authorities,
against the powers of this dark world and
against the spiritual forces of evil in the heavenly realms.

Ephesians 6:12

28

Thursday Evening — The Battle at El Rodeo

DESPITE ALL THE GRISLY sights and sounds of growing up in East L. A., I had never actually been so close to the violent demise of another human being before. Although I did not directly witness Grace's tragic end, it was obvious from RuMa's reaction and unwillingness to talk about it, that the experience was one we could never forget. As hard as I tried to put the shrieks of terror out of my mind, the gloomiest memories of the recent past were still in hot pursuit.

At the time I didn't understand why even in the face of incredible danger, Gabriel felt obligated to continue his story to the very end so that we would be adequately prepared for the battle ahead.

In addition to the authorities and rulers of that fading day, it was now becoming quite apparent that there were also a volcano and other unseen powers of darkness boiling all around us. No matter how quickly our mules raced for home, their careful steps upon wet stones were unable to outpace the approaching thunder of doom.

When we finally came to a wider path, we tried to agitate the beasts into a faster canter; however, a swifter fate behind us refused to relent, just as the pouring rain from above refused to diminish. My heart rate was definitely in the red zone as I wondered how much longer my frenetically throbbing arteries could deliver enough oxygen to keep us from being swallowed up in a cloud of dust and bullets.

Soon we realized that in addition to the sound of our pounding heartbeats and a rapidly advancing mob of fuming hoodlums, there was also a raging river right in front of us. The rio seemed so angry that it wanted to overflow at any moment and take our bridge to freedom along with it. The rickety wooden overpass didn't seem strong enough to withstand the weight of our trinity, but there was no choice other than to traverse quickly, because the impending rumble of the hoof beats was gaining upon us with lightning speed. Mounted on some of the fastest horses in the valley, dozens of men with mustaches and machine guns raced toward our bridge with nothing but mischief and menace in their eyes.

Just as my last-place burro made its way gingerly across the last few planks, the first bandit began to rapidly span the bridge. As predicted by Father Arres, my faith was about to be tested. For the first time since childhood, I prayed sincerely.

Immediately after shouting out to RuMa, "Hey got any more of that dynamite left, Butch?" I realized she wasn't appreciating the vague, light-hearted movie reference. Her confused glance slowed her down long enough for me to grasp that even if she did have a gun or some explosives left, there was no time left for that.

Suddenly, a huge explosion from the mountains behind us signaled the re-birth of an ancient volcano. The violence of that eruption startled the muscular horses on their conduit towards solid ground. Gently at first, the bridge began to sway; then so unpredictably that the lead horse fell. This startled every other man and animal behind.

Before any further panic could ensue, the aging timbers cracked and tumbled into the roaring blood red foam below. Bellowing rain waters drowned out the feeble cries for help, even as a wider wall of mud and debris rushed down from the hillside, sweeping away every last remaining horse and rider.

We were too busy prodding our rides towards the last bit of visible pathway, to notice all the death and mayhem taking place behind us. Little did we appreciate at the time that the cruel and tyrannical rain from heaven above, was actually our saving grace.

When we were fairly certain that no horse pursued us any further, we set up camp out of the rain and paused to catch our collective breath. Dropping from exhaustion, Gabriel tried to warn us that although we temporarily managed to evade our earthly persecutors this journey was far from over...

29

December 1924 —
The Battle for the Mines of Coluta

THIS WAS NO TIME for speaking. Api had plenty of time to ponder the last words Don Coronel spoke to him before they left, "Do not seek revenge, seek justice. It was your father's inability to forgive that led to his demise ,and he would be sorely angry to see you make that same mistake."

Api believed his father's pride and anger were his greatest weaknesses. He always drove too hard to make that next big discovery. Retreat was never an option for Don Rios. It should have come as no surprise that his father at some point would try to take matters into his own hands. Why couldn't I see this coming? Api scolded himself.

Then there was that mysterious message to his father from the man in black, 'Tell your father to give up El Platanar." The words were meaningless at the time, but they made sense now. The man in black also said there was 'still work to do," and Api couldn't do any work if he was dead. Therefore, even if it meant leaving El Platanar for good, he planned to follow all of Don Coronel's instructions closely.

Api led the posse to the entrance of a secret passageway. It was just at the top of a short, steep climb to the opposite side of the valley. Once inside the men could rest for a while, then travel quietly and unseen by day to the brink of El Platanar. As the horses climbed slowly towards the entry to an abandoned mine, another creature was crawling quietly towards the woman and her child.

Apolonio checked the entrance to the cave cautiously before entering. Dawn was about to break, so they needed to take cover soon. Once safely inside, he lit a torch and signaled for the others to enter. The horses were uncomfortable in the dark, but the passage was wide enough for them to enter without too much trouble. Once they were far enough into the cave to avoid being detected from outside, the torches were extinguished, and the men rested.

"This is about as far as we can go with the horses, Don Francisco," Api reported.

"If you and Father Juan Carlos will wait here with the horses, I can take the men to our positions later in the day. Then we will just wait for night to fall once again. Once we get Ismael back in here, his men will never be able to find us. Even if they try, I have a few surprises for them."

Api reviewed his plan again with Francisco just to reassure him that there was no need to worry. Even without torches, he knew the inside of this cavern like the reins of his horse.

Inside the mine it was often difficult to tell time and Api was afraid he might have overslept. Father Juan Carlos was keeping track of the hours and sat up watching the horses to make sure nothing startled them back towards the exit.

Although most of the men following Api were a few years older than he was, they quickly gained confidence in his leadership and followed without question. Wherever he pointed out a boulder, or a pulley, or a lever, they took notice and when everything was where he expected they moved forward more quickly.

Apolonio knew exactly how long it would take to wind through this obsidian honeycomb, and when they were all within a few hundred meters of the Coluta exit, he halted the group for a break. Taking just a few of the lead men with him, he extinguished his torch and moved forward. Connected to his fellow scouts by only a short, knotted rope, their language was limited to a combination of tugs and twists.

When Api knew he was just within a few meters of the exit, he signaled for the other men to wait. The plan was adequately rehearsed, so they knew exactly what to expect. Apolonio would leave them for a few minutes to determine whether the passage was clear. If it was, then the trailing scout would return to the main pack and lead them back to this staging area just inside the mouth of this cave. Api knew this was not a highly utilized entrance to the mines so he didn't expect anyone would be tending to it.

Sure enough, as he peered out into the moonlight, there was not a sound. Checking above and below, he exited the cave slowly and kept low to the ground. On his belly, he crawled to the ledge where he could peek over and see El Platanar below.

Unfortunately, due to the nature of the original gold-mining business conducted at the turn of the century, the Rios hacienda was one of the most heavily fortified compounds in the state. Getting over the ten-foot rear wall would be hard enough; avoiding detection from the watch tower at the same time would be even more difficult. There was still a lot of noise coming from the main hall, so Ismael was probably up entertaining guests or playing cards with some of his apple polishers.

As long as everyone was inside, this would be a great time to begin moving into position without too much silence in the background. Apolonio craftily slunk back into the cave and signaled to the men that it was time to move out. One by one they formed an obscure human chain from the cave entrance all the way down to the back wall of El Platanar. Twenty-five men, including Api at the front, staggered themselves about 10 meters apart so that there was always a quick way to communicate from one end to the other if necessary.

Once the line was in place, Api scaled the thick adobe with the assistance of the scout behind him. Inside he was able to quickly unlatch the back gate to allow four more men into the compound. So far, so good. Api quickly became familiar with these four men, because bringing any more inside the walls was just too risky. They took cover under an archway and kept a pair of eyes out in every direction. No one was in their sleeping quarters yet, so the men were able to rapidly advance to their point of entry.

Judging from the cacophony coming from the main hall, Api was guessing Ismael probably had about a dozen guests. Most were men, but there were a few female voices in the crowd also. The windows on the east side of the master bedroom faced a huge grass courtyard, but the one solid door leading out from an adjacent hallway was always kept locked from the inside. On the west side however, there was another smaller and more private courtyard that had a glass door that was usually left unlocked and led directly into the master bedroom.

The only problem with entering from the west door was that it would require scaling another wall to get up on the roof and then over into the small courtyard. Api knew that getting on the roof wouldn't be too difficult, but he would be exposed to the eyes of the tower guards, if they were still awake. Then once inside the courtyard, assuming the drapes weren't pulled shut, he could be exposed from any eyes inside the master bedroom. Since no one was likely to be in the bedroom now, there was no better time to make the climb.

With the boost from one of his partners, Api took a quick peek to see if the tower appeared occupied. There were two shadows in the candlelight, but they did not seem particularly interested in anything going on outside their lookout. Waiting for the right moment, Api took a deep breath and pulled himself onto the roof and quickly took cover behind a foot or two of adobe rising along the borders of the flat roof.

After waiting a few minutes to listen to the voices in the tower, he could tell they were playing cards. This gave Api the opportunity to poke his head over the adobe bordering the courtyard for a look inside the master bedroom. The curtains were open, but no one appeared to be in the room. Perfect! he thought.

This was it. The time had finally come to drop down into the small courtyard and rush into the bedroom. He hoped the door would be open and he could hide inside until Bertran finally tired of his games. Api had to jump down into the courtyard quickly, and when he did, the sentries heard the noise. They stood up and swept their torchlight around in circles to see what they might spot, but found nothing. Api was tucked too tightly and quietly into the shadows for anyone above to notice. When the shadows stopped swaying, he could tell they went back to their card game and he crept slowly towards the bedroom door to see if it was open. It was.

This was almost too easy. Once inside he felt right at home again. He noted that there was no one else in the room then proceeded to quickly enter the adjoining hall where the nearby door led to the larger courtyard on the east side. The ruckus inside the main hall drowned out any slight creaking of Api's sandals as he carefully opened the door to the east courtyard and spotted his partners. Forming an *O* with his thumb and forefinger, he signaled the group to let them know that the east door was now propped open and everything was going okay.

Suddenly, he heard someone approaching the far end of the corridor. Without any cover, he needed to get back into the bedroom. A figure crossed the hallway at the far end, but Api hoped the darkness would protect him as he slipped back into the master's chambers. If anyone saw him come into the room, there was no exit now. Even if he could make it back to the small inner courtyard, he'd never be able to get back on the roof by himself. There was plenty of room under the king-sized bed to squeeze underneath, but he'd be easy to spot there if someone were looking. The closet was another dead end.

Time passed, and prayers were answered. No one was coming. Api decided that the best place to hide out would be under the bed, so that if he were discovered he could confront the enemy and overtake him quickly enough to get him down quietly. Hiding in the closet would make too much noise, both climbing in and out. Forever seemed to pass before voices started to leave the main hall on a more regular basis. The chaos subsided, the torches went out in the courtyard and finally the master's footsteps were heading for his chamber.

Fortunately, Bertran was alone and the stubby man didn't waste any time collapsing into his bed and falling asleep. Apolonio suffered through several minutes of snoring before he finally decided to make his move. Slithering silently from beneath the bed, Api prepared his black jack for one sharp blow. Just as he had stunned dozens of sheep in his youth, the leather found its mark and the snoring ceased instantly. Quickly he gagged the tyrant's mouth and tied his hands. The thug was so cleanly walloped that there was even time to secure a blindfold around his head before he began to stir at all.

By then Api was able to signal his partners for help. They quickly crossed the east courtyard and entered through the open door. Complete silence now was not so important as speed. Two of the men wrapped Ismael in a blanket and carried him out on their shoulders like a huge burrito. The other two opened the doors and watched for sentries as Api covered the rear. Before leaving, he propped a few pillows under the sheets to make it look as though Bertran was still sleeping there just in case someone was to check in later. He exited the room and made his way quickly to the eastern exit door. The lead pair signaled that their path was clear, and the procession moved forward.

They reached the back gate and found it locked. Everything had been going too well. Someone making the rounds must have noticed that it was open and took the extra precaution of latching it from the outside as well. Some of the bishop's men must have seen the door closed and would certainly have returned to open it again . . . unless?

Unless, someone was still patrolling the grounds. The heavy handle made a slight rattling sound as they tried to force it open one more time, but that was enough to alert the hounds. Their barking in the distance rose faintly at first at the far north end of the compound. How could they hear such a small sound from hundreds of meters away? Api wondered. Maybe they were just barking at a cat or something.

That hope faded as the barking grew louder. They were definitely heading in their direction. The dogs picked up their scent, so there was no time for stalling now. Api had to climb back over the wall and open the gate from the outside. If someone was around, he hoped they could get some help. As soon as he started climbing onto the wall, the torchlight in the tower came on and whistles blew. The panicked leap caused Api to land awkwardly and he twisted his left ankle. With no time for pain now, he quickly opened the gate and the four men plus the big human wrap came storming out. Api locked the gate again from the outside and that held off the dogs for a short time.

The main gate was opened, and at least six men on horseback headed out. The two with dogs made their way out the front gates and around to the east side as Api tried to keep up with his four accomplices. Once they reached the trees and steep terrain behind El Platanar, the chain of communication reappeared and quickly contracted toward the escapees. It didn't take long for the horses to make their way around to the steep hillside where the bishop's chain was now quickly relaying their prize up the precipice towards the mouth of the cave. Even with one bad ankle, Api was motivated to climb quickly. The pace was brisk but cautious until a shot rang out from below.

The horses couldn't climb, but their riders could shoot. The night was so thick, though, that even with torches the men had no idea what they were aiming at. Api was the last man to reach the entrance to the cave and a few of the braver sentries were climbing quickly. They might have reached the top before Api if he hadn't paused to roll a good-sized boulder down in their direction. It wasn't enough to end their pursuit, but it did slow them down just enough for everyone to make it safely inside the cave.

Now the odds were much better: a posse of 25 versus two. The beaned burrito didn't count. Ismael was still out cold. Although the two pursuers probably each had five or six shots left in their revolvers, they were not carrying torches, so the darkness in this instance favored the posse. The chain of command quickly became a chain of rope. Api had to hobble his way to the opposite end of the rope before their escape could continue. There he gave quick instructions to his second in command to follow a rope along the wall. Now with the train moving quickly again in the right direction, Api was able to drop back to deliver his first surprise from the caboose.

The posse was moving forward, and the two pursuers became four. Api could tell they were a bit disoriented, but everything would have been a lot better if one of them hadn't decided to take a proverbial shot in the dark.

"Aye! That was close!" Api shrieked to himself.

The lead ricocheted a few times off the black walls before falling to the ground. The second shot missed its mark too, but the third came so close that Api could feel the breeze as it whizzed by his left ear. This was war. Fortunately, the enemy arrived unprepared.

Every good miner is never without his dynamite. Api had several sticks stashed away just for the occasion. Once the pursuers came within firing range again he lit the fuse and tossed his first surprise.

¡¡KaBooom!! That blast echoed all the way to Spain. Walls of rock were raining down everywhere behind Api as he jumped for joy on his good ankle, back towards the safety line. You didn't have to see the dust to taste it. Whoever was chasing them would certainly be thinking twice about continuing now, if they were able to think at all.

Most of Bertran's men got the message, but a few managed to squeeze through the debris and sustain their pursuit. Although the bishop's men were moving at a brisk pace now, the blast had awakened Ismael, and his squirming made it more difficult for the pair carrying him. With great precision, they kept exchanging the wrapped villain from one pair of fresh arms to another. When the catch became too animated, a free hand would take a quick punch at the stuffing or else Ismael would get dragged until he got the message. A few orders to "shut up and lie still," followed by an ample thump kept the load manageable.

Apolonio was beginning to feel like they were putting a little distance between their line and the persecutors when all of a sudden, another shot rang out. This time the bullet found a softer mark. At first Api though he had been struck in the left shoulder by a sledgehammer. The blow knocked him forward to the ground so quickly that he didn't have time to keep his face from grinding into the granite floor. Quickly he staggered to his feet and called for help. A few men toward the back of the line heard the shot and fell back to catch their fallen leader. He still had one more surprise left in him, if he could just keep from passing out.

With the help of those last two men, Api made his way to the lever he had set up in advance to release a huge boulder from a track above. If everything worked properly, the stone should have been large enough to seal the tunnel behind them. The only problem was Api no longer had the strength to pull the pry bar. With the aid of the two trailing men, Api finally had enough weight to push down the handle activating the man-made rockslide.

The trigger worked! the boulder rolled down and sealed the cavern perfectly! There was still a bit of space left near the ceiling for air and shouts to seep through, but that was all. A good thing, too, because just then Api lost consciousness and needed to be carried out like a giant bag of rice.

The bishop's men worked hard and reached the guiding torchlight of Father Juan Carlos and Don Coronel in great time. Before the sun began to rise, the team of 25 approached their horses and prepared to ride. Apolonio should have been at the head of the line, but he was not.

"Where is Api?" Francisco asked, as one after another the unfamiliar faces appeared from the darkness. Finally, at the very back of the chain, two dog-tired men dragged Apolonio to a flat spot beside the campfire. The blood loss from his shoulder was evident now through his shirt, but it was the gash on his head from falling face first into the slab that made the worst first impression.

Initially, they thought he might have been shot in the face, but it was his shoulder that was shattered by the bullet. Miraculously, by applying pressure and makeshift bandages to the major wounds, the men were able to stop the bleeding and get Api quickly up on his horse. It was his most uncomfortable ride ever.

Don Coronel kept the pace brisk so that he could get Api to a doctor as soon as possible. Occasionally, they'd take a quick pause to apply a clean wrap and rinse the wounds with water, but the young man was in shock and really didn't notice the pain much anymore. When all the horses made it safely down from the hillside most of the party proceeded southward with Father Juan Carlos and their prisoner of war towards Culiacan.

A few of the bishop's men stayed with Don Francisco and Api just for additional support in the event that news had scattered Bertran's small remaining army in their direction. The ride was long and hard, but their pursuers were far enough behind that Francisco was able to get Apolonio to the best doctor in the valley right away. It was a very hard test, but Api survived.

30

December 1924 —
The Battle of La Caldera

THE RIDE UP TO the crater flew by for Miguel. One night of rest did wonders for the young man, and even Tronido seemed refreshed and eager to climb the Espinazo. Another fresh young colt named Aguila (Eagle) was also prepared with a native-style travois for Victoria's comfort on the way back.

Inside the mountain, however, there was one more creature climbing with great enthusiasm. As the Alichan approached the upper chambers of this massive labyrinth, it warmed up to the idea of finally capturing and devouring the woman and her child.

Since Miguel knew he was the only man on this ride and that danger could always be around any turn, he made sure his revolvers and rifle were loaded and ready to fire. Since he got a late start and it was an uphill trip this time, it was already dark by the time Miguel reached the crater.

The cave entry was like a giant ear that magnified every reverberation from above. Dionicia knew that horses were approaching long before Miguel poked his head over the rim and called down, "Dionicia, its Miguel. Is everyone all right?"

"Yes, mi hijito, we are all fine. Are you alone?"

"No, I have Tronido and Aguila with me. We will be right down," Miguel said.

That did not sit well with Dionicia. While Miguel prepared the horses for the long steep descent into the crater, Dionicia thought that since Francisco was not with them the news was not going to be favorable. She did not want to go home without the forgiveness of her husband. She also wondered where Apolonio was and why he didn't return with Miguel. The answers to all her questions would have to wait a bit longer.

It took a few minutes for Miguel and the horses to make it all the way down into the rounded bottom of the Caldera formed by the meteorite of 1910. Their reunion was once again warm and lively, but this time there was even more trepidation in Dionicia's voice as she asked the all-important question:

"Well mi hijito, what did Francisco say?"

Tears formed in her eyes as she prepared herself for the blow. Tears began to form in her daughter's eyes as well just before Miguel announced: "He still loves you! Yes, he can't wait to see you again!"

Victoria cheered out loud. It was almost more than she could imagine. For Dionicia to be forgiven for all her misdeeds; all the misguided sins that seemed like pleasures at the time. Could she finally be leaving all this darkness behind forever?

Miguel unpacked the horses as the ladies prepared one last supper in their huge celestial amphitheater. The evening was one of great expectations for all five cave dwellers. The Alichan heard the celebration above and knew he was getting close to his prey.

Victoria unpacked a few small toy soldiers as gifts for Manuelito. He was excited too about discovering La Galancita. Dionicia had been telling him all about it as well as Tamazula and the schools there where he could learn with children his own age. It was quite an exciting prospect for a young boy who only on a few very rare occasions saw other children in the village of Dolores.

Manuelito wondered if it was possible that a place existed where many people of his same height lived? The toy soldiers were interesting, but why were they dressed in such strange uniforms? Why did they have long knives at the end of their rifles? Manuelito was somewhat acquainted with guns and rifles, but the concept of war was something new to him. Miguel tried his best to explain why men organize in large numbers to overtake one another, but it wasn't easy. World War I was recently over, and of course Manuelito wanted to know why? Miguel struggled to explain exactly why, but together they found no good answers as to what the war had accomplished.

He just couldn't understand, "Yes but why do we have to kill them? Killing is wrong, isn't it?"

The ladies all overheard their conversation and they were at a loss also to explain the events of their recent history. "Mi hijito," Dionicia tried to explain her observations, "sometimes bad ideas can take over good people and then we see them as bad people. It's not people we have to kill; it's the evil spirits inside we need to overcome. Your . . ." she paused because she wasn't sure what relationship her husband would assume with Manuelito.

"My husband, Don Francisco Coronel is a very wise man and he will be able to answer these questions for you better than I can."

Dionicia concluded that she was out of her league when it came to spiritual matters. The world above, the world of her people and the world of Francisco's God were all so different and mysterious to her; yet Francisco never had any doubts. Whatever the cause or reasons for war, Manuelito would finally get to hear a reasonable explanation from the Don himself.

Dionicia enjoyed hearing herself refer to Don Francisco as her husband once again. Even though she hadn't seen him in several years, she hoped that it would be like putting on a comfortable pair of old shoes. It would probably feel strange at first, but certainly it would help her wipe away all the memories of living under Bertran's tyranny.

As the fire crackled and blazed, new dreams and visions reflected in five pairs of eyes. Miguel was still trying to comprehend the loss of his father, and Dionicia shared her sympathies with him. Life would be much different now for all of them without the firm guidance of Don Rios.

Although Miguel wouldn't miss the occasional painful whippings his father could deliver, the steadfast direction and style with which he conducted his business would be sorely absent. Miguel knew that whenever he felt his father's leather, it was justified. Miguel's painful loss would have been amplified in this void if it weren't for the distraction of his escalating love for Victoria. The loss was further distanced by the idea that his brother might be in grave danger at that very moment. So, he had no time to grieve; only time to pray.

When the right moment came, Miguel revealed his father's map to Dionicia and asked if she might understand the directions to the golden sword noted as the secondary objective of this quest. Although she was somewhat disturbed initially by the news, she was aware of the fabled treasure that was apparently not too far away. As the quiet conversations and campfire started to fade, it was time to retire from the past and prepare for a brighter tomorrow. Perhaps there really was an El Dorado to be revealed.

The silence was alluring to the beast. He sensed that he would be within striking distance soon. The woman had company now, but she was not going to get away this time. The Alichan decided to sleep for a while and dream of victory, a long-awaited conquest over the wretched organisms that killed one of its own; the beings that resembled the image of his own maker.

***

When the stars faded, and weak sunlight filled the expansive crater opening, the Alichan resumed his quest. Miguel and the ladies were awake and making their final preparations for departure. It was such a chilly morning that they could sometimes see their breath. They were all eager to get back out into the warm sunshine.

Miguel awoke early to search for the spot where the golden sword was, according to the map, supposedly located in a relatively nearby passage. When he first spotted the treasure in its own grotto, he pulled the long blade from its ornately jeweled sheath and marveled at the most brilliantly sharp and highly polished oro (gold) he had ever set his eyes upon. However, it immediately cast a spell upon him and he thought about going further into the darkness to see if he could follow its path to even greater prosperity. He began to envision the Spanish coins described on the map.

Just then, a strange noise startled him. It sounded something like a low snarl, but it was not a familiar sound. Instead of pursuing golden ambitions, he decided to return to his people. As he began climbing back up toward the surface, the growling became a roar and his pace became a flight.

Rosita reminded Dionicia about her serpentine glass cross.

"Don't leave your cross here, Mama. Where is it?"

"Oh yes," Dionicia recalled. "It's up there, I'm glad you reminded me."

The Alichan spotted the woman with the baby pointing upward towards a crucifix high upon a ledge towards the back of the huge chamber.

"How did you get that up there?" Rosita wondered aloud.

"Manuelito climbed up for me and put it in the highest place he could reach," Dionicia said.

"I'll get it for you, Mama," Manuelito said.

The child rushed forward to retrieve the cross, but Rosita would not allow it.

"No Manuelito that's too high for you. I'll bring it down. You stay right here."

She knew Manuelito was probably a better climber, but she just didn't feel as though it would be safe for him up there; plus, she just felt like climbing that day for some reason.

Miguel arrived just then and stepped forward insisting that they needed to leave soon, and he would be best suited for the climb.

"No, no," Dionicia insisted, "let Manuelito bring it down. He knows how to climb like a monkey. And if he does fall, I can catch him. If you fall, I cannot catch you."

Mother knew best. Manuelito was already scurrying up his customary path to the cross. The others gathered below him just in case.

The Alichan was observing all this and couldn't stand the sight of the boy climbing towards the cross. He had to attack now. The trio of Miguel, Dionicia, and Rosita did not notice the huge shadow as they focused intently on the climber above.

Slowly the creature crept towards them without being noticed. The child was just about to reach the crucifix when Alichan let out it's blood curdling "Vvvaaauuuwww!"

The wretched guttural blast rumbled throughout the entire chamber like a feast of trumpets. Manuelito looked down and spotted the hideous beast just as he grasped the cross and began to fall.

Dionicia was the only one still focused on the boy. At first Rosita and Victoria were so startled by the abominable sound that they cowered against the wall and hid their faces. Dionicia was able to break the boy's fall enough to protect him from serious injury, but their ordeal had just begun.

While the girls scooped up Manuelito and scrambled for cover, Miguel was the only one left to face the demon directly. This infuriated the Alichan, as this worthless mortal was now standing between evil and its objective. The leviathan was just about to charge when Rosita reached for her pistol and raised her arm quickly to fire. It was in close range now and an easy mark. The hammer came back, but just as she was about to pull the trigger…

"Vvvaaauuuwww!" the Alichan roared once again. From this distance, the sound was paralyzing. Rosita was frozen and could not command a single muscle to contract. In the dim morning light, she could see death slowly encroaching upon her with its mouth gaping wide—hypnotic. The next few moments seemed to last forever as Miguel noticed every scale, every crack on the creature's hideous face.

From head to toe, the Alichan was absolutely horrifying. The teeth in its mouth were long and sharp, much more menacing than the ones his father had carved into spoons. Its nostrils flared, and vapor billowed forth. Spines on the top of its head fanned out like jagged peaks upon its bulging crown. Its backbone was long and thorny with a tail that disappeared into the blackness.

But all the Alichan's horrific features paled in comparison to the endless void of eternal darkness in its eyes. Miguel once said they were gloomier than the deepest tunnel he ever descended, and he was falling into them fast. Just as he was about to fall forward into the gaping maw, Miguel prayed for mercy. If there was any doubt left in his heavenly Savior, he had to overcome it in that moment. He did not have the power to save himself from this much evil.

Little Manuelito whimpered in fright as the ladies shivered into a protective mass around him. Victoria could not bear to lift her head to see what was about to happen next. As Rosita turned to look for Miguel, she noticed a glint of morning light reflecting off the glass cruciform clutched in Manuelito's hands.

Rosita quickly recognized that Miguel and the Alichan were locked in an epic battle. As the young woman stood frozen before eternity, the beast suddenly ceased its advance. Rosita remembered the tales of her youth and decided to have faith in the cross. There were no other options, Miguel was about to be consumed and they would all be devoured if someone did not act immediately.

Without another word, Rosita placed her hands upon little Manuelito's. Somehow, he understood the need to hold the cross at once. Invigorated by the power in her hands, she rushed towards Miguel and wrapped her arms around him from behind, waving the crucifix between their eyes and the gaping abyss.

The Alichan did not understand what was happening. It clapped its jaws shut for an instant and Rosita quickly regained her soul. The trigger finger worked, the hammer fell, and one heavy bullet glanced off the monstrosity's skull with little, if any effect. The shadow winced then crept forward slowly and with more anger than ever before.

There was no time left for hope or prayers or visions. It was time for action. Miguel leaped forward and drew his newly discovered sword. The blade was heavy, but with a singular mighty blow, he sent the menace staggering backward to the far end of the chamber where it stumbled once and fell far below into a seemingly bottomless flue. A faint splash was heard a moment later. Was the Alichan finally destroyed by its own malice?

Victoria hobbled over to her love. His hands trembled with the realization that he was not in a dream. Dionicia rose from her protective crouch over Manuelito to be sure that all were safe. The nightmare was over. The chamber was quiet once again.

The feelings of strength and pride that Miguel felt while holding the sword were so powerful that they frightened him. Dionicia warned him to step away from it as she had been warned by her Curandera friends and relatives that only the power of God could overcome evil and anyone who attempted to conquer death with the sword of Michahel would eventually be consumed by its power. So, when no one else was paying attention, Miguel took the sword back and buried it within a shallow cove along with the map to the unfound trove of riches.

The idea of returning for the mapped-out treasure never occurred to Miguel or Dionicia as they scrambled to the safety and comfort of their Galancita. On the ride home, they all vowed to each other that they would never tell anyone of the golden sword or any treasures it may protect . . .

XII
WARS TO WIN

*"Too often, the way taken is the wrong way,
with too much emphasis on what we want to have,
rather than what we wish to become."*

—*Louis L'Amour*

31

Friday Morning —
Somewhere near El Rodeo

GABRIEL BUILT A WARM fire and concluded his storytelling in the wee hours of the morning. Though we couldn't converse calmly over the last several miles, it became obvious that the young man was never romantically involved with RuMa. We still had many more bridges to cross, but it felt as though Rue was warming up to me as she snuggled into my ribs and fell fast asleep.

When the rain finally ceased, the sun came up and a bright rainbow appeared. A monarch floated above the meadow where we recovered beside still waters from our long unexpected journeys. Lying next to me in the damp, warm grass, RuMa stared into the lapis heavens above as I wondered out loud where the future would take us next.

"So where am I now?" I asked.

"Gabriel!" She cried out. "How far are we from Tamazula?"

"No, that's not what I meant." As I poked her playfully asking, "I mean where am I in your life now?"

She let out a long sigh and stared at the sky again for a while, but before she could answer that I had to say, "This trip has really shown me a lot about myself, and Gabriel gave me a whole new perspective of how little I really know about my past; especially what I believe about things we can't see with our own eyes."

"Like your anger and depression?" She asked, not so sweetly.

"Yes! That is exactly what I'm seeing now. I'm not saying we should rush back into anything right away, but if my grandparents were able to swallow their pride and walk away from a fortune in gold, maybe we can make a go of it again."

"I don't know, Alan, marriage is hard work, and I'm definitely going back for that treasure someday." She said it with a smile, but not jokingly.

"Well, guess we should get moving again. The Federales probably won't be too happy when they find out they're missing a whole bunch of their horses. Good thing I've been training for that big race in Durango."

"Yeah," she said. "And I need to figure out how I'm going to explain the loss of Grace to Ron."

We sighed in harmony. Cautiously, she began to educate me on what took place in that dark crater buried now in rubble.

"I'm glad you're laying down, because what I saw in that pit is beyond anything I'll ever be able to explain to my benefactors back on campus. When one of our Rarámuri scouts told us that the Federales and their druggy pals were heading in our direction, Grace went back down to see if she could snag any treasure to bring out as evidence of our findings, but I knew we had to get packing. That's when I heard Gabriel's shofar and well . . ."

She paused then and began bawling into my shoulder. She was not one to get emotional very easily, but whatever she saw was too much to bear.

"I've never seen anything like that, Alan. When we first found the fresh Gorgon tissue, our tests were inconclusive. For a while, it looked like part of the skeleton was Permian, like over

260 million years old, but then other parts of the same skeleton we dated at closer to 80 years old. It didn't make any sense, so we assumed it was a mistake.

Then we started hearing noises and just thought it was bats or rodents of some sort. I'm really sorry now that I used so much explosives on that cave. We will have to recover Grace someday, but I hope that creature never escapes from that place."

Trying to recover some composure she finally caught her breath and smiled. "Probably gonna need the number for your therapist too."

Gabriel began packing quietly nearby without interrupting her. He seemed to already know this next part of the story.

"So basically, most of the text inside the Scroll they call, Daniel's Scroll is just a Mixtec version of John's Apocalypse from the last book of the Bible's New Testament. They call it the Daniel Scroll because apparently it was your great-grandfather Daniel Rios who found it in a mine one day and threw it into a deep hole because he didn't understand it and didn't think it was worth anything.

For the next few minutes she explained the long story of how she discovered the Scroll and how my mother ended up inheriting the Palabra for her museum years later. "Back at the University, they were only able to decipher part of the Scroll for me, so they had to send it on to our astronomy department to figure out the rest of it."

"Ok, you lost me on that one, so what does astronomy have to do with the Scroll of Daniel or the Apocalypse of John, or whatever?" I asked.

"Well, that's where Gabriel stepped in and really threw our archaeology department for a loop. Because apparently the ancient Mesoamericans had a better handle on astronomy than some of our European ancestors and they had their own spin on what they read in the Apocalipsis."

She paused momentarily for dramatic effect before continuing in an excited and light-hearted manner.

"So . . . are you ready for this? Are you still lying down? Based upon what Grace and I have been able to figure out from Gabriel's interpretations of the Scroll, the scientists at your old school think that maybe as early as 400 BC to AD 200, the Monte Alto (high mountain) culture figured out that there is another Planet X way out in our solar system that appeared at the time of Christ's birth and will be returning to our solar system. Guess when?"

I had no idea what she was talking about, so just for laughs I said, "TODAY?"

"Right!" She bolted upright shouting. "How did you know?"

"Ummm, just brilliant I guess."

"No, I am totally serious," she said. "Today is the beginning of the Feast of Trumpets, right Gabriel?"

"Yes, that is true," our impartial observer replied.

"And there is a Day of Atonement coming in about ten more days, correct?"

"Yes, that is also true, Ms. RuMa".

"So, if anyone can add one plus one together, we should be able to figure out that God is trying to tell us something here."

"According to Daniel's Scroll, there is going to be a juncture between this Planet X, which they called ne-bi-ru, and our inner solar system sometime soon and the word Neberu or Niburum means, equinox or a junction point, especially of rivers."

She had her notes out now and was reading verbatim from some emails recently received from a colleague.

"All of our prior research has shown that there is no factual basis for belief in this mythical planet. Plus, the Bible clearly says that the Day of the Lord will come like a thief in the night. But there are just too many coincidences lining up now to ignore. Listen to this quote from La Palabra that Gabriel just shared with me. Using his boustrophedon interpretation of the ancient Rarámuri symbols on that old sword from your mother's garage it basically says:

She read this part verbatim from a note in her pocket.

"The sun will be turned to darkness and the moon to blood before the coming of the great and dreadful day of the Lord."

"That's Joel 2:31! And," she continued, "tomorrow also happens to be the autumnal equinox."

Being a fervent Libra, and seeking greater balance in my life, RuMa had my complete attention.

"So, what are you saying Rue? Is Jesus coming tonight? Tomorrow?" I was thoroughly disoriented.

"No," she said "but these are all things that have to come to pass before our Lord will return. For example, next year on January 31st there will be a super blue blood moon. That's what Joel 2:31 was talking about."

Gabriel further added to my confusion when he said, "Sir, the Bible teaches us that we cannot know the day or the hour of Christ's return. But I did have a dream the other night that we were trapped in a dark tunnel and couldn't get out. When I finally found an opening, there was a huge fire in the cavern behind me and we couldn't get everyone out. A few of us escaped into a church above, but I just remember saying over and over. . . 'We have to get the others out.' So many people were still trapped in the darkness when I awoke."

His voice trailed off into a somber realization that something real was about to happen to the world as we know it. Something unprecedented and inexplicable. For a moment, the joy always upon his face departed.

"Yes, there have been many clear signs, but probably the most frightening thing we will all discover soon is the revelation of an Antichrist." She paused to catch her breath before continuing because this revelation really seemed to disturb her train of thought.

"Alan, I know you've never believed your mom's stories, and you didn't actually see what was down in the bottom of that Caldera, but I have to tell you honestly, if the Alichan is not some sort of sign of the end times, I don't know what it is."

And with that cheerful thought she added, "Son of man, we are still alive, and that means we still have a chance to share this good news with anyone who is willing to listen: There is a Savior who will forgive all our sins and offer us eternal life if we only believe in Him."

Gabriel seemed anxious to finish telling his story and get us moving again. But RuMa lingered over that green pasture briefly before sharing one last thought for the road, "Take a look around boys, this is just a glimpse of what heaven is going to be like. Let's get back home and start telling people that it's time to come out of the darkness."

The monarch butterfly fluttered by again in that moment, and I wondered if it had any concept of what it would become when it was crawling around somewhere in its recent past as a hideous larva. Quickly climbing back upon my nameless steed, I asked Gabriel, "Hey is it okay if I name this mule after my bike?"

"Sure," he said. "What is your bike's name?"

"Joy," I replied.

32

December 1924 — La Galancita

THE POSSE RODE LIKE the wind towards Culiacan. Circumventing El Rodeo once again, Father Juan Carlos didn't want the bishop's men to encounter any resistance from the workforce of the Purple Moon. By now, Bertran's men were certainly in hot pursuit of their missing leader and his captors. Once word reached town that Ismael had been kidnapped, his legions crept from every crevice to restore their sustenance to power.

The more Juan Carlos thought about it, so many people in the valley relied upon Bertran for their feeble existence that without him there would be a huge void to fill. Bringing the kingpin to justice would not be enough. Restoring El Platanar to its rightful owners might not be so simple without Don Daniel around.

Juan Carlos prayed as they rode. Apolonio was a strong young man with a good chance of surviving his injuries, but if not, what then? Would Miguel be strong enough to take over as the leader at Coluta? Obviously, Don Coronel could be relied upon for some support but could he, with all his own dilemmas, run two haciendas at once?

The Espinazo valley suffered for too long before Ismael finally offered the people some hope. It was a false hope, but still it was hope. El Dorado was alive again in the hearts of every inhabitant of the dell. Now with their savior in custody, the Rios name, Juan Carlos and the church could likely become the new villains of the valley. In fact, it was only a few years later that a national attack began against the Catholic Church known as the Cristiada or Cristero War.

Father Juan Carlos couldn't remember ever riding so fast for so long. The bishop's men were extremely skillful horsemen and they navigated the back forests with remarkable agility. If any of Bertran's men were on their trail, they would have a hard time catching up now. The bishop gave Antonio Rincon specific instructions on where to deliver the outlaw. The cathedral would not be an appropriate place, and the jails could possibly be compromised. Bertran would have to be taken directly to the state capital building, where a loyal judge would take custody of the prisoner and see to his immediate trial.

The posse only had to stop a few times to trade Ismael from one rider to another just to give the riders and horses a break. Rincon carried the baton on the final leg as the procession finally arrived at the state capitol.

Father Juan Carlos was so breathless that he could hardly speak after climbing the steps to present their prize criminal to the judge and governor. The unwrapped Bertran was barely conscious but essentially unharmed except for his ego. The only pride he had left came from the fact that he was a big enough criminal to warrant presentation to the governor. Several state officers accompanied the governor and they quickly took him away to a secure cell in the basement.

The priest enjoyed his brief visit with the governor, but there was still much work to be done back in the high Sierra. Father Juan Carlos needed to return to La Galancita to check on his new best friend, Don Coronel. The bishop agreed to send his men back up to La Galancita with Juan Carlos for protection until they could figure out a way to reorganize the business affairs of Coluta. Because the judge was able to annul the illegal contract between Ismael and Daniel, a new document was provided that returned El Platanar back to the rightful heirs, Natividad Rios and her sons.

There was still a long trial ahead, but Father Juan Carlos was already planning his case against Bertran. There were many things that he knew about Ismael and many things he could not say, but there were others close to Bertran that could easily be persuaded to testify against him in a murder case.

After a comfortable evening of rest in Culiacan the priest was eager to return to La Galancita to check up on Apolonio. A messenger was sent ahead to notify everyone in the valley ahead of them that Don Bertran was now in custody and no longer the owner of El Platanar. The threat of attack from his sycophants was somewhat lessened, but it was still hard to say what the reaction to the news would be.

After a brief overnight stay in Tamazula, the posse rode straight through El Rodeo in broad daylight without incident. All the regulars of the Purple Moon came out to stand on the saloon deck as the Father's procession marched past. Clearly much was about to change.

***

There was a joyous reunion at La Galancita when Dionicia returned home to be with her husband Francisco once again.

Francisco cared for Manuelito as if he were his own. When Manuelito was old enough, he moved to Tamazula to study the Bible with Father Juan Carlos.

The people of the valley of the Espinazo Del Diablo were glad to hear that the Rios family was returning to El Platanar. Once Mario and Bertran's other men realized they were never going to see Ismael return to the hacienda, they had no choice but to give up their bad habits and return to honest work for the Coronel and the Rios families.

Father Juan Carlos eventually convinced several of Bertran's insiders to testify against him. The bodies of Lazaro and Daniel were exhumed briefly to prove that it was indeed the bullets of Ismael's personal handgun that delivered the fatal blows.

Although Bertran served several years in prison, he still held enough influence to eventually win his release. However, by then Apolonio was fully recovered and soundly in charge of El Platanar and its fertile soils. Miners never did liberate much gold from El Espinazo, but Api did learn how to grow grapes there and they soon became bountiful. Once prohibition ended in the States, the new Don Rios, Apolonio, was able to bottle a popular red wine that he exported in mass quantities to the north and he grew relatively wealthy.

Greater than his financial victory was the treasure that he finally mined from Rosita's heart. There was a wedding that following spring of 1925. On a Thursday, February 26th, Apolonio married Rosita and they moved soon thereafter to further pursue their dreams in Southern California...

33

Saturday — Tamazula de Victoria

WITH THAT STORY BEHIND us, we hustled as fast as the mules would clatter us back to that seemingly empty church of my family origin. On the short ride to Tamazula, I began to realize that if there was something missing in that church, it was probably me. Before hearing our family's story, I thought I knew something about God and life. My only hope was to find RuMa on that trip to Mexico. Instead, I also discovered that this story never was about us. Though we may not always agree or see things the same way, I began to set more realistic expectations for our relationships.

On that 16th of September, we all sat down on the rooftop of a restaurant across the street from the central plaza to enjoy a festive farewell dinner together. As music played and dancers twirled, Father Arres announced to his attentive listeners, "Now that I'm rapidly approaching the century mark of my life, I hope that you will never forget the lessons learned from Rosita and Apolonio. Though they are no longer with us, we continue to enjoy the fruits of their labor. In their grapes we remember that as the branch cannot bear fruit of itself, except it abide in the vine; no more can ye, except ye abide in Christ."

With glasses held high we all toasted together: "To the Rioses! Salud!"

When the clinking finally stopped, Father Arres proceeded to the conclusion of his story.

"Of course, you know that Miguel married Victoria and took over the Durango vineyards when his older brother moved north. Rosita gave birth to your mother Leonila Rios and the rest, as they say, is history.

With the money the Rioses made from their vineyards, Rosita opened a Mexican Restaurant in 1937 on the Sunset Strip in Hollywood that catered to the movie stars and celebrities of the times. The Rios Café was so popular that she eventually opened a Rio Rosa Café, then a Rosita's Café in East Los Angeles as you may remember, Alan."

"Ahh yes, growing up in Rosita's Café. That always brings back great memories," I said. "But what ever happened to my grandfather Apolonio? He died before I was born, and no one ever says much about him."

The Father explained, "No one knows exactly what ever happened to him. It was well known that he liked to drink a little more than he should have. In his later years, some people thought he was going insane. He became very abusive and angry at the world until finally he just disappeared."

"But what ever happened to the little boy named Manuelito?" I asked.

"Ahhh, Manuelito. Don Francisco and Dionicia lived happily together in La Galancita for many more years, and they cared for little Manuelito until he grew old enough to live here in Tamazula. Father Juan Carlos visited often, and Manuelito took a great liking to him. They shared stories and books and . . ."

"Yes," I interrupted, "but where is little Manuelito now?"

"You are speaking to him of course!" The priest said in surprise.

"Didn't you know? Since I didn't have a last name, El Padre, Juan Carlos Arres allowed me to adopt his surname. He became like a father to me. When I took an interest in the priesthood, he is the one who encouraged me to cherish reading, recording and sharing all our histories with anyone who has ears to hear.

Puzzling this all together I asked, "So does that mean that you are my great-granduncle?"

"Yes, I suppose so. But please feel free to call me Father Manuelito now."

The priest could see my fatigue from the long ride in an unfamiliar saddle and still there were so many questions for us to resolve.

"There is a day of judgment coming soon for all of us," he said. "It would be a dreadful thing to fall into the hands of an angry God. But thankfully there is victory ahead for those who believe. So, you must tell me Alan, have you finally overcome your doubts about whether God is real? Christ said, 'He who believes in me will live even though he dies. Do you believe this?'"

It was time for Rosa to return home on a late flight, so she inadvertently interrupted us just at that critical moment. This was my last chance to re-engage with brave Rue, so I never got a chance to answer Father Manuelito's most important question. Instead, RuMa pulled me aside to say that when she first climbed down into the Devil's Cauldron, they dove into a deep river flowing beneath the mountain, but she was never able to recover the complete Gorgon skeleton or any of the Spanish coins that were believed to have once existed there.

However, she did find one unexpected treasure on her journey. She pulled out an old envelope from her backpack and handed it to me.

"I found this letter from your grandmother Rosita's memorial. She wrote this in 1978 and wanted us to remember it always."

She handed me the letter, which I opened and read out loud. "This is Rosita's prayer:

'May divine providence be with you today & always.
My prayers will never falter for you & family.
May our Lord and God accompany you
and watch over your home & family.
This is my wish for you,

—Mama Rosa'"

I remember the eulogy that my cousin Joey gave at her funeral about food, family and faith. These were the tenets or her life. So simple and complete, yet we continually search for more. We want answers right now to so many mysteries that we may never understand, like how does a monarch find its way for thousands of miles, navigating only by celestial clues? Why do some people believe in some strange legends and inexplicable signs above, yet not others? And, how does a man ever truly become one with his bride?

Maybe we're just not paying attention. Maybe we are ignoring some obvious signs and disasters taking place in our own lives and around the world, over and over. Maybe we really don't want to believe the news we hear every day and that something dark is going on beyond the surface of the Earth that we can't see with human eyes. The answers all seem so far away…

Then Gabriel came by to say farewell, and I had to ask him one last question, "So why does God have to make our pathway of blessing so difficult?"

Without hesitation he replied, "God doesn't, man does."

RuMa came over to give me a hug before she left and said, "I'm not sure when we'll get to talk again, but I'm afraid that we still need to do some more digging here. I think whatever is in that cave wants to destroy the Church."

"Well, maybe we can try digging for some solutions together." I suggested.

As the town continued to celebrate their Independence Day, fireworks went off in the skies above. I resolved quietly in that moment to pursue life, liberty, and happiness with a new fervor.

Gabriel sounded his trumpet to celebrate the end of the festival also known as "The Feast of Not Knowing the Day or the Hour." Then, in the twinkling of an eye, I had to go home.

EPILOGUE · EPIPHANY

"Life is like riding a bicycle.
To keep your balance you must keep moving."

—*Albert Einstein*

Race Day — Durango, Colorado

WHEN I FINALLY REGAINED consciousness, the clarion call of a klaxon horn was still ringing inside my head. One of the cyclists in an orange jersey stood talking to a 911 operator on his cell phone while pointing a handheld air horn up to his partner on the ridge. That fish logo came slowly back into focus asking that same tiring question again, "How can we pray for you?"

As the cobwebs began to clear, I vaguely recalled the events of an epic journey taken just a few days earlier. Within moments of staggering to my feet, two orange jerseys were at my side helping me back onto my bike.

"We've been praying for you, man," the first orange-clad rider said.

"Well, I'm just some kind of a sinner who's becoming a believer now, I guess," That's what I mumbled, while wiping a mud-filled mouth with my filthy jersey sleeve.

"You know, that's exactly what we were praying for, that you would stand up on your own two feet and admit you're a sinner. C'mon man! Declare with your mouth that Jesus is your Lord and Savior."

The bleeding stopped, and somehow my energy returned as though I had never taken that long detour to the bottom of the hill.

"I BELIEVE!!!" I shouted.

In that instant, I was transformed into a new creature. Soon we were all back on the trail, but my head was still reeling from the blows, so I had to let them know, "I'm not sure if I can make it to the finish line?"

"IF you can?" one replied,
"Everything is possible for one who believes."
(Mark 9:23, NIV)

They say that in cycling, as in life, whoever suffers the most wins. Whoever "they" are, they're right. And so, on that day I threw off everything slowing me down and rode the last few miles of my race with perseverance. At the finish line there was a great cloud of witnesses to the fact that I finally overcame the biggest doubts in life. Though I didn't get a medal that day, there was great victory in simply acknowledging my faults and believing that my maker is not the cause of torment in this world. But now I also know that we all need to change quickly and keep moving. Because, there is still an evil one out there chasing us and his demise is coming soon - very soon...

I love my life. Faith is healing my wounded spirit and providing the strength to pursue a joyful, purposeful future.

THE END?

ACKNOWLEDGEMENTS

MOVING FORWARD, I MUST acknowledge at least some of the major forces that helped me to arrive securely at this Start/Finish line.

First of all, thanks to God for the great *Food* of His Word. Without the daily prayers of my *Family* and friends, I'd just be spinning my wheels and unable to share the great joy that comes along with *Faith*.

So much is owed to our ancestors and the wisdom they provide. A special tribute is necessary to my parents and extended family members who were my first and greatest instructors. In third grade, I was especially fortunate to have a teacher named Dr. Diane Watanabe, who published my first book and sparked a lifelong desire to write and read.

Praise to Joel Nakamura who brought the Alichan to life with his cover artwork. More thanks to Joel's parents, Grace and Yoshio, along with all the other mentors who contributed to my appreciation of art, athletics and economics (the study of motivation).

There is a singular appreciation in my heart for brother John—for his encouragement and willingness to participate in many of my crazy ventures. Other Johns such as the author of the book of Revelation, John Leach (Pastor of Jubilee Fellowship Church), John Eldredge (author of *Wild at Heart*) and Jon Paul

Tucker (author of "Cyclist in You") have also provided many meaningful words to carry me through each day.

And especially to my family and friends, thanks for your patience during all the hours and years I've spent away from you to complete this project.

Abe Thiessen has been a special inspiration to this story, by demonstrating the fullness of life on the Pathway of Blessing.

Without Michael Klassen of Illumify and his team of coaches that have fortified me through this endeavor, the publication of this Alichan story would not be possible. Cheers to L. S. Hawker, Katie Sherbondy, Laura Lisle, and the entire Illumify team for making writing that shines.